PRAISE FOR *BRIG...*

"Maitland offers his r... a mark
of his skill as a crime w... ...ok wiser, more
knowledgeable about the... ... well as deftly entertained.'
—*Weekend Australian*

'. . . will entertain those after an intelligent, realistic crime novel.'
—*Canberra Times*

'Consummate powers of description distinguish Maitland's thriller
from the pack as he takes a break from his British police procedural
series for an ambitious exploration of loyalty, betrayal, loss of
innocence and guilt.'
—*The Advertiser*

'Maitland is one of the famous five of Australian crime fiction . . .
Bright Air shines.'
—*Sydney Morning Herald*

'. . . a compelling story in an original setting you won't want to miss.'
—*Woman's Day*

'. . . a terrific thriller . . . beautifully, leanly written; the characters
and places drawn with skill.'
—*Weekend Herald, NZ*

'. . . disarms criticism with his sparkling writing, penetrating
psychological insights and powerful story-lines. Maitland also
ruminates about risk and contingency, and there are curious parallels
with Tim Winton's *Breath* in the exploration of extreme demands on
physical and moral courage.'
—*The Monthly*

Also by Barry Maitland

BARRY
MAITLAND
BRIGHT AIR

ALLEN&UNWIN

This edition published in 2009
First published in 2008

Allen & Unwin
83 Alexander Street
Crows Nest NSW 2065
Australia
Phone: (61 2) 8425 0100
Fax: (61 2) 9906 2218
Email: info@allenandunwin.com
Web: www.allenandunwin.com

Cataloguing-in-Publication details are available
from the National Library of Australia
www.librariesaustralia.nla.gov.au

ISBN 978 1 74175 763 7

Set in Fairfield by Midland Typesetters, Australia
Printed in Australia by McPherson's Printing Group

10 9 8 7 6 5 4 3 2 1

For Margaret

And with many thanks to Annette, Angela, Ali, Kirsten and Lyn for their invaluable advice, and to Tim for sorting my Jumars from my prusiks

Heart hammering, she leaped up onto the ridge and begin to run. The rock was fractured, treacherous, and her flailing feet sent stones skittering down the steep slopes on either side, from which flocks of seabirds rose protesting into the air, swooping and squealing. The equipment attached to her harness chinked and banged against her thighs as she ran, threatening to make her stumble. From behind and below she heard the shouts of her pursuers, calling her name, pleading with her to stop, but rage and fear drove her on. How could they have done this? She thought she heard one of them cry out in panic, as if falling, and she half turned her head to see, missing her step in the process. She scrambled for a handhold as her feet slid out from under her and she found herself hanging from the rock face. Looking down she saw the huge breakers crashing into the base of the cliff, a hundred metres below.

1

ove casts a strange light over everything. I recall the
moment precisely, as if watching a loop of dazzling film
played at half speed.

Through the French windows I can see one of our regular
guests, Justice Rory McGregor of the Supreme Court, sitting
on the terrace with a fat document on his knees. It is a late
Sunday afternoon in August, the last weekend of winter, and a
warm breeze has tantalised all day with its heartachey smells
of jasmine and pittosporum blossom. The low western sunlight
flickers through the angel's trumpet tree above the judge, who
sips from a cup of tea. I have the impression that he is having
difficulty concentrating on his papers, for he's staring down
over the rooftops to Rushcutters Bay, glittering with sailing
boats being readied for spring.

My Aunt Mary has gone to her bridge club leaving me in
charge, and I am in the dining room, setting the tables for
the next day's breakfast and thinking how odd it is that I
should find such a routine chore so comforting, like placing
the pieces for a game of chess—cup, saucer, plate, knife,
fork, spoon—in which no unexpected moves are permitted.
This place—Mary's little hotel—is a refuge, an old house
screened by thick foliage from the tower apartment blocks
that have grown up around it, a place of quiet predictability,
of shady nooks and heavy dark timbers sheltering beneath a
spreading orange tile roof. I have returned to the land of cosy

abbreviations—the garbo, the ambo and the firey—and I just want to sink into it and disappear.

The reception bell sounds from the hall and I put down the cutlery to go and see, and there, standing at the counter, is Anna.

The sight of her jolted me, an Alice-in-Wonderland moment, as if I might be drawn back down some long vertiginous tunnel to the past. She wasn't aware of me and I was tempted to step silently back behind the shelter of the dining-room door, but that would have been absurd.

'Anna!'

She spun around, the smile forming immediately on her lips, not at all surprised to hear my voice. Clearly she had expected to find me here.

'Josh!'

As she came towards me I was momentarily at a loss, not sure how to greet her. We were old friends, but time and circumstances had formed a yawning gap, and though it was only four years since we'd last met, we both hesitated to cross it. She reached out and held me at arm's length for a moment, examining me, then ducked her face forward to kiss my cheek. I held her for a moment, feeling a little surge of affection alongside the foreboding.

'You've changed, Josh,' she said. Her smile was genuinely warm, that familiar ironic grin threatening to break into a laugh of pleasure at seeing me, and I felt ashamed that my initial reaction had been to run.

'Oh?'

'Mm.' Her head cocked to the left. 'You look more serious, a man of the world.'

'It's good to see you again, Anna. Is this a chance visit?'

'I heard you were coming back.'

'Really?' That surprised me. 'How was that?'

'I ran into your aunt in town a month ago. Didn't she tell you? She said you were coming home. Is it for good, or just a visit?'

'We'll see,' I said vaguely. Mary hadn't mentioned meeting Anna, but I'd noticed other signs of forgetfulness. 'Glass of wine?'

'Yes, please.'

We settled ourselves in the comfortable armchairs by the windows of the empty lounge. I'd been back ten days, but the place still had an air of unreality about it, as if I might jerk awake at any moment and find myself in a crowded tube train. I relished the abstraction of it, the invisibility of the stranger, knowing that it wouldn't last, especially now that Anna had come.

The smile faded from her face, and without that sparkle I realised how much she, too, had changed. She'd lost weight, and her features seemed to have become a little harder and, in the process, to have developed more character. There was a small scar on her temple that I was sure hadn't been there before, and shadows around her eyes, and I wondered if she might have been ill. Certainly she was much better groomed than in the old days, in a smart blouse and skirt, her face neatly framed by an immaculate helmet of black hair.

She turned to me with a serious look, as if trying to read something from my expression, and I felt a need to say something innocuous to head her off. 'That's our judge.' I nodded at the figure through the window, now in murmured conversation with Socrates, Mary's labrador, sprawled at his feet. 'Justice McGregor. He's due to hand down sentence tomorrow on the man who murdered those two women on the train.'

'Oh, that case. How terrible. He looks as if he's discussing it with the dog.'

'Could be. They have a lot in common. The same sense of humour, for instance—the judge likes to hide the dog's rubber bone, while Socrates steals his gloves. And though the judge spends his time wrestling with complex moral issues while Socrates can't spell cat, I'm not sure that there's such a fundamental difference between them, actually.' I stopped abruptly, realising that of course it was Luce who'd taught me to think like that.

'*Actually*.' She grinned. 'You've become English, Josh.'

I shrugged. 'Cheers. So what are you up to these days, Anna?'

She was a manager at an aged-care nursing home out at Blacktown, she said. I found it hard to imagine this. The four-year gap was shrinking again while we talked, the physical differences fading as I tuned in to the Anna I'd last known, a 22-year-old student.

'Must be a responsible job, I suppose?'

'Fairly.' She frowned, creases forming between her dark eyebrows. 'They . . . need a lot of help, our clients.' The way she said it sounded almost like a penance. 'And how about you? How was London?'

I took a deep breath and did my best to be entertaining without going into too much detail. 'It got pretty intensive towards the end,' I concluded. 'Good money, you know, but pressure, and hellish hours. After four years I felt I needed to come back, at least for a while.' I thought I sounded reasonably plausible, becoming a better liar with practice.

'Well, you've had lots of responsibility too. Can I have some more wine?'

It suddenly occurred to me that she was anxious, hesitant about bringing something up, and I thought I knew what it was, the same unspoken thing that had been preoccupying me ever since I'd first caught sight of her.

I stood up to fill her glass, and then, as if it had just occurred to me, said, 'You know, I was devastated not to make it back for Luce's service. There was a mix-up with your message— I'd moved to a new address and by the time it reached me the date had passed and there didn't seem any point in flying back. I'm sorry. It must have been terrible.' I realised I was asking her to forgive me.

'Yes,' she said simply. 'It was.' I gathered that not only was she not going to make it easy for me, but that this wasn't what she'd come about.

'Her father took it hard, I suppose.'

'He didn't show much, but, yes, I think so.'

'I . . . I wrote to him, but I didn't get a reply.'

'I don't think he replied to anyone.'

'Ah.' Although the activity of refilling our glasses meant I hadn't had to meet her eye, I was acutely aware of her watching me closely, as if straining for a false note. I found I couldn't think of anything more to say.

Finally she spoke. 'Haven't you been reading the papers, Josh?'

'Not much; I've made a point of avoiding them for as long as I can. Why?'

'About Curtis and Owen?'

I shook my head, intrigued, wondering how they might have got into the news. 'What have they been getting up to?' I said with a laugh.

She didn't smile back, but looked down and traced a finger around the base of the glass. 'A couple of weeks ago I got a phone call from Suzi.'

'Owen's wife? Oh yes? How are they both? Any more children?

I didn't keep in touch.' In fact I hadn't kept in touch with any of them.

'I did, with Owen and Curtis. We used to catch up from time to time. They still went climbing together.'

'Really?' I gave her a look, which she avoided.

'Yes. They'd gone to New Zealand for a week. Suzi had just heard that there'd been a bad accident on Mount Cook. Curtis was killed.'

I felt the impact of the words like a physical blow, wiping the stupid smile off my face, pinning me back in my chair. 'Curtis? Dead?' An image of him came vividly into my mind, red curls spilling out from under his climbing helmet, a big cheeky grin on his face.

Then I remembered I had noticed a newspaper item, not long after I'd got back: two Australian climbers hurt in the Southern Alps, names withheld. I'd read it with a kind of shiver, thankful that all that was behind me. I must have missed the later reports.

'. . . Curtis's parents.'

'What? Sorry, Anna, I didn't catch that.'

'They were abroad, Curtis's parents, and they were having trouble tracing them.'

'What about Owen?' I felt disoriented, unable to think clearly.

'Yes, he was very badly hurt. Suzi was hysterical. They wanted her to fly out straight away, but their new baby was sick, and she couldn't go . . .' Another image, Owen beaming through his glasses, a small child perched on his shoulder.

'Dear God.'

'You've heard nothing of this?'

'No, no . . . Go on.'

'Well, I said I'd go. I caught the next plane to Christchurch, where the boys had been flown. I made it just in time to be with Owen when he died.'

'He died? Owen too?'

'I thought you must have seen it in the news. It was on TV too.'

No wonder she'd been looking at me strangely. 'God, that's just terrible, Anna. I can't believe it.' I reached out my hand to grip hers. It felt cold.

She nodded sadly, knowing the arithmetic that was going through my head. There had been six of us at university, six friends who went rock climbing together. Now three were dead: Luce first, and now Owen and Curtis.

'Just three of us left,' I said. 'You, me, and . . . I suppose Damien is okay?'

'Oh yes. I spoke to him on the phone yesterday.'

I felt dizzy, unable to breathe properly, and suddenly I couldn't stand it, sitting there talking calmly like that, and jerked abruptly to my feet. 'I think I need something stronger than wine. Can I get you a brandy, Scotch?'

She shook her head and I headed out across the hall to Mary's private sitting room, where I took a deep breath and poured myself a whisky from the bottle in her sideboard. The clock on the mantelpiece softly chimed the hour, and I stood for a while staring dumbly at the pattern in the Indian carpet at my feet. I felt physically shaken by the news, yet I didn't seem to feel anything for them. I tried to picture the two of them, Curtis and Owen, but my brain didn't respond. Finally I thought of Anna sitting out there alone and I straightened up and opened the door. The judge, his report under his arm, was crossing the hall with Socrates, perhaps bent on a game of hide-and-seek. They looked at me and something seemed to strike the judge. He gave a guarded smile and gestured at the drink in my hand. 'Just the thing.'

I had the ludicrous idea that he was accusing me of stealing Mary's Scotch. 'I've had some rather bad news,' I blurted, and began telling him about Curtis and Owen, and about climbing, and about Lucy too, and I could feel the tears stinging the insides of my eyelids. Then Anna appeared at the door across the hall, and I shut up.

The judge said, 'My dear chap, of course I read about it. They were close friends of yours, those fellers? I'm so sorry.'

He sensed Anna behind him and turned, and I introduced them. We commiserated for an awkward few moments before I escaped with Anna, leading her out to the terrace, now deserted, where we sat down with a sigh. Across the bay deep shadow was rising like a purple tide so that only the tops of the buildings on the far ridge were glowing in the golden evening light.

I gulped at my drink. 'Sorry. These past weeks must have been dreadful for you. Have you seen Suzi?'

'Yes. Her mother has moved in with her. And Curtis's parents flew back as soon as they got the news. The funerals will be held on Tuesday. I'll give you the details.'

'Thanks.'

I tried to remember the last time I'd seen the two of them. It was the night before I left for London, my farewell party. I could remember Curtis, pissed, standing on a table to sing a farewell song, but not much more, for Luce had been there too, and the evening was a blur of booze and guilt.

Anna was very quiet.

'Is there something else?' I asked.

Her eyes met mine for a moment, then slid away. It was such an uncharacteristic gesture that I was disconcerted. Anna was sometimes stubborn and over-earnest, but never shifty.

'Something bad?'

'Maybe I should leave it for now. You seem pretty shaken up.'

'No.' My voice was off-key. 'No. You'd better tell me. What on earth is it?'

'It's about Luce, Josh.'

'Luce?'

'Yes.' She shifted uncomfortably in her chair. The light was fading and the evening air had suddenly lost its warmth. 'You have to imagine what it was like, when I arrived in Christchurch. I caught a taxi straight to the hospital as soon as we landed. It was dark, and there was a lot of activity outside—TV crews, reporters. At first the staff wouldn't let me see Owen, but eventually I persuaded them that I was representing his family, who couldn't get there for a day or two. From their reaction I gathered that that would be too late.

'It was hard to make him out at first among all the tubes and dressings, just a few pink and purple bits of his face visible. He was so still, eyes shut, as if he was completely absorbed in what the machines were doing to him, pumping, dripping, measuring. The nurse said they were amazed that he'd survived the flight to the hospital, and didn't expect him to last the night.

'The room was warm and after a while my attention drifted. I felt exhausted by it all, the journey, the emotion, and the knowledge of how it was going to end. It was almost like a physical thing, like gravity, the drag of death on life.'

Anna hesitated, glancing at me, and I nodded encouragingly.

'Anyway, I got up and stretched and walked around, and when I glanced at him again I was amazed to see that his eyes were open, looking straight up at me. I spoke to him, told him who I was, and how Suzi would be there to see him soon, and

11

he listened and seemed to understand. His mouth made a smile and then he said in a whisper, *Tell her I love her*.

'I wanted to hold his hand or something, but there was nothing of him that I could touch. Tears filled my eyes. He must have registered this because his lips moved again. He said, *No regrets*. You remember how we used to say that?'

'I remember.'

'I repeated it back to him, No regrets. They felt pretty hollow now, those stupid words. He closed his eyes and I thought he was gone, but the machines were still pumping away. Then, after a long while, his lids flicked open again and his eyes were wide and bright. *Only one*, he said. I asked him what that was, thinking he'd say something about his children, but instead he said, *Luce*.

'I wasn't sure if I'd misheard, and I repeated, Luce? *Yes*, he said. *I thought I saw her on the mountain, just before I fell. Snow dazzle . . . But what if I do meet her again? What can I say?* I didn't know how to answer. He gave a sigh and said, *We killed her, you know*.

'I thought he was getting confused, and I said, No, Owen, it was an accident, like this, the same as you. *No, no*, he said. *That's what we told everyone, but it wasn't true*. He was staring straight into my eyes and he seemed quite coherent. *It didn't happen that way, Anna*. You see, he knew my name, he knew who I was.'

'He actually said "We killed her"?' I asked, incredulous. The story made my skin creep, even though I simply couldn't believe it. I sensed myself edging away from it, something that I really didn't want to hear.

'Yes, exactly as I've told you. I started to tell him he was wrong, but he just closed his eyes and gave another big sigh and said, *Forgive me, Luce*. He didn't speak or open his eyes again. At about two in the morning the machines let off an alarm, and the nurses made me leave. He died soon after.'

We sat in silence for a while. Lights were coming on in the windows across the bay, and I said, feeling how incongruous the words were, 'I have to switch on the hotel lights, Anna. Hang on, I'll be back in a minute.'

As I went around the house I thought about what she'd said. It was awful, surely too awful to be taken seriously. Yet Anna clearly did. I tried to imagine what it must have been like to listen to Owen's words, and then to dwell on them all through the following traumatic days. No, Anna wasn't now the same girl I'd known as a student. Thinking about the way she'd handled this, I realised how much she'd changed in those four years. There had been no trace of melodrama in her telling of it. She seemed so much more serious, more deliberate—more adult, I supposed.

I returned to the terrace with the bottle of wine and refilled her glass.

'Who else have you told about this, Anna?'

'No one. I've been wrestling with it for the past ten days, quietly going mad.'

'I can imagine. You haven't spoken to Damien, or Marcus?'

She shook her head, but didn't elaborate. 'The other day I remembered your aunt saying you were coming back, and I had to come into town today, and I thought, if you were here, I'd mention it to you.'

I thought it odd, not only her not talking to Damien but also not phoning the hotel to make sure I'd be in, as if she were so reluctant to share this that she had left it in the hands of fate.

'I'm glad you did, Anna. Look, he was delirious, surely. His brain would have been scrambled by the fall—how far did they fall anyway?'

'About forty metres.'

'There you are then.'

'Into snow. No, his brain was about the only bit of him that they didn't seem too worried about. And he really did sound clear-headed, just for those few minutes.'

'Doesn't mean he wasn't hallucinating. He'd have been stuffed full of drugs, massively traumatised, on the point of death.'

'I've tried to convince myself of that, but you weren't there, Josh. You didn't hear the certainty in his voice.'

I decided to try another tack. 'There was an inquest into Luce's death, wasn't there? Did you attend?'

'Yes, every day.'

'Was there any suggestion of doubt? Any hint of foul play?'

'No. But they never found a body, and the rest of the group all told the same story, so there was no reason to doubt it.'

Curtis, Owen and Damien, the three who'd been climbing with Luce, and the organiser of the trip, Marcus Fenn. That was about all I knew of what had happened, that and the place—Lord Howe Island, out in the Pacific, five hundred kilometres off the New South Wales coast. Of the six of us who used to climb together, Anna and I were the missing pair. I wondered if she felt as guilty about that as I did. But then, she had no reason to.

'It's preposterous, Anna, to suggest that they would have deliberately done anything to Luce.'

'I know . . .' She shook her head helplessly. 'How much do you know about her accident?'

'Not a lot. Mary sent me a newspaper cutting.'

'I remember she came to the service.'

'Oh, yes, that's right. She told me about it, how so many people were there.' But not me. Not me.

Anna reached into her shoulder bag and pulled out a blue plastic folder. She handed it to me. 'I kept some cuttings.'

'Ah.' I stared down at the file but didn't open it. It only weighed a few grams, but it felt much more, and I understood why she looked so tired.

'Have a look—not now. Read it and maybe we can talk again.'

'All right, but I'm sure there's nothing to worry about. I mean, you just have to remember how we all were, Anna. There's no way . . .'

We swapped phone numbers and she got to her feet and began to make for the door. I followed, thinking that the hotel felt strangely quiet. It was as if the place were under a spell.

I opened the front door for her, and she turned and gave me a little smile, sad and wistful. 'I'm sorry, Josh. I had to tell someone.'

'Oh sure, of course. I'm very glad you did.' But that wasn't true.

We walked together across the forecourt of the hotel, what had once been a front garden but was now brick-paved to provide a few parking spaces for guests. Cars hummed past in the street, their headlights on in the fading twilight.

At the pavement she glanced back at the hotel. 'This is a wonderful place, isn't it? We all came here once, didn't we? Your aunt gave us lunch.'

'Yes, I remember.' The memory tugged at me, a warm and happy day, and on an impulse, as she turned to go, I added, 'Look, apart from this business, Anna, we should catch up, have a drink or a meal or something.'

She nodded without much enthusiasm, and I realised that she must have been as reluctant as I to make this contact, to cross that chasm back to the past.

2

A nna was right, it was a fine old building, though it seemed somewhat forbidding now as I returned to the front door, its upper floor balconies dark like empty eye sockets. Mary had carefully researched its story, and had a summary printed in little pamphlets she gave to guests. She had also had a number of old photographs illustrating its history enlarged and framed and hung along the hall, and I paused over these now as a distraction, hesitating to approach the file that Anna had left for me.

The first picture was of the architect, an elderly man with a white beard in the Edwardian style, and I imagined him deciding to let rip on this final grand commission, for he chose an extravagant version of the Federation Queen Anne style that was already going out of fashion at the time. The house's two storeys were a pattern book of wall finishes—shingles, roughcast render and tuck-pointed brickwork—and its roof was embellished with extravagant chimneys, attic windows and ridge tiles. It had oriel windows, bay windows and dormer windows, and its many balconies were draped with ornamental brackets and posts elaborated with curvilinear Art Nouveau decoration.

It was in fact a wonderful tour de force, and deserved the spacious leafy surroundings it had once enjoyed, and which were apparent in the second picture, taken almost a hundred years ago. It showed the building newly completed as The

Moorings, the home of a broker and financier and his large family, who were all posed outside the front. They looked immensely pleased with their grand new house in the best residential suburb of the inner city, on the ridge of Potts Point, high above the boats in the bays of Sydney Harbour all around, but I knew that disturbances were on their way. Within a year, Kingsclere, the first Manhattan-style apartment building in Sydney, was being erected nearby in Macleay Street, and the character of the leafy suburb would begin to change forever. And a couple of years after that the war in Europe would be under way. I wondered how many of those teenage boys, ranged in ascending height next to their father, ended up on the Western Front.

But it was the Depression that did for the owners of The Moorings, apparently, and they had departed by the time of the third picture, taken at the start of the Second World War. The house had clearly gone downhill, turned into bed-sits for dockyard workers and navy people, and its decline continued into the 1960s, when it was photographed by Gordon Harris, newly arrived in Australia and armed with a small inheritance and some experience in the hotel trade in Inverness. The Moorings became the Harris Hotel, and almost immediately Gordon met and married my Aunt Mary. There was a picture of them both outside the hotel soon after their wedding, and it was clear that Gordon, something of a dreamer, had made a very astute choice in the practical and hard-working woman at his side. Together they turned the place into a refuge for visitors to Sydney, its reputation passed on by word of mouth between naval administrators visiting HMAS *Kuttabul* at the end of the point, lawyers attending the Family and Supreme courts, and country politicians with business in state parliament. When Gordon died, Mary just kept on going. The final photograph showed her at the front door, the house now shouldered by much taller, blunter neighbours, inner-city apartment blocks that overshadowed the remnants of its old gardens.

It had always had a magical, enveloping character in my mind, a true sanctuary, and it was the first place I'd thought of when I returned to Sydney. But, for all its sheltering homeliness, it couldn't keep out the world, nor, it seemed, my own past.

There was some roast beef in the kitchen fridge, and I carved a few slices and made myself a sandwich. I took it to Mary's sitting room, leaving the door slightly ajar so that I could hear anyone coming into the hotel. Helping myself to another Scotch from her bottle, I sat down in one of her plump armchairs with the folder on my knee. I didn't want to open it because I could guess what would confront me, but eventually I had no choice. I turned over the flap and there it was, a picture of Luce. Even though I'd anticipated the effect, it still punched the breath out of me. As I stared at that familiar face, a happier version of the one I'd said goodbye to, a detached part of my mind coolly told me that I'd avoided this moment for four years, taken every kind of evasive action to put it off. In the matter of Luce's death I hadn't even got past stage one of grieving. I was still in denial.

Perhaps it was the same with all the deaths I'd experienced—Grandpa's, Uncle Gordon's, Mum's—all numbed, blanked out, never really confronted. But Luce was different, the first really important relationship in my life not framed by family ties, but freely chosen, miraculously given, then tossed aside.

The picture was an enlarged photocopy from a newspaper report, captioned *Climbing tragedy: young scientist named*. I think they'd got the picture from her father, taken probably at the time of her twenty-first birthday, for she was wearing a gold locket that had belonged to her mother and which he gave her on that day. She had a slightly cheesy smile as if for a special photo occasion, and the corners of her eyes were creased with love. And so alive, so brimming with life. I couldn't bear it and quickly turned the page.

To be met by the same picture again, smaller this time, with the accompanying report below.

> Police today released the name of the young woman missing on Lord Howe Island after a climbing accident and now presumed dead. Lucy Corcoran, 22, was a member of a university scientific field-study team surveying seabird breeding colonies on the steep cliffs below Mount Gower at the south end of the idyllic island. The team leader, biologist Dr Marcus Fenn, described how Corcoran, a very experienced climber, had become separated from her companions on the afternoon of Monday 2 October, before falling to the ocean, a hundred metres below where they were working. Islanders were joined yesterday by crews from boats in the Sydney to Lord Howe yacht race, recently arrived at the island, in searching for Lucy's body. However, local fishermen say that strong currents around the island, as well as recent shark activity, make it increasingly unlikely that her remains will be recovered. A police officer from Sydney has arrived on the island to assist local police in preparing a report for the NSW Coroner. The university has issued a statement expressing deep regret and announcing that it will hold its own investigation into the circumstances of Miss Corcoran's accident.

Recent shark activity . . . Didn't that seem a bit gratuitous? How would her family have felt, reading that? And what did it mean, *had become separated from her companions*?

I read on, through several other pages of photocopied press cuttings, from the first tentative report of an accident to the summary of the coroner's findings six months later. Much of it was repetitive, some contradictory, but as I read I also began to recall things Luce had told me about the expedition at the time. I remembered her explaining that birds migrating down the Tasman Sea between Australia and New Zealand really only had two islands available on which to rest, feed, mate and breed—Lord Howe and Norfolk. They were thus the focus of intense bird activity, and important centres for scientific study. Marcus Fenn had led teams to Lord Howe in previous Septembers as part of an ongoing research program, mostly comprising honours and postgraduate students from the zoology courses he taught at the university. In that particular year he had the unusual circumstance that three of the students in his honours tutorial group—Luce, Curtis and Owen—were Alpine-grade climbers, and he had decided to use them to extend the study into areas that had previously been inaccessible, on the southern cliffs. The fourth climber, Damien, who was doing a joint science/law degree, had joined them for the final two weeks of the four-week field trip, so as to make up two climbing pairs.

From what I could gather from the press accounts, as well as some notes Anna had included from the inquest she'd attended, the accident had happened on the final day of the expedition. Damien had been sick that morning and stayed behind, while Marcus Fenn and the three other climbers were taken by a local fisherman, Bob Kelso, on his small boat to the foot of the southern cliffs below Mount Gower, where they had been studying a colony of masked boobies and other seabirds. The climbers were put ashore and began to scale the cliffs, while Marcus returned with Bob Kelso to the main settlement of Lord Howe, at the north end of the island, where the scientists were renting a cottage. At about two o'clock that afternoon Marcus received a radio message from Curtis, saying there had been an accident. He later described how the climbers had been working on a rocky shelf a hundred metres up the cliff, where the birds were nesting. The shelf appeared stable and safe, and they had worked on recording details of the colony with their body harnesses unattached to the climbing ropes, because of the risk of snagging and disturbing the nests. After lunch Luce moved off on her own to check some nests further across the cliff face. She had rounded a stone outcrop, out of sight of the other two, when they heard a cry, followed by the sound of falling scree. Hurrying over to the place, they discovered that a section of the shelf appeared to have collapsed, sending Luce down into the ocean below. There was no sign of her in the water or on the rocks.

A slight noise disturbed me, and I sat abruptly upright, conscious that I had no idea how long I'd been sitting there.

'Josh? Are you all right?'

I blinked, and saw Mary register the empty glass at my elbow, the half-empty bottle beside it, and the folder on my knee.

'What is the matter, dear? Are you upset?'

'Oh . . . no. It's all right.' I took a deep breath and closed the folder.

She looked closely at me, then slowly sat down in the armchair on the other side of the fireplace. 'What's happened?'

21

Mary's sister, my mother, died when I was ten, and I think there is perhaps some residual confusion in my mind between the two of them. From photographs it's apparent that they did look very alike, although not twins—Mary was the elder by fourteen months—and I transferred some of my feelings for my mother onto my aunt. More death-denial, I suppose. At any rate, this transference was not entirely one-sided, and on occasions such as this Mary was quite capable of assuming a maternal role.

'Come on, tell me.'

So I sighed and told her about Anna's visit, and about Curtis and Owen's deaths.

'Those two climbers in New Zealand? Oh, Josh, I read about them, but I didn't make the connection. I met them, didn't I? They came here once.'

I nodded.

'Oh, you poor thing. No wonder you're upset. That's shocking, especially after . . .' Her eyes dropped to the folder on my knee, and a small interrogative furrow formed on her brow.

'It's sort of more complicated than that,' I said, and told her the rest, about Anna's story of Owen's confession and her file on Luce's accident.

I handed it to her and she turned the pages, pondering on it in silence, then said, 'You knew them, Josh, but it's very hard to believe.'

'Exactly. I knew them all well, really well, and I just can't believe it. I told her so. Owen was badly hurt—he must have been incredibly confused.'

'But . . .' she gazed at me, sympathetic but probing, 'Anna thinks there's something in it?'

'Maybe. Yes.'

'What does she propose to do?'

'She doesn't really know. She asked me to read that file, and think about it, and then talk it over.'

'I always liked Anna. The quiet plain one, but very loyal, I always felt, to Luce especially. Sensible, I imagine?'

'She had her moments, but yes, today I'd say . . . sensible.' What I was thinking was that Anna had seemed almost weighed down now by being sensible, the old flights of fancy firmly in check.

'Yes. I remember wanting to slip a bottle of shampoo into her bag that day they came here. But when I met her a few weeks ago she was very smartly turned out. Quite the young business-woman. And this file . . . it's brought it all back, about Lucy?'

'Yes.' It was the drink, I suppose, but I felt a desperate need surge up to talk about this, to confess. 'I . . . I don't think I ever really faced up to the reality of it at the time, you see. I went to London that August, remember, the month before they left for the island? Then, when the accident happened, Anna tried to let me know through Dad, who sent me a letter, only he used my first address in London and I'd already moved on. So it was actually early November when I heard, and by then it was all over. I was very shocked, of course. I felt helpless, but also . . . Well, it just seemed so unreal. I mean, people don't tend to plunge a hundred metres into shark-infested waters in London. It seemed preposterous, somehow. I couldn't really talk it over with anyone, talk through how I felt. So I just smothered it up, tried not to feel any-thing at all.'

This was getting sticky, and I warned myself to shut up.

'Lucy was very special,' Mary said, and the warmth in her voice, and the use of her proper name, felt like an unconscious rebuke, as if to say that my appreciation of her had been rather inadequate. Well it had, and I felt the tears climbing up the back of my throat again. I coughed, and tried to pull myself together. 'The service was very moving,' she went on. 'So many people.'

'Where was it?' I realised I had no idea.

'In Orange, where she came from. The family seemed to be highly regarded. Well, the country, you know, they stick together at times like that.'

'I remember you told me you went.'

'Yes. It was a good trip. I stayed overnight. I thought I should, well, represent us.'

Me, she meant, and I began to suspect that she had understood more about me and Luce, and about what I should have felt and should have done, than I had realised.

'What do you think I should do now?' I asked her.

'Is there anyone else you can talk to?'

The obvious people were Damien and Marcus, of course, the remaining members of the group, but I wasn't sure how they'd react to revisiting what must have been a very painful experience. 'Not really.'

'I think you need time to come to terms with this, Josh.'

'Yes.' What I really wanted, I suspected, was for Anna to just go away and leave me alone. 'Curtis and Owen's funerals are on Tuesday. I'll be seeing Anna again then.'

'It must have been very hard for her, dealing with this on her own. I'm sure it will reassure her to be able to talk it through with you. And maybe vice versa, eh?'

She patted my knee and I nodded. Mary's sympathy was consoling, but part of me resented it. For four years I'd made my own way in the world, about as far from home as you could get. One thing I felt I didn't need was mothering.

'Fair enough,' I said gruffly, and got to my feet, correcting for a slight unsteadiness.

In the hall we encountered the judge and Socrates again.

'Ah, Mary. How was bridge?'

'A bit strained tonight, Rory, I'm afraid. My usual partner didn't turn up and I had to play with someone who had some rather odd ideas about bidding.'

'Oh dear.' He regarded me suspiciously, frowning at the empty glass in my hand, and it occurred to me that perhaps the judge didn't like me. Maybe I was in the way.

'I'll make your warm milk, Rory,' Mary said, and he beamed. I thought of the murderer in his cell at that moment, awaiting the fate that Rory would perhaps finalise over his warm milk, and felt a little chill. 'Why on earth are you only wearing one slipper?' Mary added.

'Ah yes.' The judge gazed at his feet in some bemusement. 'I seem to have mislaid the other one. I rather thought I might check Socrates' basket.'

'Good idea. Come along.'

I found it hard to get to sleep that night. My mind put images to the bald descriptions in the newspaper cuttings: the cliffs of Mount Gower, the rocky shelf, the projecting outcrop behind which Luce had disappeared, the scramble when they heard her cry out . . . And Owen's words, *It didn't happen that way*.

Finally I wept a little, for Luce. It wasn't like a dam breaking. More like something frozen beginning to melt.

3

There was a big crowd gathered in the forecourt of the church when I drove past, and I had to go on several blocks before I could find a parking space. I didn't recognise anyone as I joined the queue at the foot of the church steps to sign the attendance book. Then, turning away, I found myself facing Damien. He seemed larger, more forceful, as he gripped my hand and pulled me into a bear hug, slapping my back.

'Fantastic to see you, Josh. I didn't know you were back. Isn't this just sickening? What did they think they were doing? Crazy bastards. God, I'll miss them.'

He *was* larger, by half a dozen kilos at least, and smoother somehow. When we were students he'd had a beard and had seemed quite rugged, but the beard had gone now and the look was much sleeker. But the change was to do with his personality, too, or his projection of it. He'd always stepped in when our group needed a bit of leadership, but now I had the impression that he didn't wait to take charge.

Something over my shoulder caught his attention and he said, 'I'm going to have to shoot off straight after this, but we must catch up.' He slipped a business card out of his top pocket. 'Here.'

'You're a lawyer?' I said, noting the name of a big law firm in Martin Place.

'Yes, I gave up on science the year you left, concentrated

on law. Commercial mainly, up your street. Who were you with in London, by the way?'

'BBK, a German bank . . .'

'I know them, they're clients of ours. So you're working for them in Sydney now? With Victor?'

'No. I'm looking around first.'

'Okay. Who was your London boss?'

I hesitated. 'Sir George Henderson.'

'Don't know him. Well, look, give me a call. Soon.' He clapped me on the arm and moved off. I felt as if I'd been strip-searched. I joined the crush moving into the church. I couldn't see Anna anywhere.

It was a good service, I suppose you'd say, very professional. Parts of it moved the people around me to tears, especially when Curtis's brother delivered a heartbroken eulogy, but I couldn't feel anything. It all seemed so remote from the two blokes I'd known. Only the pair of caskets, side by side on the altar steps, stopped me short, metonymy in spades.

But afterwards, outside the church, I had to face Owen's wife, Suzi, and that was painful. She was weeping and looked totally washed out, as if she hadn't slept in days. We hugged each other and she whispered her thanks to me for coming. I hardly knew what to say, and mumbled some platitude. Really, there are no words, are there? She was twenty-five, a pretty but not very bright girl with few options. A little boy was clinging to her hand, looking confused.

'Do you remember Thomas?' Suzi asked, sniffing and wiping her eyes.

'Of course. I used to babysit you. Can I have a hug?' I bent down and the boy gave me an awkward peck on the cheek.

Ranked behind Suzi were the families, her parents and Owen's holding the second child, a baby, and then Curtis's next to them, with Curtis's brother. I shook all their hands, and they said they recognised my name and knew I'd been a good friend to the two young men.

Anna was outside the church, standing in the shade of a large tree, the morning sun turning hot.

'Hi,' I said. 'You okay?' I saw that she'd been crying too, a little smear of make-up in the darker skin beneath each eye.

She hunched her shoulders. 'Did you see Damien?'

'Briefly. He seemed in a rush. He said a few words about the boys and then grilled me on my CV. Very focused.' I was remembering a more carefree Damien, a lad with an eye for the girls, who fell for him with bewildering speed. We never understood why because he wasn't particularly good-looking. We'd quiz the women afterwards, but they didn't seem to know either.

'That's what happens to us,' she said. 'A couple of months filling in six-minute charge-out time sheets and calculating his Christmas bonus, and Damien has turned into a wage-slave like the rest of us.'

'True enough. Want a bite of lunch?'

'I haven't got long before I have to get back to work,' she said, checking her watch. 'Let's talk over a sandwich, then you can drop me at the station.'

We found a café not far from my car, and sat at a window table. She ordered turkey on Turkish with a mineral water, and I a large cappuccino and a ham sandwich.

'Did you get a chance to read the cuttings?'

'Yes, and I've been thinking a lot about what you said. It seems to me that Curtis and Owen felt that they'd been negligent in some way. Maybe they persuaded Luce it would be easier if she unclipped her harness, or maybe they had an argument about something that made her go off on her own.

I don't know, it could have been a dozen things, but when she fell they blamed themselves. They were ashamed and didn't mention it at the inquest, and so, in his dying moments, Owen felt compelled to say that they'd killed her, and that it hadn't happened exactly as they'd said. But they didn't *murder* her, for goodness' sake. Nothing like that.'

She stared at me for a long moment, considering this, and then she said quietly, 'Are you really sure about that, Josh?'

I had a sudden feeling that I'd underestimated Anna all those years; that, from within the shadow of more glamorous friends, she'd learned to observe and become rather more perceptive than I'd given her credit for.

I shrugged. 'I just think, maybe that's the best thing we can believe.'

She frowned, then shook her head. 'I want to know the truth. I owe that to Luce. I think we both do.'

I winced, bowed my head. 'Yes.'

'The thing is, if we can't rely on what Owen and Curtis said afterwards, then we really have no idea at all what happened to her. All we can say for sure is that she disappeared.'

I was struck by her choice of words, *disappeared* rather than *died*. 'But is it possible to know the truth now? What can we do? If you go to the police with your story of Owen's last words, I'm sure they'll just tell you to forget it.'

'I know.'

'Tell me, why didn't you speak to Damien about this?'

She looked uneasy, poking at her food. 'Maybe I've been letting my imagination run away with me, I don't know. But if we can't rely on what Owen and Curtis said, can we believe Damien and Marcus either? They all stuck together at the inquest, told exactly the same story. Perhaps . . . there was some kind of cover-up.'

I gaped at her. 'A conspiracy? Oh, come on now, Anna. That is getting a bit wild.'

'Yes, probably.'

We ate in silence for a while. When we were finished I wiped my mouth and said, 'So, what can we do?'

'I was thinking—the police prepared a very detailed report of the case for the coroner. It contained transcripts of all the interviews they conducted, diagrams, timelines, everything. I saw it at the inquest, a big fat document, the coroner referred to it all the time. If we could get hold of that, we might find something.'

'Okay, yes, we could try.' I was trying to sound encouraging, just to satisfy her, but it sounded pretty hopeless to me. 'Any idea how we could get hold of a copy? Do we apply to the coroner's office or something?'

'I thought we might ask Damien to get it for us. I thought it might be a sort of test.'

I laughed. 'You devious . . .'

'Only it won't work if I see Damien on my own. He'll just laugh at me and brush me off with some condescending remark.'

I thought she was probably right about that. There had always been a slight undercurrent of antagonism between them, something to do with Damien's rather cavalier approach to the opposite sex, I assumed.

'He gave me his card.' I reached into my pocket and showed it to her. She nodded and looked expectantly at me. I hesitated, then decided that Damien was probably the only one who could reassure her. I took out my phone and dialled his mobile number.

'Stokes.'

'Damien, hi, it's Josh.'

'Oh, hi, Josh.' I could hear the surprise in his voice.

'I met Anna at the funeral, in fact I'm sitting having a cup of coffee with her now. We've been talking things over and there's something we'd like to discuss with you.'

'Oh yes? What is it?'

'It'd be better if we sat down together, the three of us. Have you got a half-hour you could spare in the next day or two? We'll come to you.'

He laughed. 'Mysterious, Josh. Well, of course, if it's important. Stirred up a few memories today, did it?'

'Yeah.'

We waited, then he came back on. 'How about this evening, six-thirty? There's a little bar across the street from where I work—Sammy's Bar.'

'Fine. See you there.'

As soon as I hung up Anna thanked me and said she had to go. We got in Mary's car and I drove her to Central to catch her train back to work.

'See you tonight,' I said, and she waved and ran off into the crowd.

I arrived at Sammy's Bar with ten minutes to spare and saw Anna already there, sitting at a corner table with a glass of mineral water and a look of lock-jawed determination. I bought a beer and joined her.

'Your clients all tucked up for the night?' I asked.

She smiled, looking tired. 'They're watching a movie, which means they'll all be asleep.'

'So, what's the approach?'

'Will you tell him? I think it'll work better that way.'

'Fine.' I took a welcome gulp of cold beer and looked around. The bar was filled with clusters of corporate warriors, young men and women making quick sharp judgements on the action of the day. They were the same as the people I used to know in London, and as I picked up snatches of their insider chatter I felt like a deserter, absent without leave. There was one table with four girls sitting together. A spotlight overhead caught the hair and face of one of them and she reminded me of someone. At first I couldn't place the memory, and then it came to me, a girl I'd met not long after I'd first arrived in London. I remembered feeling guilty with her, as if I was being unfaithful to Luce, not realising that Luce was already dead. What surprised me now was how long it had taken me to make the connection, as if my London experiences were already being packed away in mental drawers of long-term memory. Soon it would be as if London, all four years of it, had never happened, and I felt a stab of resentment that Anna was dragging me straight back to the time before I'd left.

'How's your love-life these days, Anna?' I asked. 'Do you have a partner?'

She shook her head. 'Not at the moment. You?'

'No. There was someone in London, but . . .' I shrugged. 'How about Damien? Do you know?'

'Oh yes, rather predictable really. He married the senior partner's daughter. Captured her heart within three weeks of joining the firm, I believe.'

'As soon as he'd mastered the six-minute time sheets, eh? Were you invited to the wedding?'

'Yes, but I couldn't go. Owen told me about it afterwards. Very plush apparently.'

'Kiddies?'

'I don't know.' She glanced over my shoulder. 'Here he is now.'

I got to my feet and went over to intercept Damien, feeling the need for a little foreplay.

'Hi, Damien.' Another firm handshake. He was in shirt sleeves rolled up to the elbow, his thick silk tie unfastened, a sheen of sweat on his face as if he'd just walked out of a heavy meeting. 'You look as if you could do with a beer.'

'Too right, but better make it a mineral water, mate. I'm in the middle of a conference.'

'Oh, sorry. Listen, Anna's just told me you're hitched. Congratulations!'

He grinned. 'Thanks. We wanted to invite you, but I didn't have your address.'

'What's her name?'

'Lauren. Look, I'm sorry, but I can't stay long. What's this all about, Josh?'

'Oh, just something that came up when we were talking after the funeral.' I paid for his drink and we made our way between the gesticulating combatants to our table. I noticed that Damien, too, seemed unsure how to greet Anna, then braced himself and bent to kiss her cheek.

They exchanged brief compliments about how they both looked, Anna reserved and Damien expansive, trying to gauge her mood.

'So, what do we need to discuss?'

'The funeral got us talking about Luce's death, Damien,' I said.

'Oh?' He looked wary.

'Yes, about how the two of us weren't there, with the rest of you, when it happened. And then the fact that she was never found . . . We discovered that we've both been left with a sense that it's never been resolved.'

'Resolved? But—'

'Oh, I know it has in a legal sense, but emotionally, you know? For us. We feel a kind of guilt.'

'We all do.'

'But you went through it all at first-hand. It must have been terrible for you, but at least you can feel you did what you could. We just weren't there.'

'So, what, you want me to tell you about it?' He glanced pointedly at his watch.

'We'd like to get hold of the police report to the coroner. The full report. That way we can understand exactly how it unfolded.'

He looked startled. 'Really? Well, I suppose you could apply—'

'We don't have a direct interest,' Anna broke in. 'I mean as far as the coroner's concerned. I understand the Coroners Act provides that an interested person can apply to the registrar of the local court for a copy of all or part of the coroner's file, but they have to show sufficient cause.'

This sudden display of homework, delivered in a low rapid voice, was rather jarring, and undermined my attempt to sound casual. 'I don't think we'd be successful,' she went on. 'But you could get it. You're a lawyer.'

'Commercial lawyer,' he murmured, frowning at a coaster on the table between us.

'Still, you must know people who know people. Your father-in-law's very highly regarded, I believe. I'm sure you could get a copy for us.'

He looked from one to the other of us. 'Is that really necessary? I can show you newspaper cuttings I kept . . .'

'We've seen the cuttings,' Anna persisted. 'We'd like more detail.'

He took a deep breath, thinking, raised his glass to his lips, placed it carefully back on the table, then said, 'All right, I'll see what I can do. I can't promise, but I'll do my best. Okay?'

'Thanks, Damien,' I beamed, surprised.

'And now I really must get back. Great to talk to you both again. You look as if you're working too hard, Anna. Maybe you should do a bit of climbing with Josh, now he's back. I'll be in touch.'

We watched him leave, and I took a deep breath. Anna gave me a tight, expressionless look and said, 'Now I'd like a vodka tonic. You?'

'Yeah, me too.'

I made to get up, but she waved me down. 'I'll get them.'

When she returned with the drinks I said, 'Sounds like you've been doing research, about the Coroner's Court.'

'One of our residents worked there for thirty years. She filled me in.'

'So, did he pass the test?'

'What do you think?'

I shrugged. 'He was reluctant, but that's understandable. Yes, I think he passed. You?'

She sipped her drink, staring into the far corner of the bar, then said, 'No. I didn't think he passed at all. I bet he finds it's impossible to get hold of that report.'

4

The hotel became busy again that week and into the next, and I put in a lot of time helping Mary with the daily routine, filling the hours in between with overdue maintenance work. I cleaned out the gutters and repaired a section of uneven paving in the small garden below the terrace at the back, and as the days passed and I heard nothing I began to think that the whole thing had fizzled out. But I still had Anna's file of cuttings, with their photos of Luce and the others, and when I went up to my attic room at night it was impossible not to turn them over, again and again.

I first set eyes on her at a summer wedding on a beach. It takes a lot of organising to have a wedding on a Sydney beach, and friends and relatives had been out there since early morning, roping off the designated area, raking the sand, setting up flowers. I didn't really know the couple, but had agreed to accompany my then girlfriend. Unfortunately our relationship had unravelled in the interval between the invitation and the event, so that things were a little tense by the time we arrived at what we both agreed would be our last outing together.

Everyone was dressed up for the occasion, the men of the wedding party in their fancy shirts and ties, the women in elegant gowns and hairdos, but everyone was barefoot on the sand, the celebrant included, and this gave everything a rather startled air, as if someone had played a practical joke. One of the bridesmaids particularly caught my eye, a slender girl with flowers in her short bobbed blonde hair. She stood very erect and was self-contained while everyone around her twittered and fussed. When she smiled her face came tremendously alive, and I thought from the economy and poise of her movements that she might be a dancer or an athlete.

After the ceremony we retrieved our shoes and went to the reception at the nearby surf club. At some point I found myself queuing at the bar next to one of the other bridesmaids, a raven-haired girl who struck me as rather shy. In fact it was only as I remembered this that I realised that my first contact with them wasn't with Luce, as I'd imagined, but there in that queue with Anna. She didn't seem keen to talk at first, but there was a crush at the bar and I was chatty, and she gradually became more open. We were both at the university, although we hadn't met before, and with the academic year about to start she told me the subjects she was taking. I showed more interest in her than I really felt, because I realised she was a friend of the blonde girl I'd noticed—whose name, she told me, was Lucy, or rather Luce. By the time I'd given her the three flutes of champagne she wanted she was quite animated and seemed enthusiastic about the idea of meeting up again. I suppose this was the first small betrayal in our story, my misleading Anna into thinking I was interested in her rather than her friend.

The following day, feeling a little bored, I checked the timetables for the subjects she'd mentioned, and two days later stood outside one of the large lecture theatres for an introductory lecture in STAT 303, a subject I'd taken two years before. There had just been a torrential late summer downpour, and the air was thickly humid, the trees dripping, students peeling off steaming rainwear. The girls were late, and the mob outside the auditorium had mostly moved inside by the time they came running along the concourse. I jogged up beside them as they joined the end of the queue, and called out, 'Anna! Hi.'

She turned and gave a bright smile of recognition and introduced me to Luce. I'd meant to be very casual and indifferent, but up close I found her smile even more compelling than before. I think I blinked rather stupidly, and then we were climbing up the stairs and into the back of the theatre, which was packed. The two girls squatted on a step of the side aisle, and I followed suit immediately behind them. Luce's hair was drawn up in a simple ponytail, while the back of Anna's head looked rather untidy, as if she'd had a go at cutting it herself. From where we were it was difficult to see the lecturer's podium, far below us. He strolled in ten minutes late—this was the Faculty of Management, after all—turned his back on the audience and proceeded to mutter inaudibly at the formula he began to scrawl across the board.

'What?' Anna hissed to Luce. 'What did he say?'

'I've no idea.' Luce shrugged with a movement of her head that revealed the most beautiful ear I'd ever seen.

I leaned closer, mesmerised, and whispered into it, 'That's the two-mean hypothesis test for large samples.'

She turned and our eyes met, just centimetres apart, and that was it, I think, at least as far as I was concerned.

'Is it?'

'Yes, here.' I wrote the formula on my pad, tore the page off and handed it to her.

'Thank you,' she said, and gave me the most wonderful smile, as if I'd written her a brilliant sonnet.

At the end of the lecture we got up, stiff from sitting on the concrete floor, and Anna said to Luce, 'Well, I didn't understand a bloody word of that.'

I said, 'If you're interested I've got the notes. I already did this course.'

Anna regarded me suspiciously. I think she'd already guessed what I was up to. 'Why, did you fail?'

'No, I got an HD. I thought this was something else.'

Luce smiled. 'You sound like just the person we need.'

I thought so too.

We went to a coffee shop and chatted. Luce was doing a Bachelor of Science, majoring in biology, Anna sociology, and I'd hit on the one subject they had in common, statistics. It seemed the two of them were old friends who'd been to the same school, and I sensed Anna's resignation that I was clearly more interested in her friend than her, as if this had happened many times before. But I didn't pick up any hint of competition between them, and felt that the slight belligerence that began to surface in Anna's manner was rather protective of her friend, as if she was used to fending off the attentions of unworthy males like myself. They both struck me as pretty fit, Anna slightly softer and slower than her friend, but still tanned and physically capable. I asked if they surfed or played a sport and Anna replied, with a touch of bravado, 'Yes, we climb.'

'Rock climbing?'

'Yes.'

I sensed from the decisive, almost challenging way Anna said it that this might be a key test of our fledgling relationship.

'Oh, great,' I said boldly. 'So do I.'

She looked deeply sceptical. 'I haven't seen you at the climbing club.'

'No, I don't belong. Actually, I'm a bit rusty. I've been thinking about joining.'

'You should,' Luce said. 'We meet most Wednesday evenings at the gym.'

'Where have you done your climbing?' Anna demanded, obviously not at all convinced.

'Oh, mostly in the Blue Mountains,' I said airily. 'A bit around Nowra.' It wasn't entirely bullshit; I'd done rock climbing as a sport at school, training on an indoor climbing wall and going on a couple of camps, one in the Blue Mountains where we did mainly bouldering and abseiling, and a longer one on the crags along the Shoalhaven River. 'What about you?'

'Yes, we've been to the Blue Mountains quite a lot,' Luce said. 'Diamond Falls? Bowens Creek?'

'Ah, yes,' I nodded. The names meant nothing to me.

'Last year six of us spent a month climbing in California, at Yosemite and Tuolumne. That was fantastic, if you like granite.' I found it hard to decipher her expression. She seemed amused, but whether she was just being friendly, or was thinking what a phoney I was, I couldn't tell, but if it would have helped I'd have gladly told her I was besotted with granite. The mention of the California trip should have alerted me, but I went on nodding eagerly, captivated by that smile.

'We did the DNB,' Anna added, in a tone that sounded like a warning.

'Really?' I hadn't a clue.

'We're planning to go to Nepal next.'

That did register. Wasn't that where the Himalayas were? Wasn't Everest somewhere around there? 'Oh wow, that would be fantastic,' I said.

Later, as I went back over this first meeting, unpicking every half-remembered phrase and gesture for its hidden meanings, I came to several preliminary conclusions. The first and most important concerned my chances with Lucy, or Luce as Anna called her. Were they gay? Was their double act some kind of game they played with dopes like me, attracted to Luce? I could believe it of Anna, protective of her friend and antagonistic to at least this male outsider. But all my experience of reading the signals given off by women told me that it wasn't true of Luce. I was convinced that she was as warm and sincere and *interested* as she appeared to be.

That was my first conclusion. My second was that these two women were out of my class. Their accents had told me that straight away. I imagined that the school they'd both gone to had been one of the better Sydney private schools, that their fathers were city businessmen or doctors, and that swanning off to California for a month hadn't been that big a deal. This wasn't necessarily a problem, just something that set off some well-tuned early warning signals. It's not that I was ashamed of my family, I told myself. In my heart I knew that Dad and Pam were good people, the best. And successful in business too. You may have seen their business, out on the Great Western Highway—bright and clean, with a five-metre wide meat pie tilted jauntily on the roof. Ambler's Pies won the Best Aussie Meat Pie national award three times during their thirty years of trading, and I know from extensive market research that they deserved it. My childhood memories all revolve around the central tableau of Dad labouring over the big stainless-steel table rolling and folding the dough, rolling and folding, to make that special flaky pastry which is so accurately depicted at gigantic scale on the roof, and of Mum in the kitchen nearby preparing her special rich beef recipes for which she was known to every truckie and rep on the highway. Just before she died, Mum passed on those recipes to Pam, the help they'd taken on when Mum first fell ill, and in due course Dad sealed the business partnership by marrying her. It all seemed very straightforward and admirable to me. And yet, the first time any of my new friends at university asked me what my parents did, I fudged it, mumbling something about hospitality and tourism, and later mentioning the Potts Point hotel as if it was theirs, rather than my Aunt Mary's.

The third conclusion came to me as soon as I looked up *Yosemite climbing* on Google. It seemed the DNB was climbers' shorthand for the Direct Northern Buttress of Yosemite's Cathedral Rocks, a six-hundred-metre granite cliff described bluntly as 'hard, with some scary loose flake in the middle'. The pictures looked absolutely terrifying to me, even without the scary loose flake. I decided that Anna had been exaggerating in order to frighten me off. Of course they hadn't climbed *that*.

So I turned up at the climbing wall the following Wednesday evening and Luce seemed pleased to see me, in an underplayed, almost shy sort of way that I stored away for future contemplation. She introduced me to some of their friends, including Damien, Curtis and Owen, then to the club secretary, who gave me a questionnaire to fill in and signed me up. Anna pretty much ignored me.

It didn't take long for me to realise that I was seriously out of my league. Apart from my lack of recent practice, my gear was all wrong, my thick-soled shoes clumsy and my shorts hampering my movements. As I struggled painfully up the easiest routes I watched the rest of them racing up ahead of me. The only good thing was that, clambering to keep up, struggling not to look like a total idiot, I didn't have time to worry about my fear of heights, which had been a recurring problem on the school climbing camps.

After a while I collapsed, humiliated, on a bench. My arms and fingers had lost all strength and I was soaked in sweat. Luce came and sat beside me, looking as if she'd used up no energy at all.

'Sorry,' I panted. 'Really am out of practice.'

'Don't worry, it's often like that after a gap.'

'But you're absolutely brilliant.' I couldn't hide my astonishment. The others were good, but she made them look ponderous. Smooth and balletic in her movements, she had seemed weightless. 'Did you really climb the DNB?'

She laughed. 'Didn't you believe us?'

'It's just . . . that's pretty advanced, isn't it? Maybe I should stick to statistics. I've brought those course notes, if you're interested.'

She studied me. 'But you won't give up, will you? I mean, I wouldn't mind some help with STAT 303, but this is . . .' she looked up at the people hanging in space above us, '. . . it's what I do.'

'Right,' I said, still waiting for the feeling to come back into my fingers. 'No, no, of course I won't give up. I'll bring my proper gear next time. These shoes are hopeless.'

Later, in the changing room, I overheard a snatch of conversation from two blokes in the next aisle. One said, '. . . won't see him again.' I caught the words 'bloody hopeless' in the reply, and they both laughed. When they left I saw that it was Owen and Curtis.

5

A week after our meeting at Sammy's Bar, Damien gave me a ring. He asked where I was living, and when I told him he said he'd call in at the hotel that evening after work for a chat.

He looked more composed that evening, in his expensive suit. I led him through to the bar and got us both a beer. He slipped off his jacket and dropped into an armchair.

'Sorry I was so rushed last week,' he said. 'I must have seemed rude. I was just preoccupied. Aaagh . . .' He stretched out in the seat. 'Trouble with clients is you have to listen to all the crap they come out with. We didn't get a chance to catch up. So how are things, now you're back?'

I handed him his drink and told him about what I was doing at the hotel.

'I remember you bringing us here,' he said, looking around. 'Lovely little place. As a matter of fact I've recommended it to several people since. Amazing it's survived, though. The site must be worth a fortune. You'd have thought someone would have snapped it up by now. Your aunt's well?'

'Very. And so you're really married, Damien.'

'That's right. Lauren. Wonderful girl, you must meet her. We'll have you for dinner soon.'

'Is she a lawyer too?'

'Yes, and a very bright one. Much sharper than me.'

'Same firm?'

'No, she works down the street. I sometimes look out of my window and see her walking past and I think, how was I ever lucky enough to catch her?'

I laughed. 'You were always good at that.'

He laughed at the compliment. 'Oh, now, I was no Don Juan.'

'I rather thought you were.'

'What? I never pinched one of your girlfriends, did I?'

'No, but I did wonder if you were after Luce at one point.'

'Did you? No, I may have harboured lustful thoughts early on, before you came on the scene, but I decided she was too tricky for me. That's got nothing to do with this business with Anna, has it?'

'Of course not.'

'Ah.' He didn't seem completely convinced. 'Well, I do know how it is with Anna.'

'How do you mean?'

'Oh, the dogged way she is when she gets some idea in her head. I gather this was her idea, wanting to get the police report?'

I made a noncommittal gesture.

'Anna and I haven't really kept in touch,' he went on. 'I was trying to remember if she came to our wedding, but Lauren says not. I can't remember how I heard about her breakdown. Maybe Curtis or Owen . . .'

'Breakdown?'

'Mmm, two or three years ago. Didn't you know? Perhaps a delayed reaction to what happened to Luce, I'm not sure. I'm guessing that's what this is really all about, getting you on side to help her work things out.'

'Was it serious, this breakdown?'

'I think so. Not that she was hospitalised or anything. Least as far as I know . . . Ah!'

Mary had heard our voices and put her head around the door. She recognised Damien, giving him a warm smile, and he got to his feet and stretched out his arms.

'Mary! How wonderful to see you again.' He kissed her cheek. 'I was just saying to Josh how it brought back so many memories coming here. I remember you made us all so welcome and gave us a fabulous lunch—roast lamb.'

'Did I?' She laughed, flattered by his charm.

'And tell me,' he went on, 'how are you coping with Mr Chang?'

'Mr Chang? From Hong Kong? Do you know him?'

'He's a client of ours. When he wanted to know where to stay in the city I told him he had to come here. I knew it would be perfect for him. Didn't he tell you?'

'Well, no. But he's one of my regulars now, Damien. I should thank you. He's such an interesting man.'

'And very rich.' Damien chuckled.

I poured Mary a glass of her favourite sauvignon blanc and she took it without shifting her eyes from Damien's.

'But I'm so very sorry about your friends, Owen and Curtis, Damien. You must be as devastated as Josh.'

'Yes . . . But at least they died doing something they loved.' I thought that sounded rather glib, and then he added, 'It's the people they left behind I feel most sad for, Curtis's mum and dad are devastated, of course, and as for Owen's family . . .'

'Ah yes.'

'I went to see them the other day, Suzi and the kids. It was Thomas's birthday at the weekend, you know. Six. He kept talking about his daddy. Heartbreaking. I felt so inadequate, taking him a little present. What can you say?'

'Oh, I know. And will they manage financially, now?'

'I'm helping Suzi with that, negotiating with Owen's employer and their super fund to get her the best possible deal.'

Mary put a hand on his forearm and gave it a squeeze, a glint of a tear in her eye. I thought guiltily that I might have gone to see Suzi too, but it hadn't occurred to me. I had no idea it was the boy's birthday. Frankly, I was amazed at Damien's thoughtfulness, and began to wonder if I'd misjudged him. Mary was obviously impressed. She said she had things to do in the kitchen, and gave him a big hug when she left.

'Anyway,' he said with a sigh, 'I've done what you asked.' He opened the briefcase he'd been carrying and handed me a thick spiral-bound document. The title read INQUEST INTO THE DEATH OF LUCY CAROLINE CORCORAN. I hadn't heard of the Caroline before. 'This is a copy of the complete police report to the coroner. It wasn't that easy to come by, but anyway, I pulled a few strings and managed in the end.'

'I really appreciate it, Damien.'

He sat back and took a deep draw on his beer and wiped his mouth. 'Well, good luck, but don't let Anna drag you into some morbid soul-searching is my advice. It was a shocking thing, but there's nothing we can do about it now. Oh, by the way, I ran into one of your old mates the other day. One of your BBK London pals, Brian Friedland.'

'Oh yes? I didn't know him well. He's in Sydney, is he?'

'Passing through. No, he said you hadn't been in the same office, but apparently he's moved over to Risk Management now, working as right-hand man for Lionel Stamp, your old boss, under Sir George whatsisname.'

I felt a chill deep inside me. His voice was casual but he was watching me closely, and smiling. 'Small world, isn't it?'

* * *

After he left I sat on the terrace with the report. It weighed heavily on my lap, hundreds of pages, tens of thousands of words devoted to Luce's last hours, but I just couldn't face it. What was I supposed to make of all that? I remembered the judge sitting in this same cast-iron chair, as reluctant to open the report on his knee, as uneasy perhaps at the futility of finding some needle of truth in such a haystack. I compromised with myself, reading the index. It listed the dozens of statements, diagrams, medical reports, telephone records and other documents compiled by Detective Senior Constable Glenn Maddox of the Homicide Unit, Major Crime Squad, based in Kings Cross, Sydney. Even allowing for the press interest in the case, he seemed to have been extraordinarily thorough. I wondered if it was usual for an accidental death to be investigated by someone from the Homicide Unit.

Then Mary called to me from the kitchen window, having trouble with a blocked sink, and I closed the report thankfully and went to help. Later I decided to take it to Anna at her work the next day. I was curious to see her in that setting, imagining her at the hub of a smoothly operating enterprise, surrounded by crisply uniformed minions and genteel clients. It took a few phone calls to track her down to the Walter Murchison Memorial Nursing Home at Blacktown, and the next morning I drove out there. I didn't warn her I was coming. I thought I'd surprise her—it was what she had done to me, after all, that first Sunday evening at the hotel.

The original house had been enveloped by a confusing aggregation of new wings and extensions, and these so filled the site that car parking was pushed out into the surrounding suburban streets. I found a space, eventually, and walked back to a driveway that seemed to lead into the nursing home. It ended in a yard blocked with two skips and a row of bins smelling of kitchen waste. Beside them was a large clear plastic bag, filled with shoes. To one side a ramp led up through a small densely planted courtyard. There was a steel gate at the top with a locking mechanism designed to foil the infirm. Eventually I managed to open it without dropping my bulky package, and stepped onto a broad veranda. Clearly I hadn't found the main entrance. After following the deck around the building for a while I came to a set of glass doors, through which I could make out elderly people seated in a lounge room. There was a keypad beside the doors and a sign that said RING BELL FOR ENTRY. I couldn't see a bell.

Eventually a tiny grey-haired woman appeared through the glass and tapped in the entry code on the pad on her side. The door opened to a gust of Elvis Presley from a loudspeaker somewhere inside, and I said, 'Thank you. I seem to be lost. I'm trying to find the manager.'

'Mr Belmont?' The woman was smartly dressed in a white blouse and dark suit, and I took her for a member of staff.

'No, my name's Ambler.'

'No, I mean you're looking for Mr Belmont, the manager?'

'Oh.' I wondered if I'd come to the wrong place. 'No, Anna Green.'

The lady chuckled. 'Ah, you mean our *activities* manager. Do you have an appointment?'

'No. I'm, er, here to deliver something she's expecting.'

'Follow me.'

I stepped into the room, my eyes adjusting to a dimmer light. The old people, seated in a circle of assorted armchairs, seemed either asleep or deep in thought, and oblivious to both my arrival and Elvis's 'Heartbreak Hotel'. There was a doorway on the far side, but to reach it we had to cross the circle of vinyl floor, in the middle of which lay a large white blob of something wet. A very shrivelled old man was hunched forward in his chair staring at it, white dribble running down his chin.

'Oh, Stanley!' the lady said. 'What have you done?'

Stanley didn't respond. At that moment a woman in a green apron passed the door and my helper called out, 'Maureen, Stanley's done it again.'

'That'll be right.' The woman swept in with a mop and set to work while we skirted the circle and made for the door.

'I'll take you to the library,' my friend said. 'I'm Rosalind, by the way.'

'You work with Anna, do you, Rosalind?'

'Not exactly.' She gave another chuckle. 'I'm seventy-nine—I'm one of the residents. But I do work with her in a way. I help her look after the library.'

'And Anna's in charge of activities, is she?'

'Yes, she organises the bus outings and bingo and sing-alongs. She's very efficient. I don't know what we would do without her. Are you in the aged-care business, Mr Ambler?'

'No, no. I'm a friend of hers. We were at university together.'

'Really!' She stopped and turned to examine me more closely, obviously intrigued. 'How very interesting. Do you see a lot of each other?'

'Not exactly. I've been abroad, and I'm just catching up with old friends.'

'Ah. We love Anna dearly, but she is something of a mystery to us. We'd like to learn more. For instance, is it true she was a mountaineer?'

'Yes, we used to go rock climbing together.'

'Ah! The two of you?' She gave me an eager glance.

'A group of us.'

'With a rather striking blonde girl?'

'That's right. How did you know that?'

'She used to have a photograph on her desk. You weren't in it, though.'

She was leading me through a confusing labyrinth of corridors in which every wall seemed to be painted a different colour and none of the furniture matched. In places we came across seated figures whose appearance shocked me, as if a Nazi doctor had administered some grotesque experimental poison that turned people into shrivelled wrecks. Naive of me, but I just hadn't seen anything like this before. The Nazi doctor was Nature, of course, and the poison was old age and its crushing diseases. There was nothing like this in EverQuest. My guide must have noticed my reaction, because she smiled at me and said, 'Don't worry, not much further.'

Finally we reached a door marked LIBRARY, and she stopped and indicated another door nearby with a label ROSALIND on it. 'My room is close by, you see? So convenient.'

The library door opened into a small room lined with bookcases on three walls, the fourth with tall French windows leading onto another veranda and dense greenery beyond.

'The library is Anna's special baby,' Rosalind said. 'There were no books here before she came. We used to sit like zombies in front of the TV, but now we have a reading group. We have a section of normal-print books . . .' she indicated one wall, 'as well as large-print books, and over there audio books.'

There were several armchairs, one occupied by a silver-haired woman wearing headphones, who seemed marginally less comatose than the folk in the corridors.

'Wait here and I'll see if I can find Anna for you.'

While I waited I idly scanned the authors on the shelves—Sayers, McDermid, Paretsky, Christie, Walters, Lord, Cornwell,

Evanovich . . . It took a moment for the penny to drop. When I opened the covers I found 'A. Green' written inside many of them, some yellowing with age. I remembered a conversation with Luce years before, joking about her flatmate's choice of reading matter. Anna had three kinds, strictly segregated into separate piles on her floor, as if she were afraid they might contaminate each other—coursework textbooks, feminist theory and crime fiction.

'Anna will be along in a moment.' Rosalind had reappeared at my side. 'Do you like murder mysteries, Mr Ambler?'

'Er, not much. Do you?'

'Oh yes, I'm an addict—many of us are. And the wonderful thing is that, at our age, we can read them again and again without remembering who done it. Why do you look puzzled?'

'Well, don't you find the idea of murder, death, a bit . . .' I was embarrassed, but she helped me out.

'A bit close to the bone?' She laughed. 'Not at all. Bring it on, the more gruesome and gory the better. Goodness, I worked for thirty years in the coroner's office. I saw plenty of the real thing.'

'Is that right? I bet Anna's interested in all that. Do you talk to her about your time there?'

'Yes, of course. She's always checking forensic details with me to make sure the authors have got it right. Can you tell time of death from stomach contents? Can you fit a silencer to a revolver? That kind of thing.'

'But what exactly attracts you to stories like this?'

She cocked her head and fixed me with her bright eyes, and said, 'Resolution, Mr Ambler. Something sadly lacking in the real world, you might say.'

Over her head I saw Anna standing in the library doorway.

'Thank you, Rosalind,' she said, 'it's time for your rest now,' and my guide smiled sweetly and left.

Anna looked at me cautiously. 'What are you doing here, Josh?'

'I've brought you the police report. Damien came good; he dropped it in at the hotel.' I handed her the package, which she took, hesitating for a moment before opening it and reading the title of the report.

'Have you read it?'

'Not yet.'

'Made a copy?'

I shook my head, then followed her to an office further down the corridor. On the way I caught a glimpse of an entrance hall with a receptionist's counter.

'What on earth were you doing, coming in the back way?' The office was tiny and crowded with machines and files. She opened the lid of a photocopier and slid the report in.

'The entrance wasn't clearly marked. Where's your office?'

She shot me a rueful glance. 'This is it.' She turned the page. 'Want a cup of tea?'

'Where's the cocktail bar?'

She smiled. 'Four blocks away. The cluey ones sometimes make it there. Take a seat anyway.'

I cleared a pile of magazines from the only chair and squeezed onto it. 'How long have you worked here?'

'A couple of years. I had an aunt living here I used to visit. I started to help out with the bingo games and the outings, and next thing they offered me a job.' She glanced at my face. 'What? You think I'm mad?'

'Well, no, I mean, obviously this is very valuable work. But how the bloody hell do you stand it?'

She bowed her head to the copier. 'It has its rewards.'

Then she added softly, 'I'm embarrassed.'

'Why?'

'You're comparing this to the exciting life you've had, making piles of money in London, and wondering where I went wrong.'

'Not exactly. It was exciting at times, but also a bit scary, and lonely, too, sometimes. The truth is, things didn't quite work out as I'd planned—nor did the piles of money.'

'Oh? What happened?'

'I'll tell you one day.' I cleared my throat and changed the subject. 'Rosalind showed me the library. She said it was one of your innovations. I'd forgotten how keen you were on detective stories. Still read them?'

'Mm.'

'You don't think, well, that they might be colouring your judgement about what happened to Luce?'

She looked up sharply. 'How do you mean?'

'Well, life isn't like that, is it? Things are left hanging, unresolved. Like with Luce—no reason for it, just a stupid accident. No body to farewell, no resolution.'

I thought for a moment she might be going to throw the report at me. Instead she turned the page, thumped the document back down onto the machine and said tightly, 'I heard a dying man confess to killing my best friend, Josh. I'm not fantasising or mixing up fiction and reality. I heard it.'

'Okay, okay. Sorry.'

'Anyway, when I've finished doing this we can both go away and read it and see what we think, and you can make sure that my judgement isn't *coloured*.'

I sat in silence while she finished the job. She handed me the copy and showed me to the front door. As I stepped out into the fresh air I said, 'What's with the shoes?'

'What shoes?'

'Outside in the service yard, there was a bag full of shoes.'

'That's the incontinents. It runs down their legs and they have to get new shoes.'

I hurried away, thinking that Anna's grip on reality was probably pretty tight.

6

In other circumstances I'd have just put my humiliating experience with Luce and her friends on the climbing wall down to experience, and gone on to find a new girlfriend somewhere else. But the remarks I'd overheard in the changing room really annoyed me. Those blokes were a couple of years younger than me—I was just starting my master's, while they were in the third year of their first degree—and I thought they were up themselves. Also there was Luce; I found I couldn't stop thinking about her. So I decided I'd better get serious.

The following day I went to a climbing equipment shop and blew my budget on some essential items. The most important single thing I would ever own, according to the fanatic who served me, was my rope. We settled on a kernmantle nylon sheath and core, 10.5 millimetres thick, 50 metres long, weighing 3.45 kilograms. Next were the shoes, a pair of all-round, glove-tight lace-ups with sticky rubber soles that would be the next best thing to climbing in bare feet, I was assured. Then there was the harness (a waist belt with separate padded leg loops for a less intrusive fit), the helmet, the chalk bag, carabiners and a book. I decided to leave the slings and quickdraws and all the other arcane devices for another day.

Later I enrolled at an off-campus gym with a climbing wall, where hopefully word of what I was doing wouldn't get back to Luce and her friends. I started weight training, climbing lessons and jogging, and in the evening memorised the book and practised knots, until I knew my prusik from my klemheist and could tie a figure-eight follow-through in the dark. In my room I fixed up a fingerboard, a piece of timber with strips of wood nailed to it to hang from, to strengthen the grip of my fingers. Later my climbing instructor told me of a concrete retaining wall in a secluded corner of a nearby park, where climbers had glued artificial holds to the surface for bouldering practice. According to my book, bouldering—that is, solo climbing on low rocks or walls without ropes—was the best way to sharpen technique, and I became a regular visitor to the place.

Looking back now, I can barely recognise myself in all this secretive and rather obsessive activity. Although I saw Luce from time to time in the following weeks, helping her with her statistics assignments or going out to the pub, I didn't mention anything about my training. I avoided seeing her with her friends, and made excuses for not going to their next climbing sessions while I desperately tried to get fit, strengthen the peculiar muscles that seemed to be crucial, and develop some minimal expertise. After a few weeks of excuses I could see that she was losing interest, and I realised I was going to have to make an appearance. They were all clearly surprised when I turned up, and more so when I put on my no-longer pristine shoes and made a reasonable showing on the wall. I was still hopelessly inferior to the girls, and to a lesser degree Curtis and Owen, but I actually outpaced Damien, who was probably still hung-over from lunchtime, and he generously conceded that I might be okay and said he'd shout us all at the bar.

We sat around a table together, Owen, Anna, Luce and I, with Damien and Curtis returning from the counter with beer, and they were friendly enough, but I still felt uncomfortable, the outsider, their conversation and humour full of references I didn't know and which they didn't bother to explain. I remembered Luce saying that six of them had gone climbing in Yosemite together, and I wondered who the other one had been. Then Curtis raised his arm and waved to someone at the door, and I turned and saw a tall lean man wearing a black shirt and jeans. He had shoulder-length black hair swept back from his face, and as he made his way towards us I saw that he was limping heavily, putting his weight on a stick in his left hand.

Curtis jumped to his feet and pulled another chair into the circle, and the man sank into it with a grunt, handing Curtis a fifty-dollar note which he took up to the bar.

Luce said, 'Marcus, this is Josh. Josh Ambler, Marcus Fenn.'

I got up and stretched my hand out to shake his. His face was deeply lined and tanned, his hair touched in places with grey, and I saw that he was much older than us, maybe mid-forties. He regarded me impassively.

'Josh has been climbing with us this evening, Marcus.'

'Really?' His voice was soft. Curtis returned and placed a large Scotch by his hand, and laid the change beside it. 'What do you do, Josh?'

'I've just started an MBA.'

His expression registered an involuntary wince and he took a quick gulp of whisky as if to clear a bad taste. 'Merchant banker, eh?' This caused general merriment.

'That sort of thing. How about you? What do you do, Marcus?'

'Oh, I work for this godforsaken institution, I'm sorry to say, and occasionally try to squeeze a little understanding into these guys' heads. Fairly unsuccessfully, I'd have to admit.'

I couldn't pin down his accent—Australian, certainly, but with what might have been an American flavour. His attention turned to Owen. 'How's Pop bearing up?'

Owen shook his head wearily. 'Bushed. If you have some dope for crying babies, please can I have some.' This was the first time I'd heard that Owen was a father. Apparently he was also married. 'Suzi's going spare.'

'If she needs a break,' Luce said, 'I don't mind doing the odd babysit.'

Owen seized on the offer. 'We'd really appreciate that, Luce.'

Marcus was observing this domestic exchange with a sardonic smile, as if he found the whole idea vaguely pitiful.

There was karaoke in the adjoining room, and everyone looked up and listened as the next song began. It was an INXS track, and they all joined loudly in the refrain, *Falling down the mountain*, all that is except Marcus, who leaned forward, shaking his head as if some kind of joke was on him.

They were all big INXS fans, apparently, still grieving for Michael Hutchence who'd died just over a year before. Trying to get more of a handle on each of them, I asked what else they liked. Curtis was toying with heavy metal, Owen nominated Silverchair, Damien Shania Twain, Anna U2 and Luce Savage Garden (possibly for the name). Marcus said nothing, but I'd have put him down for Leonard Cohen. Seeing my lip curl at this selection, Luce said, 'Well, what about you?'

'How about The Fall?'

They looked blank, then sceptical, as if I'd made it up following on the INXS number.

'Never heard of it,' Owen said.

'But you've heard their music. Remember that last scene in *The Silence of the Lambs*, when Clarice Starling stalks the

Buffalo Bill/Jame Gumb character through the dark house? The background music was The Fall, from their album *Hex Enduction Hour*. The track was called . . .' I hesitated as if pondering, then looked straight at Marcus, '. . . "Hip Priest".'

He stared right back at me, and there was a moment's silence. They still thought I was making all this up, and probably taking a poke at their crippled guru.

Then Marcus suddenly tossed his head back with a short bark of a laugh. 'You know, I believe he's right.' He slid the cash lying beside his whisky across the table towards me and said, 'Get us another round in, merchant banker, eh?'

I grinned and got up. 'Sure, Marcus.'

After that the evening went just fine, and when it was over Luce and I walked back to her place while the others got a lift in Marcus's old Jaguar, which he was able to drive with his good leg. I asked Luce what had happened to him, and she confirmed that he had been the sixth member of their climbing group in California, fifteen months before, and that it had been on that trip that he had taken the fall that had shattered his left leg, just a month or so after Hutchence hanged himself, hence the references.

'What happened?'

She shrugged. 'He just tried to push himself that little bit too far. He was a really good climber, and he'd have been able to make the move without any problem ten years earlier, but I think he was trying to prove something to himself, or to us, and got taught a nasty lesson. It was a terrible thing when it happened, right at the end of our trip. We had to climb up to him and bring him down. He was in shocking pain. He was in hospital in San Francisco for a week before they could fly him back, and then in Royal North Shore for another six weeks.'

We walked on for a while, and then she said, 'What did you think of Marcus?'

'I don't know . . . You all seemed rather overawed by him.'

'He's become more sombre since the accident, more angry. He used to be great fun. But he's brilliant, Josh, the most inspiring person I've ever met. Look, I'll show you.'

We had reached the door of the flat she shared with Anna, and she took me inside, where Anna was setting up an ironing board.

'We were talking about Marcus,' Luce explained to her. 'I want to show Josh the Oslo tape.'

'Fine.' Anna turned to me. 'We were debating in the car whether you made that up about The Fall. Marcus said no, but the others thought you were.'

'What about you?'

She narrowed her eyes at me. 'I think you told the truth. I can usually tell when people are lying.'

'Clever you.'

Luce found the tape she wanted and we sat together on the sofa as the picture came on. The scene was a stage with a lectern, large letters on the wall behind proclaiming OSLO ECOSOPHY SYMPOSIUM. A lone figure took his place behind the microphone to some scattered applause. I recognised a younger Marcus, vigorous, bright-eyed. His speech was in English, but I can't remember much of what he actually said, and what I can remember—something about the ancient Greek word for house, *oikos*, being the root for economy (stewardship of the household), ecology (knowledge of the household) and ecosophy (wisdom of the household)—didn't sound very exciting. But his presentation was inspiring, riveting in fact, as became apparent from the murmurs of approval from the unseen audience, gradually building to bursts of spontaneous clapping that punctuated his impassioned speech. The end was greeted with a huge wave of applause, and a second, rather elderly figure came striding onto the stage and grasped Marcus in a hug.

'That's Arne Naess,' Luce said, in a tone that suggested Moses himself had appeared.

'Who?'

'Arne Naess—you must have heard of him.'

'Sorry.'

Anna made a sort of clucking noise behind me, accompanied by a hiss of steam from her iron. 'He's just about the most important philosopher of the twentieth century, that's all. He invented deep ecology.'

I hadn't heard of that, either.

Luce said, 'He's also a great climber. The day after this he took Marcus onto the Troll Wall at Romsdalen. That is awesome.'

'Looks a bit old for that.'

Anna butted in again. 'His nephew, also called Arne Naess, led the first Norwegian Everest expedition. He's married to Diana Ross.'

I turned and stared at her. 'Now you are having me on.'

She shrugged, poker-faced, enjoying herself, and went on with her ironing.

When I left the flat I lingered with Luce on the doorstep, giving her a kiss, and was gratified by the response. Suddenly she was interested in me again, really interested it seemed, and I wondered if there was some quirk of wiring in her brain linking climbing and sex. I said, as if the idea had just popped into my head, 'Hey, how about I come and help you babysit Owen's kid?' I imagined a quiet romantic evening, a sofa or even a bed, free of Anna, there being no privacy in the primitive flat that I was sharing at that time.

She looked at me in surprise. 'You don't want to do that.'

'Yes I do. We can work on your statistics.'

She laughed. 'All right. I'll speak to Suzi.' Then she slipped away, giving me a beautiful smile as she disappeared through the door.

Memories of those times came painfully back to me when I finally sat down on the terrace with a stiff whisky to read Detective Senior Constable Maddox's weighty report. He had been sent out to Lord Howe on the third of October, the day following Luce's disappearance, to support the sole police officer on the island, Constable Grant Campbell. Together they had examined the scene of the accident and taken statements from just about everyone who had had contact with Luce during her month there. There are some three hundred and thirty permanent residents on the island, and visitor numbers are restricted to about four hundred. At that time of the year, mid-spring, Maddox reckoned there were three hundred and twenty visitors, their numbers boosted a few days before by the arrival of a dozen yachts taking part in the annual Sydney to Lord Howe Island race.

Maddox paid closest attention, naturally enough, to those nearest to Luce, the group from Sydney, interviewing each of them several times. They began by expressing their shock at what had happened and their dismay at the loss of such a wonderful friend. Their accounts of the accident were consistent, and they described the relationships within the scientific study team as harmonious and Luce's mood as happy. However, a shadow was cast over this rather bland and comforting story by some of the other people that the police spoke to. A young woman, Sophie Kalajzich, a temporary resident on the island working as a waitress and cleaner on a twelve-month contract, had become friends with Luce, and described her as being withdrawn and depressed on occasions, especially towards the end of her stay. She also said that Luce had referred to some disagreement among the research team, and that she felt that Luce had seemed isolated and marginalised as the only woman in the group. She mentioned that Luce had been to see the island's doctor several times. Dr Richard Passlow confirmed that he had seen her twice, treating her for diarrhoea, nausea and insomnia. He described her mood as subdued rather than depressed.

Faced with these comments, the others in her party modified their statements. Luce had seemed a bit down lately, Curtis said, and Owen agreed that she hadn't been her usual cheerful self, though they denied there had been a disagreement with her. Curtis put it down to the time of the month. Finally Damien, no doubt sensing the way things were going, came out with the fact that she had broken up with her boyfriend shortly before coming on the trip, and he attributed her moodiness to that. Maddox had added a note in his report that the boyfriend, Joshua Ambler, had moved to the United Kingdom and he had been unable to contact him at the London address provided. But when Maddox bluntly asked them if Luce might have taken risks on those cliffs, or even deliberately jumped, they were all adamant that that was impossible.

As I read through these statements I felt I saw Luce emerge as if through a mist, vague and unfamiliar at first, then in sharper focus, a sadder, darker version of the woman I'd known. This glimpse of her, over the gap of four years, made me feel terrible, and for a while I pushed the report away and couldn't go on with it.

My eyes strayed to the morning newspaper on the table at

my elbow, folded to an article on the sentencing of the double-murderer on the train. Rory had sent him down for thirty-four years. It struck me as an odd figure—why not a nice round thirty-five?—until I realised that the victims had been aged sixteen and eighteen. Also, the murderer was aged thirty-three and Rory sixty-seven. A methodical and precise man, our Rory. I wondered how he might calculate my guilt.

Mary came out onto the terrace, carrying a plate of savoury tidbits that she'd been experimenting with in the kitchen. As I tried a couple, she took in the coroner's report and the whisky.

'I thought you were a beer man, Josh. I never saw you drink Scotch until that day Anna came.' She tilted her head so that she could read the title on the report. 'Where did you get that?'

'Anna and I persuaded Damien to get hold of it for us.'

'Ah.' Mary sat down facing me, a worried frown on her face. 'If you need help I could always ask Rory, you know. I'm sure he could arrange for you to talk to the policeman who went out there, if it would make you feel any better. I think his name was mentioned in the press at the time.'

'Thanks. Maybe later.' It was a kind thought, but the last thing I wanted was to get Rory involved.

'I wonder if this is such a good idea, Josh, raking over the past like this.'

I looked at her in surprise. 'I thought you were for it.'

She gave me a sad smile. 'I didn't realise then that you're still in love with her. You are, aren't you, dear?'

I blinked at her, and remembered a crack my father had made one Christmas, that Mary was a witch, with the gift of second sight. I think she'd caught him out over something to do with Pam, while my mum was still alive.

She reached forward and squeezed my hand. 'We're all just ships that pass in the night, Josh. For a brief time we make friends, we fall in love, and then we're alone again. We all have to cope with that.'

'Sure.' I shrugged, embarrassed by this bit of homespun wisdom. Four years before I would have said coping wasn't a problem, but I seemed to be getting softer with time. 'With a little help from these . . .' She thought I was reaching for the whisky, but instead I grabbed a couple of her savouries. She laughed and clipped my ear as she went back to the kitchen.

I was drawn back to the report by a lie. In one of his statements Marcus, the leader of the team, had described Luce as being a 'highly skilled but impetuous climber'. I supposed he'd said it as a precaution, as a first small step to protecting himself and the university against any future accusations of negligence. But it was a lie—Luce was never impetuous. That was the amazing thing about her, that she could do the most breathtaking things with such control and deliberation.

That got me thinking about Marcus again, the most enigmatic and, for me at least, the most perplexing of our circle. For although he was one of us, it was never quite possible to forget that he was also a member of staff, a senior lecturer and director of the university's Conservation Biology Centre within the Department of Zoology, and tutor to Luce, Curtis and Owen. He elided the two roles, teacher and friend, in a way that I hadn't seen before at university, allowing him to slip from one to the other, so it seemed to me, according to the circumstance. His social life seemed to revolve entirely around his tutorial students, with whom he would be viciously funny, putting down his academic colleagues and deriding the ways of the university—then he'd abruptly assert the authority of his position and turn on one of them with some scolding remark.

That wasn't the only ambiguous thing about him; it was hard to be sure how old he was, dressing young, usually in black with his hair often pulled back in a ponytail. And then there was his sexuality, a continuing topic of discussion among us. He'd never been married, and though his manner seemed mildly camp he was reputed to have once got a female student pregnant. He seemed to exercise a hold over both male and female students that to me seemed sexual.

Luce disagreed with me about this of course, putting his charisma down to his brilliance and his standing in his field. There was that; after watching that video of him in Oslo I could imagine the impact he must have had on his students. None of my lecturers were inspiring, and the idea of any of us wanting to own a video of one of them giving a conference speech was laughable. We all needed our heroes, and his green credentials were impeccable. He'd done his doctoral and post-doc studies at Oxford and Caltech, and he had an endless store of anecdotes about the great figures he had drunk and argued with—Richard Sylvan on anarchy, cannibalism and deep green theory, and Peter Singer on animal liberation, as well as the mythical Norwegian Arne Naess, with whom he claimed to have debated the eight principles of deep ecology in a sauna in the Arctic forests before falling into a vodka- and heat-induced coma.

To add to this intriguing background, Marcus lived in a very strange house half buried into a rock face in the northern Sydney suburb of Castlecrag, to which we were occasionally invited to celebrate some triumph over the reactionary establishment where he worked. He was very generous with booze and other more exotic stimulants, and after that first bemused encounter with him it seemed quite natural that he should always be around, a magus with a droll wit and a savage contempt for the university, the government, the country and pretty much everything else.

I set the coroner's report aside and had a look for Marcus on Google. I found an old conference website that listed some of his publications, papers on the conservation biology of declining seabird populations, the distribution of certain species of invertebrates and the ecology of the double-header wrasse, whatever that was. But he wasn't listed on the university's website any more.

7

I did go babysitting with Luce, but the rewards weren't quite as I'd anticipated. Suzi answered the door of their tiny flat, and my immediate impression was that Dracula had already paid a visit. She looked deathly pale, hair lank, nails bitten short, wearing a milk-stained overall. Owen, cradling the whimpering baby in the room beyond, looked robust and reasonably unscathed by comparison.

'Oh,' she whispered. 'Is it that time already? Sorry, we're running a bit late. Come in, please.'

Luce immediately took charge. 'No worries, we'll take care of everything. You just get yourselves ready. You haven't met Josh, have you, Suzi? Don't worry, I won't let him touch Thomas without proper supervision.'

I took a limp hand and reflected a wan smile. From the sudden increase in baby-noise it seemed to me it was Thomas rather than me that was going to need supervision, and I was interested to see how Luce would deal with it. And she did a pretty good job, after Owen and Suzi had finally been hustled out the door, of calming the little beast. For about ten minutes. Then it started again. We followed every procedure that the exhausted parents had suggested—a bottle, change of nappy, expression of wind and vomit down the back of my shirt, singing, rocking, patting, tight swaddling, liquid Nurofen and a call to a 24-hour help line—until there was only one left. This was infallible, they'd said. It involved putting the baby in his pram and going out into the night and walking the streets—on and on, without stopping. It worked all right, but it wasn't what I'd had in mind for our evening together, though it was a kind of bonding, I suppose, of a rather different sort.

'I feel so sorry for Suzi,' Luce said. 'She looks close to collapse. Her family are no help at all, and I think she's pretty depressed.'

'Did they plan this?'

'No, it all happened very fast. One day Owen turned up with this pretty first-year arts student on his arm and a goofy grin on his face, and the next she was pregnant and they were putting a brave face on it, rushing to get married. Owen's devoted to them, crazy about the baby, but it's easier for him. He has his coursework and his climbing as a relief, whereas she gave up uni and has nothing else but this twenty-four hours a day.'

Then she said, 'Would you like to do a bit of climbing with me? I practise on the sea cliffs at Clovelly and Coogee. There's some good bouldering, and one or two stiffer climbs, if you're interested.'

And so it became a regular thing, over the following weeks, going out along the coast with Luce, and sometimes Anna too, getting tactful help from the most brilliant climber I'd ever come across, and mixing more frequently with the other members of their group. We even babysat for Owen and Suzi a few more times, and I developed a grudging affection for little Thomas, who seemed to be suffering so much. Owen doted on his child; I thought of him as the quintessential scientist, peering thoughtfully at the kid through his glasses, and it seemed ironic that it had been he, rather than Damien with his multiple dates, or Curtis the wild-haired party animal, who had got himself a pregnant girlfriend.

One evening at the pub the others made plans to head out of the city for a weekend climbing in the Watagans National Park north of Sydney, and I found myself included in the arrangements, as if this was now a natural assumption. We set off early the next Saturday morning in two cars up the F3 freeway, me in the back of Marcus's with Curtis and Owen, and the girls with Damien in a four-wheel drive he'd borrowed from his parents. Marcus's driving was as erratic as his veering walk, and we were thrown about a bit on the ancient cracked leather seats. He revealed that one of his many areas of interest was old pubs, in one of which, a grandly verandaed Federation hotel in the Hunter Valley coalfields, he had booked us rooms.

We turned off the freeway into the bush, and as the road turned into a dirt track, winding higher and higher into thick forest, I became apprehensive. This was the first real climbing that I'd done with them all, and I hoped I was up to it. I wasn't much comforted by Curtis and Owen's assurances that, although we were heading for the largest crag in the park, the climbing would be moderate and the routes short at around only twenty metres. What was twenty metres, after all, compared with six hundred on the DNB? The equivalent of a six- or seven-storey building, that was all. I felt my palms go sweaty, and wondered if it wouldn't be better to be a non-participant like Marcus, and spend the day with him drinking in the bar of the Hibernian Hotel. Curtis added that unfortunately most of the climbs had been assisted with permanent bolts fixed into the rock, which seemed an excellent idea to me but not to the others, who tended to be purists on this question. Moreover, many of the bolts weren't the modern stainless steel sort glued into place, he said, but old mild steel types hammered into lead, and liable to pull out without warning. Also, I should be wary of the sandstone rock face itself, which could be a bit crumbly. I said thanks.

We reached the car park in thick bush at the base of the crag and tumbled out of the cars, taking in big lungfuls of the fresh forest air, the others loud and cheerful at the prospect of the day ahead. It seemed that Marcus wasn't going to spend the time in the bar after all, but had brought a folding seat and table as well as a bag of gear, including a camera with tripod and assorted zoology field equipment. We got these out of the boot and set them up for him, then changed our shoes, strapped on our harnesses and helmets, and shared out the wedges, carabiners and slings that would secure us and our ropes to the rock face as we climbed. Then we took the track up the slope to the base of the cliff. Along the way we disturbed a wallaby, as black as the fire-charred tree ferns in the bush around us. It hurtled away down the hill, weaving and bounding among the rocks.

We came to the crag, and the others selected the pitch, three parallel routes to the top of a cliff creased with cracks and wrinkles like an ancient petrified brown face. I had hoped I might climb with Luce, but it quickly became apparent that I was to be paired with Damien, which I saw made sense, for we were about the same weight and strength.

He said he'd lead for the first half of the climb, and I took my stance as his second at the foot of the crag, paying out his rope while he worked his way steadily upward. After five metres or so he jammed a wedge into a crack in the rock, and clipped his rope to it as an anchor in case he fell. Then he continued across what looked like a difficult section with few apparent handholds, until he reached a ledge on which he found a steel bolt that he used as a second anchor and tied himself to it. Then he called down to me, 'On belay,' the signal to let go of his rope. I released the belay brake at my waist and shouted up, 'Belay off,' and he began to haul up the rope until I felt it tug at the carabiner on my harness to which I'd tied its end with my much-practised retraced figure-eight and stopper knot. Up above, Damien was feeding the rope through his belaying plate, then shouted 'On belay,' again. I called out, 'Climbing,' then dug my hands into the chalk bag hanging in the small of my back and stretched for the first hold.

By the time I reached the first anchor, I was breathing hard and sweat was trickling down my back. I'd grazed my cheek and scraped my fingertips on the hard granular rock. But I was moving all right. I eased the wedge out of the crack and clipped it to my belt, then looked up at the smooth bulge above me. From here it swelled out much more than I'd realised from the ground, like a pregnant belly, and I couldn't see Damien at the end of the rope that stretched up across it. For a moment I was at a loss, unable to read the surface for places to grip, but then I noticed the traces of chalk where he'd placed his hands, and I stretched out across the warm rock to the first. There was a small indentation, and I pressed my fingers in and shifted my weight upwards.

'You all right?' Damien asked as I finally hauled myself up onto the ledge beside him.

'Sure,' I panted. Even after such a short climb, my hands and shoulders were aching, with tension as much as effort.

'Let's keep going then.'

I looked across the cliff at the others, Owen leading Curtis on their second pitch, and Luce beyond them already nearing the top of her climb. I glanced down and caught a glimpse of Marcus in his camp chair, watching us through a pair of binoculars, and felt myself sway. I turned back and gazed up at the cliff rising above us, and my heart sank. Climbing isn't just about stamina and technique, it's also about reading the rock face and understanding its possibilities. With time and experience this becomes second nature, matching your body's abilities to the subtle variations in the rock's surface. I didn't have that experience. There were no chalk marks to follow now, and my mind went blank. I thought I'd have to ask Damien, but I felt his eyes on me, waiting, and I guessed that might be a mistake.

Then I noticed a series of shallow depressions leading up to the left, followed by a thin vertical crack. I knew that if I stopped to think about it I'd never go, so I abruptly tied onto the anchor, took the gear he offered me to hang on the rack around my waist and set off.

The important thing was to maintain momentum, I thought; momentum and focus. And not to look down. This wasn't like the gym—I was suspended in an airy void, with no well-designed grips thoughtfully placed by human hand and no safety rope ready to support me from above. If I made a mistake now, I would fall twice the distance that I was above Damien before the rope caught me, assuming that the bolt held. If it didn't, that was me gone.

Arms aching, I reached the base of the crack and fumbled a small wedge into it. I tugged, it held, and I hooked on and breathed a sigh of relief. After that the going became easier, and I finally scrambled over the lip and rolled onto the broad flat rock at the top of the pitch, heart pounding.

As I waited for Damien to follow me I gazed out over the treetops to the hazy horizon, then looked down. The snapping whoop of a whipbird sounded far below. I felt the nauseating tug of the void, the familiar weakening in my knees and stomach as if it were literally sucking at my insides. But I had made it, and a sense of relief flooded through me.

Perhaps the shot of adrenaline cleared my brain, for as I pulled in Damien's rope a very obvious thought occurred to me. For most purposes you climb in pairs, one supporting the other with the safety rope, but without me—and without Marcus—they had been five. Later I learned that there had been a sixth during the previous year, but he hadn't fitted in with the group and had moved on. When I came along they must have been looking for someone to even the numbers. It was a sobering thought. Was that all that Luce had seen in me? You could tell, just by watching them, that the other pairs, Luce and Anna, Curtis and Owen, understood exactly what their partners were going to do without a word being spoken. Damien and I, however, clearly had a relationship to work out. We abseiled back down to the foot of the cliff and moved on to another route, neither commenting on the other's performance.

Again he took the first pitch, and as I waited for him to move off I looked up and saw the dark shadow of a substantial overhang, a 'roof', halfway up the cliff. Damien climbed to about five metres below it and anchored himself on a shallow ledge. I followed.

There was little room to manoeuvre on the ledge, and the roof above us now projected alarmingly.

He repeated his earlier question, expressionless. 'You all right?'

'Sure.'

Luce and I had practised on overhangs on the cliffs at Clovelly, but I hadn't attempted hauling myself over an obstacle like this before. I set off cautiously to the base of the shelf, then stretched out beneath it, clinging to the surface like a bat. If I lost my grip now I'd drop clean past Damien to bounce on the cliff face beneath him. As I reached one hand out to the lip of the roof I felt one foot lose its purchase, then the other slipped away, and in a moment I was swinging on my fingertips, dangling helplessly. The momentum of my fall took me out and then back, and I arched my back, straining every muscle, and brought one foot up over the ledge, and hauled myself over. It wasn't the most elegant of moves, but it got me there.

I was shaking with effort as I reached the next belay point, and collapsed back against the rock for a moment, catching my breath. Down below I saw the glint of Marcus's binoculars. Though he was roped, I was pleased to see that Damien wasn't too smooth on his manoeuvre over the shelf, and his face was red, his beard bristling and gleaming with sweat, by the time he stood beside me, breathing heavily. I asked if he wanted me to lead the final pitch to the top, which looked straightforward enough, but he shook his head impatiently, annoyed with himself I think, and set off without taking a break. He should have done, though. He'd gone barely a couple of metres before he made a mistake with his footing and began to slide. He scrambled to correct his balance but couldn't, and now he was falling. I caught him, hauling his rope tight before any damage was done, and he clambered back onto my ledge.

'Aah . . .' He stood gasping for breath, face turned up to the sky, then muttered, 'Thanks, mate.'

After he'd recovered a little he set off again, much more cautiously, and I followed without further incident. I felt pretty good.

Later we returned to the foot of the crag for some lunch. I was the first to get out of my gear, and went down to the cars to get the esky with our sandwiches and cold drinks from the boot of the Jag. There was no sign of Marcus by his chair and bag of equipment, and I wondered where he might have got to. I went over there, peering around, and noticed his stick lying at the top of a steep bank leading down to a dark pool in a stream. Then I saw his foot, almost invisible beneath an overhanging bush.

I scrambled halfway down the slope and dropped to my knees and made out his prone body, face almost in the water. The bush tore at my arms as I grabbed hold of his leg and desperately tried to haul him back up the bank. The earth was damp and slippery, his body awkward, and I slipped and struggled to get him to the top when I became aware of his muffled cursing. I was relieved that he was conscious until I realised that he was cursing me. I fell backwards and we sat facing each other in astonishment, covered in dirt and wet leaves. He was still cursing me when the others arrived.

They hauled him to his feet and brushed him down, while I recovered his stick, still not sure what was going on. Finally, grasping a stiff shot of whisky in a plastic cup, he told us that he'd discovered what he believed to be the entrance to a platypus burrow, hidden behind a tangle of roots on the opposite bank of the pool. From his pocket he produced a tiny triple-cusped tooth which he'd found at the waterline, which he said had belonged to an infant platypus, discarded at the time of its leaving the breeding burrow. My rescue efforts caused much predictable amusement, and I had to put up with a good deal of ribbing while we ate lunch.

Afterwards, as the others moved away, Marcus waved me over and proceeded to give me a detailed critique of everything that was wrong with my climbing technique. He was quite merciless and I felt humiliated as I stood there, staring at the ground. It was all no doubt absolutely true and invaluable, but I found it hard to absorb those quiet, relentless words. Then, when he had finished, he asked me to help him up, and led me to a clearing nearby. I didn't notice anything at first, but then I made out a small area in the middle that had been demarcated by plastic strips driven edge-on into the soil.

'A square metre of forest floor,' he said. 'What do you see?'

I shrugged. 'Nothing.'

'Nothing. And what would it be worth?'

I looked blank, not sure what this game was all about.

'Come on, Mr Merchant Banker. What would this fetch on the market? What's its dollar value, would you say?'

He was pissing me off now, so I said again, 'Nothing.'

He smiled. 'Right. Now, go and do some more climbing, and remember what I just told you—especially the way you're handling that rope, otherwise you'll end up hanging from the ankle upside down.' Then he added, 'I should know.'

The way he said it made me look at his face, and I saw a smile, and had the sudden vivid impression that he cared and that it was as if he'd been lecturing his own younger self. The trick of a good teacher, I suppose.

At the end of the day's climbing I stood beside Damien watching the two women on a final pitch. We had gone well that afternoon, becoming much more effective as a pair, but nowhere near as intuitively understanding of each other's moves as Anna and Luce. As always, I was captivated by the grace and speed of Luce's ascent. Although, being smaller, her reach was less than the men's, her strong slender fingers were able to grip narrow fissures and creases on which we could get no purchase. Her strength-to-weight ratio was about perfect, and she seemed to glide across the rock, as if she had some innate knowledge of its inflexions and could effortlessly match her body's movements to them.

'Climbs like a bloody angel, doesn't she?' Damien murmured at my side, and I realised he'd been watching me, engrossed in my study of Luce.

'Yes, amazing. What's she like in the lab?'

'Marcus says she's the best student he's ever had.'

I encountered Marcus again when we'd descended to the valley floor. He was in the clearing, half crouched, half lying beside his square metre of dirt. I knew better than to try to rescue him this time.

'Ah, the merchant banker. How did it go?'

'Good,' I said. 'We're climbing better together, Damien and I.'

'Yes,' he said absently, entering something in his notebook, as if we were an experiment he'd already disposed of. There was a field microscope and a magnifying glass lying beside his square metre, which I saw had been excavated to a depth of twenty centimetres or so. 'How about you?'

'Yes, I've been studying your patch of worthless nothing. This is what I've got so far.'

He showed me his book with its entries and calculations under a series of species headings. As he explained the scribbles I began to understand his point—that the area had been teeming with life: ants, lice, spiders, mites, and then increasingly minute specimens, their numbers meticulously totted up, amounting to a whole township, a city quarter of thousands of inhabitants. And then he outlined their mutually intersecting roles, their conflicts and alliances, right down to the personal narratives and dramas the debris scraped out of the shallow hole revealed. There were the fragments of a tiny marsupial vole that had died there, for example, and the traces of a nest of centipedes that had been eliminated by the fiercer ants.

He didn't have to spell out the equation he was making, between money-value and life-value. It was a little demonstration, a masterclass, for me, the barbarian economist. I understood this, and even felt rather privileged to have had this effort expended on me. But I also felt that the passion behind the message was not what it had once been, that I was maybe one dumb student too many.

That evening we retired to the Hibernian Hotel, a massive monument to coalminers' thirst, built in 1910, and the largest building in the little village it occupied. There Marcus entertained us, while we wolfed down large steaks, with an erudite account of the improbable sexual practices of certain snakes and stick insects, but given the sleeping arrangements—we had four rooms, Luce with Anna, Curtis with Owen, me and Damien, and Marcus on his own—I saw little opportunity to investigate if they might be adapted to humans. Instead his flagrantly grotesque descriptions seemed designed to draw attention to my increasingly desperate longing for the girl on the other side of the table, who seemed oblivious to my surreptitiously yearning looks. However, as we started making our way towards the stairs, Anna came to my side and whispered, 'Wanna swap?'

I looked at her in surprise. 'Eh?'

'Beds.'

'Um . . . Did Luce . . .?'

She looked at me as if I was being a bit slow, and I quickly nodded, feeling a sudden agitation in my chest, a brightening in my gloomy mood.

She said, 'Use the veranda. Marcus'll be roaming around the corridor.'

The pub was on a street corner, with deep verandas around two sides, onto which all the bedrooms had shuttered doors. By the time I'd cleaned my teeth, Damien was already fast asleep, snoring softly. I turned the key in the veranda door and pushed it open with barely a squeak, and stepped out into the chilly night air. Down below in the street a group of locals was spilling out of the bar, yelling cheerfully at each other as they made their way to their utes. I padded softly along the deck until I came to what I thought was Luce and Anna's room. Now what? My bare feet were freezing and I had the sudden sickening thought that this was some kind of prank, a trick to maroon me out on the balcony all night. Then the door in front of me clicked open, and Anna slid out. Like me she was wearing a shell jacket over a T-shirt and pants. She grinned at me, gave me a quick peck on the cheek and padded off. I stared after her, then a voice whispered from the door, 'Hurry up, I'm cold.'

Luce was wearing a coat, but nothing else. I stepped inside and took her in my arms, and decided that this was just about the best of the eight thousand-odd days I'd spent on the planet.

I think it was fairly apparent to the others over breakfast the next morning what had happened between Luce and me. I thought I was playing it pretty cool, but each in turn, coming down into the dining room, blinked at the pair of us, then grinned and winked, as if we had neon signs on our heads. I couldn't read the signs with Anna and Damien, though, and as we carried our bags out to the cars I got a chance to speak to her.

'You okay?'

'Yes.'

'I mean . . . good night?'

She gave me a patient smile and turned away, me none the wiser.

We returned to the Watagans and, in an unspoken agreement, Anna, Luce, Damien and I switched climbing partners, so that I spent the day climbing with Luce, a breathtaking experience. In the mid-afternoon we made our last ascent together, me exhausted, and I staggered into her arms on the scrubby plateau at the top. She pulled me away from the edge, out of the line of sight of Damien and Anna making their way up below us, and I told her she was beautiful and that I loved her. She smiled and took my hand and led me back into an area of huge boulders and thick clumps of tall grass. We rounded an outcrop, searching for a place to settle, when we were suddenly presented with a sight that stopped us dead. Curtis and Owen were together in a sheltered nook, their climbing helmets and harnesses discarded on the ground nearby. Curtis was on his back, groaning, eyes closed, while Owen knelt over his midriff, head down.

My shoe sent a stone skittering noisily away and Owen opened his eyes, pushed himself marginally upright and stared at us. For a moment we were frozen, the four of us, then Owen said, 'Aw, fuck.'

I muttered, 'Sorry,' and turned away, following Luce, already retreating around the outcrop.

I followed her back to the cliff edge, where Damien was standing now, pulling in the rope on which Anna was secured. I reached for Luce's hand, feeling the tension in her, not sure what to say. Finally I whispered, 'Things happen.'

She turned slowly and stared at me. 'Poor Suzi.'

Anna called me the day after I'd visited the nursing home to arrange to discuss the report. We settled on Saturday afternoon at the hotel. I said it'd be private and convenient, but the truth was that I wanted Mary to have time to meet her, and tell me if she thought Anna was making too much of this.

It was another beautiful warm spring day, the air still, but Anna didn't like the idea of working on the terrace where we might be interrupted. Instead we moved in to Mary's sitting room, Anna setting her stuff out on the table like someone preparing for a major presentation. As she was unpacking her bag Mary came in with a pot of coffee. They seemed genuinely pleased to see each other again, as if there had been some earlier bond of understanding or sympathy that they both remembered.

'Josh has told me all about your trip to Christchurch,' Mary said. 'You poor thing. It must have been a terrible experience.' I could see the appraising look in her eye. 'I'm so sorry you've had to deal with all this, Anna. You were a good friend to them, flying out like that. And then to hear that terrible confession. You're quite sure he wasn't just confused or hallucinating? People say strange things when they're drugged and in shock and as desperately ill as he was.'

'I know, I've been wrestling with that ever since. It's just that he was, briefly, so lucid.'

My aunt nodded sadly. 'Well, you were there. Couldn't you speak to someone about it, though? Perhaps the police officer who looked into the matter? We have a regular guest here—a good friend—who's a Supreme Court judge, and I was saying to Josh that I'm sure he would pull a few strings to help you get the ear of the right person.'

'That's very kind of you,' Anna said cautiously. 'But I think we should try to be as clear as possible in our own minds before we go as far as that.'

'Maybe that's wise.' Mary hesitated, unwilling to let it go. 'Of course, the other aspect of this is, what happens if what Owen said was true? They're all dead now—Lucy, Curtis and Owen. What good can it do? And think of the possible harm, the distress to Lucy's family, for instance.'

'But they aren't all dead, Mary. There were two other people in their group, Damien Stokes and Marcus Fenn. They're very much alive.'

Mary looked shocked. 'Oh, but surely you don't imagine they . . .?'

'I don't know.'

'Well . . .' Mary stared at her, then turned to go, catching my eye with a look that I took to be a warning to be careful.

'So, what did you come up with?' Anna asked as I poured the coffee.

'Not a lot.' I'd wanted to avoid talking about how Luce had been depressed, but in the end it was all I had to say.

Anna looked at me pointedly. 'Yes. They shifted their ground, didn't they? And in the end Damien put the blame onto you.'

I took a deep breath. 'Was he right, do you think? You saw her after I left, didn't you?'

'Yes, she was down. But she wasn't suicidal. She was looking forward to going on the trip. I mean, she was really fired up about how important the work was, and about doing some climbing, and what a beautiful place it was. Something changed while she was out there. Despite all their protests that Luce wouldn't have deliberately stepped off that cliff, Damien and the others planted the seed of the possibility. I think it was a smokescreen, in case Maddox found something that didn't fit the picture of an accident.'

'Could be.'

'Anything else?'

I mentioned Marcus's description of Luce as impetuous, another smokescreen.

Anna agreed, but was obviously disappointed by my lack of progress, so I asked, 'What about you, then? What did you find?'

She unfolded several large handwritten tables and charts and spread them out. One was a timeline, tracing Luce's movements on the island according to witness statements, and another was a chart showing the names and connections of all of the people referred to in the police report. A third was a large map of the island locating all the places mentioned. I was impressed. She'd obviously approached it in a methodical, scientific manner, making my casual observations look pretty thin. I put it down to a lack of mental challenge at the Walter Murchison Memorial Nursing Home.

'They arrived on the first of September,' she said, pointing to the timeline, 'moving into the same cottage belonging to the Kelso family that Marcus had rented in previous years. During the first two weeks they worked on the accessible small islands off the north end of Lord Howe. Then, when Damien arrived to make up two climbing pairs, they tackled the more difficult cliffs at the south end, below Mount Gower. Each day Marcus would go out with them in Bob Kelso's boat, and return for them in the evening. They all kept work diaries, which Marcus would compile, day by day, into the research log. The weather was generally good, although there were a number of stormy days, especially towards the end, when they couldn't go out.

'On Wednesday the twenty-seventh, the ocean-going yachts on the Sydney to Lord Howe race arrived at the island, and on the following evening the Kelsos, who are an important family on the island, threw a party for the yachties, to which Marcus and his team were invited. On the Friday they returned to Mount Gower for what was originally scheduled to be their last day in the field. However, a bad storm blew in on the Saturday, disrupting flights to the island, and because of time lost earlier Marcus decided that they would stay on for a few more days to finish their work. The weather cleared on the Sunday, and on the Monday they lost Luce. The search and police interviews went on for another week.'

I had been following her finger as she traced this chain of events across the page. Seeing it laid out graphically like that made it easier to get a feel for the pattern. It struck me that there was a sort of congestion towards the end—the arrival of the yachts, the party, the bad weather, the delayed departure—disrupting the even repetition of the previous weeks.

When I mentioned this, Anna nodded and said, 'Something else odd about those last few days . . .' She pointed to the names written against each day, referring to witness sightings of Luce. 'After that party on the Thursday night, the only people who mentioned seeing Luce again were the three other climbers, plus Marcus and Bob Kelso, whereas in the days before Thursday, lots of people saw her around—Sophie Kalajzich, Dr Passlow and his wife, the other Kelsos, the National Parks and Wildlife ranger, the people who ran the grocery store . . .'

'What do you make of that?'

'It's like Luce withdrew, kept herself to herself, don't you think? As if she wanted to be alone.'

I thought about it, then I said, 'I just can't get over the fact that she should never have been there at all on that Monday. They should all have been back in Sydney by then.'

'Yes,' Anna said.

'And they should never have tackled that cliff without Damien. I mean, it's just so bloody stupid. It shouldn't have happened.'

'So what are we going to do about it?'

'I wonder if Mary isn't right, Anna, about how we should be thinking more about the impact on Suzi and the other families if we go on with this. I mean, supposing we did discover something nasty?'

She frowned at me. 'How do you mean?'

'Did Luce ever tell you about something that happened that first time I went climbing with you all at the Watagans? Something about Curtis and Owen?'

She looked blank and shook her head, so I told her. A couple of days after that weekend, Owen had come to see me. He was in quite a state, desperate to convince me that what we'd witnessed had been a terrible mistake, a moment of madness on his part. He was utterly devoted to Suzi and the baby, he said, and begged me to keep it to myself. I said, fair enough, it wasn't my business and I had no intention of mentioning it to anyone else, but what about Luce? He'd already seen her, apparently, and she too had agreed to keep quiet, so we left it at that.

Anna was surprised, but not as much as I'd expected. She'd known that Curtis had had relationships with men, but hadn't thought about Owen.

'You're wondering—what if they didn't stop, if they were lovers when they went to Lord Howe, and Luce threatened to spoil things?'

'She was very concerned about Suzi, and she didn't believe Owen's story that it was a one-off thing. Look, it needn't have been a deliberate plan to kill her; maybe just that she got into trouble and they . . . hesitated to help, because of this problem. A second would do it, a look exchanged between the two of them, a moment holding back, and then it would be too late.'

I felt sick talking like this. It seemed all wrong, not the actions of the people I'd known. Surely Luce wouldn't have pushed them into a corner, and surely they would never have reacted like that if she had. But could I be sure?

'And then I started to wonder about the accident in New Zealand. What do we know about what happened there?'

Anna frowned. 'They were roped together, just the two of them, crossing a steep ice slope. The rest of their party could see them, but they were some distance behind. They said Owen, following Curtis, fell and pulled Curtis down with him.'

I pictured it. 'Oh, hell,' I whispered.

We sat in silence for a long while, then I said, 'I think we should talk to Marcus.'

8

I borrowed Mary's car, and we drove across the bridge into North Sydney and through the suburbs beyond until we reached the strip of shops at Castlecrag, where I pulled over to consult the map. Outside, people were walking their dogs and sipping lattes at pavement tables, enjoying the sunny Saturday afternoon. But I had a hollow feeling of foreboding in my gut at the thought of meeting Marcus again.

The area we wanted lay to one side of the main road, on the rocky bushland hillside dropping down to the bays of Middle Harbour. It's a place unlike any other in Sydney, laid out in the 1920s by the two American architects, Walter Burley Griffin and Marion Mahony Griffin, who had previously won the competition to design the new Australian capital city at Canberra. They were inspired by the dramatic site at Castlecrag, and must have seen some poetic metaphor in medieval castles, for they gave its narrow lanes, winding along the contour lines between rocky outcrops, names like The Rampart, The Bastion and The Bulwark. The Griffins designed a number of the houses in their subdivision, too, and if you think of the quintessential Australian house as being lightweight, open to the landscape, with sunny decks and a tin roof, then these were exactly the opposite—solid cubic bunkers embedded into the hillside like refuges for trolls in a strange land. Marcus's house was one of these, located at the end of a cul-de-sac in The Citadel, its rough stone blocks almost invisibly hunkered down among large boulders and overgrown by gnarled banksias and angophoras. Its walls ended abruptly at a flat roof, like a castle keep, the source of dramatic views down into the ravine leading into Middle Harbour. Seeing it again, rugged and dour, I felt an odd sense of time shifting, as if the front door might open and we'd find the others still inside, laughing and arguing and drinking as before.

We parked and walked down the narrow sloping drive, flanked by rock green with mould, to the heavy front door. I rapped the brass knocker and we waited, and waited, and then there came the scuffle of a bolt being slid, and the door opened.

It was as if all his most distinctive features had become exaggerated, eliminating the rest. His leanness had become skeletal, the lines on his face gaunt cleavages, and the long black hair shaggier and greyer. Most of all, the crippled leg had dragged the rest of his frame down around it, making him stoop awkwardly, like a damaged stick insect.

He frowned at us for a moment, then his mouth split in a wide smile. 'Anna! Hi! And . . .' He clicked his fingers.

'Josh,' I said.

'Josh, yes, of course, sorry. Great to see you.' A dank sour smell wafted past him from the depths of the house. 'Come in, come in.' I caught a strong gust of whisky on his breath.

It was dark inside the hall, the space smaller and more cave-like than I remembered it. We came to a living room, whose view out through stone-mullioned windows was obscured by dense foliage. The room was a jumble of ancient leather furniture surrounded and covered by piles of books and other debris. Judging by the stains in the ceiling the damp problem from the flat roof hadn't been fixed.

He continued through to a brighter room, with French

windows opening onto a small terrace. This room was his den, as untidy as the one before but more lived in, with an empty wine bottle and a tray with the remains of yesterday's pizza on the floor, and more books. He cleared a couple of chairs and went off to find another bottle, leaving Anna and me eyeing each other doubtfully. There was an old chintz-covered armchair in the corner by the window and I had a sudden vivid memory of another Saturday in this room, music playing, laughter from the garden, and Suzi sitting in that chair, flapping a handkerchief to try to keep the smoke from a joint in Curtis's hand away from the face of the baby on her knee.

I picked up a book lying among the remnants of Marcus's meal and checked the title—*Occult Science* by Rudolf Steiner. Anna had opened the doors onto the terrace and I followed her out. Further down the steep slope we could see a kind of amphitheatre formed in a hollow in the hillside, accessible from Marcus's house by rock steps winding down between the boulders. To one side of the terrace a shade-cloth conservatory had been built beneath the overhang of a sandstone outcrop, with ferns and other plants dimly visible inside.

We turned and saw Marcus limping into the room, and went back inside. He almost stumbled on a book on the floor, and I caught his arm and steadied him, startled by how light he felt. I took the bottle from his free hand and found three empty glasses.

He eased himself with a sigh down into another piece of furniture I remembered, a heavy dark wooden chair he called his throne. 'So how are you guys?' he said, examining us in turn. In that more haggard face his gaze seemed brighter, more intense, but his manner was less certain, almost as if he'd become withdrawn, unused to being with people, reclusive, or maybe just drunk.

'We're fine,' Anna said. 'I work over in Blacktown, and Josh has been in London.'

'Ah, the merchant banker, yes. London?'

'Right, I've just got back.'

'Four years,' he said. 'Of course, of course.' As if that was terribly significant.

I smiled. 'How's the uni these days?'

He lowered his eyelids, raised his wine cautiously to his mouth and drank. 'I don't work there any more, Josh. They decided they could do without me—very wisely no doubt.' Some wine spilled onto his knee.

Anna said, 'But you were a great teacher, Marcus. And your research . . .'

He gave a dry laugh that turned into a cough. 'After the accident, well, someone had to pay. Inquiries, suspended from teaching, research grants withheld. They made life impossible for me, drove me out.' He shrugged, wiped his knee absently.

I was shocked, by both his story and how he looked, and said, 'I'm sorry. Where are you now?'

'Um? Oh, I'm working on my own private research program.'

'No more students?'

He gazed at his feet sombrely, then shook his head.

I raised an eyebrow at Anna, who took over.

'We wondered if you'd heard about Curtis and Owen, Marcus?'

'Curtis and Owen? No, I haven't heard from them for a while. What about them?'

I hadn't noticed a newspaper or a TV in the house.

'They were killed in a climbing accident in New Zealand last month.'

He cocked his head forward, peering at her. 'No . . .' He looked confused, and I wondered if he might be on medication as well as booze. 'A climbing accident?' He shook his head, not upset but more as if this just couldn't be right. '*Another* climbing accident? Are you sure?'

'Yes. I went over there as soon as I heard. I was with Owen when he died in hospital.' Anna was leaning forward, speaking slowly, watching his reactions. 'Just before he died he told me something very disturbing. He said that Luce didn't die the way the inquest had heard. He said her death wasn't accidental.'

'What do you mean?'

'He said, *We killed her.*'

Marcus looked startled, opened his mouth to speak and then closed it again. Finally he said, 'No, that's . . . that's . . . crazy.'

'Is it? You weren't actually there when it happened, were you?'

'You're not serious.' He began tapping a finger on the arm of the chair. 'There was an inquest, a full investigation.'

'Which relied on what Curtis and Owen said.'

He hauled himself abruptly upright in his seat, glaring at her. 'This is crazy, Anna. Tell me again, the whole thing.'

While Anna did so I looked at the books lying around my feet. There was one called *Knowledge of the Higher Worlds and its Attainment*, which I thought might have been about climbing until I saw that the author again was Steiner. There were others by him—*The Being of Man and His Future Evolution* and *Cosmic Memory*—and a thick tome called *A Guide to Anthroposophy*. The books had Dewey classification numbers on their spines from the university library, and I wondered if he still had access, or if he'd stolen them.

'Thank you for telling me this, Anna. I had no idea.' Marcus drained his glass and I got up to refill it for him. 'Have you told anyone else about it?'

'Not yet.'

Marcus seemed agitated, preoccupied. 'The fall,' he said.

'Sorry?'

'Owen's mind . . . He was obviously deranged by his fall.'

'You don't think it's possible he could have been telling the truth?'

'What? No! Of course not.'

I said, 'How about Luce's state of mind, in those last days before the accident?'

'Luce? State of mind?' He focused his eyes on me in that intense way he'd had before, as if he wanted to burrow right into your brain and find out what you were hiding in there.

'Yes, I mean, was she depressed? At the inquest several people said they thought she was. The police investigator even asked you all if she might have killed herself. I just wondered what you really thought.'

'No, Luce would never do that . . . Ah, I think I can see where you're coming from, Josh. She still had a photo of you inside her wallet, and you're wondering . . . Am I right?'

I felt the colour rise in my face, but didn't say anything.

'No, it wasn't like that. A bit subdued maybe, towards the end of the trip, but not suicidal, no, no.'

Anna said, 'One of the witnesses said there was a disagreement between Luce and other members of the team.'

He turned to her, then slowly shook his head. 'No, Anna—no disagreements.'

I said, 'What about Curtis and Owen, how were they getting on?'

'Fine, we were all getting on fine.' He shook his head, impatient with these questions.

'Were they lovers?'

He glanced at me, eyebrow raised, as if reassessing me. 'You know about that, do you? No, that was over long before, as far as I know. And even if they were—what difference would it have made?'

'Luce felt protective towards Suzi and the baby. I think she felt that Curtis should have left Owen alone.'

'Was that how it went, Josh? I don't know. It was none of my business. And Luce never mentioned it. Look . . .' he waved a hand at us, pale and bony as a turkey's claw, 'this has stirred up old memories, but nothing sinister happened. I promise you that. It was just a terrible accident, terrible, terrible. If there had been any hint of anything else . . . I miss her too, you know.' He nodded towards a bookshelf on which we saw a small framed photograph of Luce. 'Every day I think of her and blame myself.'

He took a deep breath, a glint of moisture in his eyes, and then added with a kind of choked sob, 'I saw her, you know . . .' He waved his hand at the French windows onto the terrace.

'How do you mean?'

'About a year ago, out there . . . Beautiful as ever.'

Anna and I exchanged a glance of alarm.

'A year ago?' I said.

He turned his face back from the window to me and said quietly, 'Have you wondered why you've come back now, Josh?'

I looked at him in astonishment. 'Well, it was just the way things turned out, with my job and so on . . .'

He shook his head and smiled as if I was being incredibly naive. 'You were looking at my books,' he said, pointing to the pile beside my feet. 'Rudolf Steiner, a great man, a great scientist, who realised the limitations of conventional science and moved on further—much, much further. The man and

woman who designed this house were great followers of his.
They studied his books, his philosophy, his discoveries. It took
me a long time to realise . . . The people they designed it
for were my grandparents, who left it to me when they died
twenty years ago, but it's only in the last year that I've begun to
realise that they were all into it, the people who came to live
here, including my grandparents. There was art and dance,
and everyone joined in; anthroposophical festivals in the
open-air amphitheatre down below us here in The Scarp . . .'
he pointed to the French windows, 'by the light of flares. Tell
me, how many rooms are there in this house, Josh?'

His rambling was becoming more and more confused.
I shrugged. 'No idea, Marcus.'

'Seven, arranged in three overlapping suites. Now, look at
the carving of the stone window surrounds, the patterns of
glass in the French windows, the design of the fireplace—all
repetitions of seven elements in three overlapping groups, at
many different scales. You see?'

'Oh yes, right.' I looked at Anna again, eyebrows raised.

'One of the things, the fundamental things, that Steiner
discovered was that we have seven parts, seven kinds of self.
The house, you see, is the philosophy made flesh, Josh. It is a
template, a model, an embodiment of the human spirit itself,
as revealed by Steiner. He was the Darwin, the Einstein of
the spiritual world, and this was one of his great discoveries.
When we die, Josh, only the first member, the physical body,
is destroyed. For a few days its companions, the astral and
etheric bodies, cling together, after which the astral body
separates itself and goes on its way without the etheric, which
also dies. Now the person goes through a painful process of
purification, retracing his or her life experiences and purging
them in what Steiner calls "the consuming fire of the spirit",

until at last the whole of their earthly life is distilled to an extract, a quintessence, which the Ego carries forward into the spiritual world, the Spirit-land.'

He was becoming more and more excited, eyes wild, and he suddenly reached out to grab my arm. 'Josh, Steiner tells us that the process of purification takes about one-sixth of the time the person spent on earth. Don't you see? For Lucy that would be four years. Four years! That's why you're disturbed, why you've come back to this house now. You were close to her, you sense her being at the time when she must move on into the land of Spirits!

'That's why she returned here. It was a dark night. I came into this room, and switched on the light, and there she was, out there on the terrace, a pale figure, but absolutely clear, unmistakable, illuminated by the light from the room. I cried out her name and went towards her. I wanted to speak to her, ask her forgiveness, but she disappeared. She'd come back to this house, Josh, to seek out the blueprint of her future life, to find her way forward into the Spirit-land.'

'Forgiveness?' I said sharply. 'Forgiveness for what?'

'What?'

'You said you wanted to ask her forgiveness. What for?'

'Oh . . .' He became a mass of confusion. 'I felt responsible. She was my student . . .' Then he turned on me. His frown might have been puzzlement, or concern, or perhaps no more than a struggle to concentrate. He repeated my name a couple of times, 'Josh . . . Josh,' then his face cleared and he said, 'I understand— you're suffering, right? Shit, you feel guilt . . . despair, right?'

'Yes, but—'

'I felt exactly the same, until I discovered the truth.'

'The truth? You know the truth, about how she died?'

'Ha!' Now a beatific smile lit his face. 'But that's the point, Josh, that is the point.'

'What is?'

'She isn't dead.'

We left soon after, exchanging promises to catch up again another time. As we made for the front door Marcus, returned now to a more prosaic spiritual plane, said to Anna, 'On morphine, was he?'

'What?'

'Owen, when you saw him.'

'I suppose so, something like that.'

Marcus nodded, as if he knew all about morphine. 'Messes with your brain, Anna. People believe all kinds of stuff.'

We stepped carefully through the obstacles on the living room floor, and I recognised a Lloyd Rees print on the wall that Luce and I had admired on one of our visits. The memory brought back just how much energy and life there had been in this house then, and how neglected it now seemed. I felt sorry for Marcus. He'd been an intriguing and generous man to know, and he'd made our student lives more interesting, more vivid. Now he seemed utterly lost.

When we reached the front door, Anna led the way up the path between the rocks, but Marcus put a hand on my shoulder and stopped me. He was uncomfortably close, his breath foul on my cheek. 'Josh,' he murmured, 'you don't want to get into all this. Really. I understand how fond of her you were, but believe me, there's no *conspiracy* here.'

I nodded, embarrassed to see what looked like a tear in his eye. He was so close I couldn't avoid noticing the unhealthy colour of his skin, the tufts of bristle he'd missed shaving beneath his chin.

'Anna's got it all wrong, you see. You should put her straight. Don't let her make trouble. Bad for everyone.'

I didn't mention this to Anna as we drove back to Central,

where she wanted to catch a train. On the way she said, 'Poor Marcus. I can't believe how much he's altered. This thing has really done him in, hasn't it?'

'Yes, pretty much. He's a changed man all right. Did you believe what he said, about the accident?'

'Yes, I did, though he wasn't there of course, when Luce fell.'

I had believed it too, until that last little exchange at the door. Now I wasn't so sure.

We agreed we'd have a think about things and talk again soon.

9

I wanted to think about something else, and Mary helped by giving me a new list of jobs that needed doing around the place. I got stuck into them, and was rewarded later with a lobster dinner and a bottle of wine. After the meal I lay on my bed with a crime novel one of the guests had left with us. She'd recommended it highly, and the reviews quoted on the back cover were all ecstatic, but it annoyed me. It wasn't that it was unrealistic, at least concerning the technical aspects of murder—DNA profiling, gunshot trauma, the action of bacteria in buried corpses, autopsy procedures and all the rest—in these things it was grossly realistic. But I just couldn't relate to the characters. They were so incredibly resourceful and resilient; the more they were beaten up and shot and mis-led, the more determinedly they returned to the fight and the more brilliantly their brains worked. Real people aren't like that—they're very easily frightened and confused, their motives are boring and selfish, and when trouble comes they have a tendency to curl up into a little ball until it all goes away. I know, because I'm one. But of course that doesn't make for a very interesting read.

I had been confused by our visit to Marcus all right, and unsettled in ways I couldn't quite define. The house had been part of it: claustrophobic, chaotic, a chamber of memories and ghosts. And Marcus himself, diminished and turned in upon himself. I thought about that performance of his, my mind coloured by the book I'd just been reading. In crime novels, of course, every fact, every event may be significant, carrying the germ of some revelation. Life may not be like that, but the more I considered Marcus's mystic blustering, the more dubious it seemed, like an elaborate cloak he'd felt obliged to gather around himself. I began to become convinced that the cloak concealed something. A secret. And I wanted to know what it was.

On Monday morning Damien phoned and invited me to have lunch with him. It was a very swish place on East Circular Quay, with a stunning view of the Opera House, and I felt a little out of place among all the corporate suits, but pleasantly so. I really didn't want to be like that again.

Damien was expansive and friendly, but also, I felt, pointedly assertive as he ordered this and that, as if establishing a certain position of authority. I let him come to the point in his own time, as we were halfway through our fish.

'I got a call from Marcus Fenn at the weekend,' he said, dabbing his mouth with his napkin.

'Oh yes?'

'He said you and Anna paid him a visit, at Castlecrag.'

'That's right.'

'What did you think?'

'It was a bit of a shock, frankly, seeing him again. He's really gone downhill, hasn't he? The house was a mess, and he didn't look too fit.'

Damien nodded sadly. 'You're right. I've watched it happen. The university treated him very badly, you know. Really beat him up. He'd made a lot of enemies over the years, especially within his own faculty—well, you know how sarcastic he could be. The dean hated his guts and saw the accident on Lord Howe as a way to get rid of him. Rumours circulated—that he hadn't organised proper back-up for the team, that he was indifferent to safety procedures, that he was spaced out on drugs when it happened—all discounted by the police investigation, but no matter. They made life as difficult for him as they could, and when he accepted a package they refused to give him a reference. Then Luce's dad went for him.'

'What? Her father?'

'Mm, Fred Corcoran, tough old bastard. He saw Marcus's quitting the uni as an admission of guilt and when the coroner cleared him of any negligence, Corcoran took a private action against him. It dragged through the court for a year. In the end it failed, but it cost Marcus his university payout in lawyers' fees. The court sympathised with old man Corcoran, even though he was wrong, and didn't like the look of Marcus, so they didn't award him costs.'

'Hell.' I shook my head.

'What was so unfair was that Marcus really was devastated by what had happened to Luce, but he just refused to show it, and people didn't like that. They thought he was arrogant and didn't care.'

'So what is he doing now? He said he was involved in some kind of research.'

'No, no.' Damien said it with a dismissive flick at some breadcrumbs on the white tablecloth. 'He's become a recluse, living on an invalid pension. We tried to help him, Curtis, Owen and I, but he's difficult. He has these mood swings, and he hates the idea of people feeling sorry for him, or giving him charity.'

Damien put the last piece of barramundi in his mouth, chewed, and then said, 'When he phoned me, Marcus said something strange. He said Anna told him that Owen made some kind of confession to her, just before he died.'

'Yes, that's right. Apparently Owen said that the accident hadn't happened the way they told it afterwards.'

He stared at me. 'Really? You didn't tell me this before.'

'No. I was a bit sceptical. I think Owen's brain must have been scrambled by the fall, but Anna is convinced he was lucid.'

'And you really didn't think it was worth mentioning this to me?'

There was an unspoken undercurrent here, concerning our places within the group, that I'd allowed myself to overlook, or forget. He was saying that, of all people, he should have been the first to be told, for it had always been his role to take charge and get us organised, whenever that proved necessary. And equally, I guessed this was the reason why we hadn't told him straight away, because we knew he'd try to take over.

I shrugged and turned back to my fish, embarrassed in spite of myself. 'As I say, I don't know that it can be taken seriously.'

'Well, it was serious enough to confront Marcus with it.' His grip on his knife and fork tightened.

'We just wanted reassurance from him that Luce wasn't . . . wouldn't have jumped.'

But he wasn't to be deflected. 'What exactly did Owen say?'

'What I just told you, plus he said, *We killed her.*'

'*We killed her?*' he repeated through his teeth. 'I was there, Josh. I was part of that team, part of *we*, and you two didn't think it worth telling me about this?'

'I'm sorry. We would have. We just wanted to get up to speed first on how things were out there.'

He looked incredulous. 'You got me to obtain the police report for you, but you didn't tell me the real reason you wanted it. What was that, some kind of test? You thought I was involved in . . . what? A murder? A cover-up?'

His field was commercial law, but it occurred to me that Damien would have made a pretty sharp criminal lawyer.

'No, no, nothing like that.'

There was an awkward silence, during which he stared at me, then he turned away, shaking his head in disgust. 'Who else have you told about this?'

'No one. Well, Mary.'

'Don't you realise how preposterous it is?'

'Yes, I do.'

'And what motive could *we* have possibly had?'

'There was one thought that occurred to me.'

'Oh really? I'd like to hear that.'

'Do you know that Curtis and Owen had . . . a relationship?'

'A sexual relationship you mean? Yes.' He said it bluntly, as if to emphasise that he would know everything that went on in the group. 'Why? What's that got to do with it?'

'Luce was worried about Suzi. She didn't like the deceit. I wondered if it was still going on, and she maybe confronted them.'

'So they pushed her down a cliff? That's laughable.'

'Was it still going on?'

He hesitated, looked down at his knuckles. 'I'm not sure about that. Possibly.'

Another long silence, then I said, 'Well, it was just a theory.'

Finally he said, very softly, 'It doesn't matter, Josh. Not any more. Curtis and Owen are dead. The rest of us just have to live with it—Suzi, old Corcoran, Marcus, me. Christ . . .' He put a hand to his face, wiping his eyes. 'How do you think

I feel, knowing that if I'd been with them that day it might never have happened? I feel guilty as hell.'

'Yes, I can see that,' I said, not meaning it unkindly, but thinking that his tone wasn't quite right somehow, more complaining than contrite. 'In fact I don't really understand why they did go without you.'

'It was a bright sunny day, we'd already been up and down that cliff several times and they were all confident. They just wanted to finish off the job. They didn't realise how the heavy rain the day before could have loosened the scree. Look, I don't believe your theory for a moment, but even if it were true, what's to be done? Uncover the truth? Confront Suzi with it? Destroy her son's memory of his father?'

I shook my head.

'No, it's not really on, is it?'

We finished our meal in an uncomfortable atmosphere, and as we left the restaurant I asked if he had Suzi's address. He gave me a dark look.

'It's okay, I just want to see if I can help.'

He knew it off by heart, and wrote it on the back of one of his cards for me, with a final warning. 'We've got to move on, Josh. She doesn't need any of this.'

He was right, of course. The only trouble was, he wasn't the only one feeling guilty.

Risk management had been my area in London. After we parted, as I walked around the quay watching the gulls wheeling over an incoming ferry, it occurred to me that Damien would also make an excellent risk manager. He had been forceful, persuasive, working me into a corner from which I had little choice but to agree with him. But Marcus's voice kept whispering insistently in my ear, 'There's no *conspiracy* here.' I'd never heard him sounding needy and cowering before. It had been an unpleasant experience, more so than being pressured by Damien.

I stopped at a toyshop and bought a handheld electronic Spiderman games unit that the man assured me was perfect for a boy of six, then bought a bunch of roses and some chocolates next door, and made my way to the address Damien had given me. I parked outside, and stared at the blank front door, imagining all the pain and turmoil on the other side, and lost my nerve. I would have started up the engine and driven away again, but then I saw them approaching along the footpath, Suzi pushing the baby in a stroller with one hand and holding Thomas's little paw with the other. It hadn't really struck me at the funeral how like his father the boy was, with that serious, studious expression, and the same black hair. In a couple of years I expected he'd be wearing glasses just like his dad, too. I got out of the car and Suzi looked surprised, then glad. We went inside for a cup of tea, and I handed over the gifts. Thomas took to the game as his father might have to a new electron microscope, and after I'd set it up for him he sat in a corner of the room, utterly engrossed. Suzi and I chatted, mostly about London and the places she'd like to visit in Europe one day, and then I escaped. Of course I didn't bring up any difficult issues. Sitting there, the doubts and suspicions that had been going through my head seemed simply obscene, and I came away convinced that there had to be some other explanation for what her husband had whispered before he died. I went back to the hotel and began to sift through all the material again, determined to find it.

Anna rang me that evening.

'Did you read the schedule of items of evidence at the back of the coroner's report?' she asked.

'Not really.'

'Among Luce's possessions on Lord Howe they found a diary. I checked with someone in the coroner's office. Apparently it was returned to Luce's father after the inquest closed.'

'Hm.'

'I think we should have a look at it.'

'Oh look, I said before, Anna, this isn't some detective mystery with the murderer's name spelled out in the victim's diary in invisible ink. If there was anything interesting in it, the police would have picked it up, surely?'

'We won't know until we see it. It depends what they were looking for. I've told Mr Corcoran that we're connected to the research project Luce was working on, and we need to see if there was any missing data in the diary.'

'You've spoken to him? But he knows you, doesn't he?'

'Luce and I went to boarding school together in Sydney, but I only ever met him once, and again briefly at the funeral. He won't know what subjects I was doing at uni. He was all right when I called him. Bit cautious, but all right. He said he'll be available tomorrow, and I've arranged to take the day off. Can you make it? If not I'll go on my own.'

'No, it's okay, I'll come. I'll borrow the car.' Then I told her about my lunch with Damien, and visiting Suzi.

'He's right,' she said finally. 'I don't want to do anything that will make things worse for her. But I want to know, Josh. I want to know what happened.'

'Yes,' I said. 'Me too.'

I followed the old Great Western Highway early the next morning, so that I could pass Ambler's Pies. It was a pet shop now and I hardly recognised the place, the front rebuilt and the pie removed from the roof. I could see that a giant meat pie might not be the most appropriate symbol for a pet shop, but I felt sad, and wondered what had happened to it. Dad and Pam had long gone, too, their hard-earned cash reinvested in an allocated pension fund and a Winnebago Explorer motor-home, in which they were now roaming the continent with all the other grey nomads.

I turned off into Blacktown, following the directions Anna had given me, and found her waiting at her front door. At least she didn't live in the nursing home, but in a flat nearby. She grinned hello as she got in the car, and I felt a touch of warmth at seeing her again. She was wearing a dark green shell jacket that looked identical to the one she'd worn in the Watagans all those years ago.

We climbed up over the Blue Mountains and down onto the western plains beyond, reaching Orange in time for lunch before our appointment with Luce's dad. I drove along the wide main street, recently beautified with new street furniture and trees, like every other country town we'd passed through, and found a wood-fired pizza café. She chose a cheese topping and I remembered that she'd been a vegetarian. I asked her if she still was and she said yes. Like Luce, who'd persuaded her that that was the way to go. It was strange to feel the traces of Luce still present in our lives, like footprints on the sand. Luce had had no luck in trying to convert me to vegetarianism, but she did get me to stop smoking, another mute footprint.

We found Corcoran's Farm Supplies on the edge of town, housed in several large steel sheds surrounded by a car park dotted with piles of barbed wire, drainage pipes, fencing posts and water tanks. Inside, wide aisles displayed an extraordinary, and to me baffling, range of gadgets that the modern farmer apparently needs. While Anna spoke to the woman behind the counter I learned quite a lot. I had no idea what a calf puller ($59.95) was, for instance, until I saw the illustrative photo of an unfortunate beast with a metal arm stuck up its backside. Then there was the ute dog tether ($14.95), the drench gun ($129.00) and the lightning diverter ($40.12) to protect the energiser on one's electric fence ($3,447.40 to power 160 kilometres of multiwire fence). I was studying the action of the footrot shears ($54.95) when Anna came to my side. 'He's here,' she said, and picked up a castration ring applicator ($32.95) with rather too much relish for my liking. 'This place could be a supermarket for the Spanish Inquisition,' she said.

Luce's father was a gaunt and weathered man. He gripped my hand briefly, drilling my face with his eyes (bright blue, like hers) for a moment before turning and leading us up to an office built above the counter. He was wearing moleskins and R.M. Williams Stockyard boots that clumped loudly on the timber stairs. We sat around a plain wooden desk and Anna repeated her story about the research project, and how there was some missing data that Luce might have recorded in her diary or other papers. I felt that her tone, polite but businesslike, was about right. He listened with an inscrutable look on his face, bottom lip thrust forward, and I wondered how this leathery old man could have been the father of such a vital and beautiful daughter.

'So that research business is still goin' on, is it?'

'We're just gathering the loose ends.'

'That Fenn feller isn't involved, is he? They haven't taken him back at the university, have they?'

'Oh no. He's not involved any more.'

He grunted, then stooped to a cardboard box at his side, about the size of a shoebox, and lifted it onto the table.

'This is what the coroner's office sent me,' he growled. 'I haven't thrown anything away. Couldn't bring m'self to.'

It sounded like an opportunity to say something sympathetic about his loss, but Anna didn't take it, so I mumbled a few words about how sorry we were. He ignored me, and I felt stupid.

'May we look?' Anna said, after a pause.

'Go ahead.'

He didn't move, so Anna stood up, reached for the box and slid it towards her. It was roughly sealed with packing tape. Mr Corcoran rummaged in a drawer in the desk and handed her a Stanley knife, with which she cut the tape and looked inside.

'Her clothes and personal things came separately, did they?' she asked gently. This was getting a bit too forensic for me.

He nodded. 'They sent her suitcase back first with the things they didn't need.'

Anna lifted out a mobile phone, an electronic notebook and a small address book. There was also a wallet from which Anna systematically unpacked Lucy's driver's licence, Medicare and credit cards, her university student card, and a small photo of me. Her father stared at it, then at me, and I gave him a weak, pained smile. This was awful, staring at her things spread out on the table, things scuffed and worn by her fingers.

'No diary,' Anna said.

I pointed at the electronic notebook. 'What about that?'

'Maybe.' Anna turned it over. It looked old, battered and scratched. There was a loop attached, and I could imagine Luce carrying it clipped to her climbing harness. Anna found the switch and pushed it to ON, but the screen remained stubbornly blank. 'Looks dead,' Anna said, and I winced. 'I wonder . . .' she ploughed on, turning to Corcoran. 'Maybe we could take this to someone who could fix it. See if they can make it work?'

He stared at her for a moment, then shook his head. 'I reckon not. Could be personal stuff in there Lucy would prefer left alone.'

'It could be exactly what we're looking for,' Anna insisted. 'I can assure you that only Josh and I would see it, and we'd keep any personal things strictly confidential, and return it to you.'

He shook his head, unmoved.

Anna seemed about to argue, then shrugged and put it back in the box. She flicked through the address book and put that back, too, and then the wallet and mobile phone. A blue envelope I hadn't noticed before remained lying on the desk. Anna picked it up and read the name written on the front. 'It's to you,' she said, and looked at me. She handed it over. I stared at it, then at her father, and put it in my pocket.

When we got back to the car, Anna banged the car door in frustration. '*Personal stuff.* That's exactly the point. The police probably never got into it. There's no other reference to it in the report. And I know someone I'm pretty sure could get it open.'

'Not much we can do, Anna. It's his prerogative.'

She turned to me and said, 'Aren't you going to read her letter?'

'Later.' I started the engine and we moved off. As we circled to the car park exit I glanced back at the building and saw Corcoran's face at the upstairs window, staring down at us.

When we reached the town centre I said, 'Want a coffee or something before we head back?'

She shrugged, and I pulled into a parking space outside

a different café. While we waited for our coffees I reluctantly got Luce's letter out of my pocket.

It was clearly a draft, undated and with words and phrases crossed out.

Dear Josh,

I can't tell you how hard it is to write ~~to you~~ this. I feel ~~like the last phasmid.~~ so sad. There are so many things I want to tell to you, and no words to say them with ~~though I've tried so many times~~. But today when I was climbing something made me think of Frenchmans Cap. The wind, I think. ~~It broke my heart.~~ How brave we were then??? You said I was a hedgehog and you a fox, and now I have one big thing to tell you.

That was all.

Anna was looking at me with concern in her eyes. I handed it to her without a word, because my throat was so tight it hurt to swallow.

She read, then looked up and said, 'There was something she wanted to tell you.'

Yes, I thought: that she didn't love me any more or that she still did; that I was a bastard or that she wished me well.

'The fox knows many things,' Anna said, 'but the hedgehog knows one big thing. What was it?'

'Maybe that she was going to kill herself,' I said. 'That's why the police held onto it, don't you think? Because it sounds like a suicide note.'

Anna reached out her hand and gripped mine. 'No, Josh, I'll never believe that.'

'Well, we'll never know.'

'Unless it's in that bloody diary.'

The waitress brought our coffees and then Anna said, 'We were brave at Frenchmans Cap, weren't we? Fearless.'

'Not exactly. I was terrified.'

'But we did it. We had the nerve to do it, just us. I sometimes think I haven't got the nerve to do anything like that any more.'

'Damn right.'

We sipped our coffees in silence, and then she said, 'I want that diary, Josh.'

I stared at her.

She said, 'What's the roof of Corcoran's shed compared to Frenchmans Cap?'

So we found a hardware barn on the edge of town, a huge place with a vast car park scattered with utes and four-wheel drives. Though inexperienced in this field, we thought we did a pretty good job of equipping ourselves, emerging with a pair of sheet-metal shears, a crowbar, a torch, a builder's leather tool belt, bolt cutters, a big screwdriver, a long length of rope and a box of disposable latex gloves.

As we got back into the car with our loot, Anna said, 'What is a phasmid, anyway?'

'I have no idea.'

10

After the Watagans I went on a number of weekend climbing trips with Luce and her friends around the Sydney area. I was still doing the bouldering and gym work, and was gradually becoming more proficient and more confident with heights. Then, towards the end of the year, we decided to take a climbing trip to Tasmania as soon as exams were finished. I think Marcus had something to do with the decision, because he had some business to do there at the University of Tasmania. So we made arrangements to fly to Hobart, and hire a van to drive out to the Franklin–Gordon Wild Rivers National Park in western Tasmania. Our goal was Frenchmans Cap.

Just getting there was quite an effort—a two-day hike from the Queenstown road, where we had left Marcus and the van to return to his meetings in Hobart. We hauled our thirty-kilogram packs over the Franklin Hills, from which we should have got our first distant view of Frenchmans Cap, but were disappointed to find the whole horizon obscured by low cloud. This was a wet part of the world, where rain falls three hundred days in the year, and we knew that our climbing would depend on getting a spell of decent weather. We descended to the plain of the Loddon River, a notorious bog of button grass, ponds and mud, as Curtis discovered when he stepped off the trail and sank to his waist. A fine drizzle set in as we plodded through the marshland, and we no longer said much. After crossing over the pass on the far side and descending to the hut on Lake Vera, we'd been going for over ten hours and were exhausted. We were the only people at the hut that night, and after a hot meal and change of clothes we fell fast asleep.

The rain was heavier the next morning, uncomfortably so at first, then more alarmingly as the track led along an exposed ridge and the wind picked up, lashing us as we laboured under our heavy packs. At one point Anna lurched against me, blown sideways by the stinging wind, and I had to catch and steady her to stop her falling down the scree slope. Again we should have had a sighting of Frenchmans Cap from there, but could see nothing until we approached the Tahune hut, almost at its base, when the peak suddenly loomed out of the cloud, huge and scary. I had been told that these were the highest cliffs in Australia, four hundred metres of sheer white quartzite, but the immensity of the climb hadn't hit me until then, and I felt queasy all that evening, guiltily hoping that the rain would keep falling.

But it didn't. The next morning was cloudy but dry, becoming brighter as the day went on. We decided to limber up on some of the shorter routes on the north-west wall, an array of pinnacles and buttresses on the lower side of the mountain. I was paired with Luce, and after a slightly shaky start I began to get a feel for the hard, crystalline rock surface, and gain a little confidence.

The skies kept clearing until by evening there wasn't a cloud to be seen, and the others decided that the following day would probably offer the best chance to attack the long routes on the high cliffs on the other side of Frenchmans Cap, which would need a whole day's climbing. There was a lot of debate over maps and diagrams about which route we should try, and in the end we decided to go for the east face. They selected three parallel routes, just as at the Watagans, except that now the climbs would be three hundred and eighty metres long instead of twenty. Luce and I would take the middle one, rated 20 on the Australian scale, 5.10d on the American, and much tougher and longer than anything I'd attempted before.

We set off early the next morning for the hour's hike to the base of the east face, then we split up into our pairs. Luce and I climbed to the top of a grassy ramp, where we roped up and Luce set off to lead the first pitch. We had planned to take the climb in seven pitches in all, with Luce to lead most of them, establishing the belay anchors at the end of each pitch. These were long stages for me, forty or fifty metres each in length, and my heart was thumping when I finally heard Luce's cry, from far above, 'On belay.' I set off, focusing on the glittery surface immediately above me, making steady progress until I joined her in the lee of a jutting prow of rock. I was breathing heavily, my arms and legs shaky, but I'd made it, and I grinned and turned to see the view, already a broad panorama across the national park although we'd barely begun. While I rested, Luce described the next stage, pointing out the features I needed to recognise up to the next belay point, fifty metres above our heads.

We continued in this way, stage by stage, through the day. Our climbing styles were very different, Luce free and confident, swinging out into space on the end of a sling, while I stuck as close to the wall as I could. Anyone studying us would have wondered what a natural climber like her was doing with a dunce like me, but at least, slowly and doggedly, I was getting there. At each belay point the views became more breathtaking, and the sense of being suspended on a vast white vertical surface more intoxicating. By the time I climbed up to join Luce at the head of the fifth pitch we were three-quarters of the way to the top, and I was finally confident that I was going to make it, weak as my body felt, and terrifying as the void beneath me looked. She said something about leading the next pitch again, but I felt it was time I showed some initiative, and I waved her aside and moved to the first hold. She spoke again, but there was a singing in my ears and I didn't hear her properly. It was late afternoon now, and the wind was sharper up there, and cold. She repeated something about a tricky corner about fifteen metres above us, and I nodded and set off, muttering to myself, 'Balance and rhythm, focus and momentum . . .'

When I came to the tricky corner I suddenly realised what she'd meant. I looked down, and saw that it was bottomless. I had to step from one face to the other across a thousand feet of void—the height of the Empire State Building. I hesitated, trying to clear the giddiness from my head, and then my legs began to shake violently. They call this 'sewing machine leg' or 'disco leg', when your weight concentrated on the edges of your feet causes the leg muscles to spasm and convulse uncontrollably. Afterwards Luce told me that as soon as she saw it she knew I was going to fall. I urged myself to move forward, but I simply couldn't. For a breathless moment I was suspended there, and then, gripped by sick panic, I felt my feet give way, my fingers drag across the rock, and my body topple backwards off the wall.

Once I realised that I was gone, that there was absolutely nothing I could do, my terror faded. In a kind of appalled calm I watched the cliff face accelerating past me and then jerk to a violent stop as my rope caught in the highest of the three wedges I'd driven in on my way up. But the brutal force of gravity wasn't going to give me up so easily, and with a sickening *ping* the wedge flew out of its crack and I continued down, moving faster. The rope snagged the next wedge and it too failed—

ping—and the next—*ping*. All my protection was gone now, ripped out of the rock by the accelerating momentum of my fall and I was tumbling free, past Luce who was desperately trying to haul my rope through her belay brake. *Too late*, I thought, *the belay anchors will go and then she'll be pulled off too. We're going to die together on Frenchmans Cap.*

But the belay anchors, solidly implanted in the rock by Luce, didn't give way. My rope jarred abruptly tight and I bounced and spun and smacked my head against the rock, and finally was still, dangling fifteen metres below her. I'd dropped the height of a ten-storey building.

I hung there, dazed and shocked, and gradually became aware of distant shouts. Then I made out Luce's voice. 'Josh? Are you all right?'

I opened my eyes, groggily trying to orientate myself, and saw a distant haze of dull green. It took me a moment to realise that I was staring at the tree canopy far below. I was hanging upside down.

'Josh!' Luce called again.

I called back, 'Yes, I'm here.'

'Are you hurt?'

'Not much.' Blood was running into my eyes from a cut on my cheek where I'd hit the rock face, but my bones seemed intact.

'Can you climb up?'

My first thought was, how? Even if I could get myself the right way up, we weren't carrying Jumars for climbing the slender ropes. Then I remembered I had a prusik loop somewhere in my gear, though I wasn't sure if I'd be able to remember how to use the bloody thing. It took a while to twist myself upright while the others shouted questions and advice to each other. Should they try to get help? But the mobile phones didn't work. Should they try to lower me to the ground? Three hundred metres? I thought, no way. So I rigged up the ascender and began to inch my way painfully up the rope.

The evening sun had set the forest ablaze in golden light and purple shadow when Luce finally hauled me onto her ledge, and I thought how cruel of nature, indifferent to my fate, to put on such a show at a time like this. The others wanted to lower ropes and haul me up, but Luce was worried about the condition I was in, shaking with cold and shock, and also about the approach of darkness.

'We'll spend the night here,' she said.

'Sleep together?' I stammered through chattering teeth. 'Is that all you think about?'—for it was true that our lovemaking had taken on a certain intensity of late. She laughed, and began shouting instructions up to the others. One of them, Owen I think, had abseiled part-way down and about twenty metres away to the left, and Luce gave him a list of things we needed, as we'd come up with the minimum of kit. He climbed back up to the top and a couple of them set off on the summit walking track back down to the hut to fetch them for us.

I looked at the narrow ledge we were on, only a few centimetres wide, and wondered how the hell we were going to sleep on that—like bats perhaps, hanging upside down with our toes jammed into cracks. But Luce was placing wedges and flexible friends into the rock all around us, and lacing rope between them to form a sort of cradle. When she was satisfied, she perched beside me and held my hand, and we watched the great shadow of the mountain creep out across the wilderness. The dark was absolute by the time the backpack came bumping down the cliff on the end of a line—a sleeping bag, thick jumpers, a flask of hot soup, water, a couple of packs of dry rations, a first-aid kit and a torch. With them we built our nest safe inside Luce's rope cobweb, had a meal, then zipped ourselves inside the bag and fell deeply asleep.

We woke to a gleam of golden light. It was the dawn sun, rising directly in front of us. We were pressed very close, our bodies warm despite the chill wind on our faces.

'My nose is freezing,' I whispered.

'Mine too.' She turned her head and we rubbed our noses together like Eskimos, then lay there watching the world beneath us take shape in the gathering light. Small glinting lakes appeared through the dark forest, and crags, like the stumps of ancient teeth, caught fire in the morning sun. I felt enveloped by the natural world, in a way I never had before. When I thought about it, I was amazed to realise how totally insulated my life had been from this world until I'd started climbing with Luce. Nature to me had been no more than a marginal risk of hurricanes or floods that could be managed with a range of financial instruments. I had only ever seen true wilderness through the filter of a TV screen or an aeroplane window. And now I was about as fully exposed to it as one could be, suspended in a gossamer net high up a mountain face in bright air. Credit derivatives and hedging positions weren't going to be much use to me here. For the first time I felt I understood about Luce. The wilderness absorbed her utterly; she studied it, experienced it, loved it. It was the one big thing this hedgehog knew. She'd often told me about it, its beauty and its tragedy—the decimation of its forests, the poisoning of its rivers, the murder of its species—but to me it had been just another rather boring greenie lecture. Now I felt I understood. Climbing was her way of addressing it, risking herself against it, gripping it close like a lover.

There was a shout from above us, and we disentangled ourselves, had a little breakfast, and climbed out, Luce leading, as I should have let her do in the first place. The rain returned soon after, and I was spared any further tests of my overstretched climbing abilities. I had been transformed by my experience on Frenchmans Cap. I felt that Luce and I were true partners now, dizzyingly in love, constantly touching, looking at each other. The others were in high spirits after their successful climb, too, and I heard Anna say something about 'the highest ever'. I said, 'But what about the DNB? That was even more, wasn't it?' and she confessed with a laugh that they hadn't actually done the full ascent, just a short section.

I suspected that the good humour of the group was partly due to the absence of Marcus, as if we were on holiday from an admired but dominant presence. He was waiting for us at the prearranged time when we made our way back to the highway, and immediately began to reassert his influence, starting with his own students. He had to use a light touch, for we were still full of the experiences we'd shared in our week away from him, but gradually he drew our attention back towards the things that interested him. These centred on an ongoing protest against logging in the Styx Valley forest, to which we now headed. An area of pristine wilderness, but lying just outside the protection of the Southwest National Park, it had become a focus of conflict between the logging industry and conservation groups. Marcus made it clear that fooling around climbing rocks was a fairly trivial activity alongside the struggle to save this corner of the planet in which he had apparently become vitally involved.

That was all right, and so long as he kept it general I found it rather amusing, from my position of absorbed preoccupation with Luce, to watch him use this to manipulate the group.

But Marcus liked to make things personal. He really didn't like how close Luce and I were now, so that she wasn't giving him her undivided attention, and he started aiming barbed comments in my direction. This wasn't entirely new; he'd poked fun before at the degree courses that Damien, Anna and I had chosen. In his scornful opinion, the law was venal, sociology was weak science, and commerce and business studies were beneath contempt. But now the comments became more personal. Money was the underlying poison that was destroying the environment, apparently, and doing an MBA was more or less equivalent to worshipping the devil. I tried to respond with humour, arguing that money was the greatest invention of all, without which civilisation and science would have been impossible, but it wasn't really funny. When people like Marcus started lecturing me about the evils of capitalism I always heard at the back of my mind my father's voice saying *bloody wanker*.

As we trudged through the Styx Valley forest with a cluster of activists, I began to feel a distinctly new antipathy towards Marcus. I disliked the way he basked in their deferential attention, bringing out just the right coded phrases and buzzwords to make them laugh and nod in eager agreement. Apparently he'd been interviewed on TV and radio in Hobart, and had been saying wise and supportive things about the protesters, calling for greater activism. I thought he was a hypocrite, remembering that in the past he'd been scathing about most of these groups, saying they confused ecological goals with principles of social equity, for instance, and suffered from the romantic delusion that Aborigines had possessed some idyllic empathy with the land.

We came at last to a protest camp, deep in the forest. There were tents pitched in a stand of enormous trees, and a kind of ramshackle platform suspended high up between three of the eighty-metre giants (the tallest hardwoods in the world, we were assured, at least four hundred years old). Someone had been living up there for eight months in protest at the logging threat, and there was a general spirit of defiant enthusiasm, which I found hard to share. Maybe it was the melancholy damp gloom of the forest, but I found it all rather sad. So later when we all sat around a campfire with our hosts and Marcus began to hold forth about the world of money as the primary enemy of the world of nature, I began to feel apprehensive. Then he turned on me.

'Well, what do you think, Josh?' he said, in his knowing drawl. 'This is *real* passion, wouldn't you say?'

I was startled by the directness of the stab, as if to say that an MBA student wouldn't know real passion from the back end of a dingo. Someone sniggered.

'Yes, it is,' I said. 'But it seems a waste of time to me.'

I was holding Luce's hand, and I felt a warning tightening of her fingers. The rest of the group went very quiet.

'Really!' Marcus's eyes lit up. 'And why is that, exactly?'

I sensed everyone waiting for my reply. 'Well, as I understand it, the TV crews that used to film here in the early days have lost interest now, and the loggers have found another trail through the forest to bypass us.'

There was a tense stillness in the camp, made all the more pointed by the continued crackling of the fire.

'I see. And what would a *money* man do?'

I didn't really care. I was still full of the euphoria of the past days, and I was experiencing one of those moments when I felt I couldn't lose. If I'd been playing poker I'd have gone for the pot. I let the silence hang for a moment, then said, 'Well, aim at the money jugular, I reckon. The woodchips they take out of this forest are being loaded onto a Japanese ship in Great Oyster Bay at this moment. I'd go and firebomb it. That would stop the bastards.'

A stunned moment, then Curtis, bless him, gave a whoop and cried, 'Yeah! You got it, Josh.' Then everyone started talking at once.

I didn't really mean it, I just wanted to call Marcus's bluff, but somehow the preposterous notion connected with some mood of frustration in the camp and grew like a bushfire spreading. Even Damien and Anna were caught up in it, answering questions about how one might set about climbing the flank of a Japanese bulk carrier. I looked at Luce, wondering if I was in trouble, but her eyes were shining and she leaned close to my ear and whispered, 'You naughty boy.' We both knew what must have been going through Marcus's head; he'd just been on TV with this mob, advocating stronger action.

In the end he didn't have to speak, as more sober members of the camp calmed things down. They mentioned the T word, *terrorists*, and people pulled themselves together. No one wanted to be called that.

So now here I was, reluctantly agreeing to accompany Anna on her break-and-enter mission, if only because she had reminded me how exciting life had once seemed. After our bit of hardware shopping we went to a pub. She stuck to mineral water, but I felt I needed a couple of stiff drinks in order to go through with this. We had a meal in a very agreeable little restaurant, then watched a dire movie at the local cinema before driving out once more to Corcoran's Farm Supplies. There were no headlights on the long straight road as we approached the place, and no signs of life within, although the yard around the building was ablaze with security lights. I parked on the shoulder just beyond the chain-link fence, manoeuvring the car into a stand of trees so that it wouldn't be too obvious from the road. Then Anna loaded the tools into her belt and led the way to the fence, through which I cut an opening.

I had been worried about dogs, and was relieved that there didn't seem to be any. I thought Anna was going to have trouble breaking through the doors with the equipment we'd brought, but that wasn't her plan. Instead she led the way to the rear of the sheds, keeping to the shadows of the yard perimeter. There was a large steel rack built against the back wall, holding fencing posts and other stuff, and forming a convenient platform to get halfway up the wall. She rang my mobile with hers, so that we could be in constant touch with each other, and told me to return to the front of the yard to watch the road. Then she hitched her heavy belt and reached for the frame.

'Hell.'

'What's wrong?' I hissed.

'Bloody jeans. I can't climb in these. I didn't come prepared for this.' So she took off her jeans and handed them to me, and set off again. From the top of the racking she took hold of a square metal rainwater downpipe and began hauling herself up. I got a flash of frivolously polka-dotted panties disappearing over the eaves, then I jogged back to the front fence.

From there I could see Anna's dark shape move along the roof, and I guided her over the phone until she was directly above the office, with its window at which I'd caught that last glimpse of Corcoran's face.

'What now?' I whispered.

'There's a skylight . . .' She was panting, her breathing harsh in my ear.

I heard a splintering crack, and watched her outline disappear into the dark shadow of the roof. At the same time a blue light started to flash at the front of the building and an alarm began to shriek.

How long would it take? I supposed it would be a matter of luck—there could be a police car cruising on the highway nearby, or a security guard patrolling the industrial estate two minutes up the road. I bit my lip and clenched my fists as the minutes ticked by. What the hell was she doing?

Then I saw headlights on the road, coming fast towards us. When I tried to warn Anna, the noise of the alarm coming through the phone obliterated my words. I shrank back behind a big plastic water tank as the headlights swept across the yard and came to a stop at the gates. Someone moved into the beam. Whoever it was had a key, because the gates swung open and the vehicle, a white ute, lurched forward to the main doors. When the driver got out again the lights caught him, and I recognised the lanky figure of Luce's father. He transferred something to his left hand, a stick perhaps . . . no, a gun. I stopped breathing. He was carrying a rifle or a shotgun.

He unlocked the big front door and rolled it partially open, then stepped inside. The alarm abruptly stopped. Ears ringing still, I spoke softly into the phone. 'Anna, can you hear me? Corcoran's arrived. He's in the building. He's got a gun.'

I didn't know if she'd heard because she didn't answer, but I did see the office window swing open, and the thin grey lines of a rope snake down the wall. Anna followed, giving me palpitations as she struggled through the tight opening, then slid down the rope. She tugged one end of it and it fell to her feet, where she scooped it up and started running towards me at the gap in the fence. A dog I hadn't noticed before in the back of Corcoran's ute began barking furiously, and Anna half turned her head towards it, and at the same time her belt with its load of tools slid down her hips and became tangled with her legs, and she crashed to the ground. Behind her I saw Corcoran reappear at the main door, and I raced over to Anna, grabbed her and the belt and hauled them both towards the fence. There was a shout as we tumbled through, and then a loud bang. Shredded leaves and twigs pattered down on us as we reached the car and hurtled off into the night.

'Wow,' I finally said, as darkness enveloped us. 'You all right?'

'Yes.' She was panting, vibrating like a plucked string. 'I couldn't find it at first. He'd hidden it behind the filing cabinet.'

'But you got it?'

'Yes.'

'What else?'

'What do you mean?'

'What else did you take?'

'Nothing, I'm not a thief.'

I took a deep breath. 'So somebody made a forced entry into his building and ran off with his daughter's electronic notebook, and nothing else? The same notebook he'd refused to give to two visitors earlier in the day?' She didn't say anything. 'You left the wallet, with its photo of me, I suppose?'

After a long silence she whispered, 'Yes.'

Earlier, Bonnie and Clyde had come to mind, but now Laurel and Hardy seemed more like it.

'Sorry.' She was pulling on her jeans.

I said nothing. I was wondering what to tell the police who would surely be on my doorstep first thing in the morning. If they didn't catch us on the highway.

11

But they didn't catch us on the highway, nor, to my relief and surprise, did they come calling the following day. I got on with my chores and waited, but nothing happened. I did read Luce's note again and again, trying to extract its meaning, without success. And I looked up the word *phasmid* in the dictionary. It was an insect of the order Phasmida, apparently, a leaf or stick insect, which immediately brought an image of Marcus into my mind as we'd last seen him, all awkward arms and legs. Was that what she was referring to? Was that how he saw himself, the last phasmid? It didn't make much sense to me, and I wondered about Luce's state of mind when she'd written that note.

I continued going back through all the documents I had relating to Luce's accident, searching for some new angle, and a couple of days later I found it. The first hint of it was in the bottom corner of one of the last newspaper reports of the accident that Anna had photocopied. It was the small heading for another article that was off the page, and it read, LORD HOWE RACE YACHT SKIPPER QUESTIONED. It seemed an odd coincidence to me, and I decided to find out what it was about. I went to the local library and searched through their microfiche copies of the paper until I found it. It was a eureka moment, and I felt that burn of apprehensive excitement you get when you come across something really big. It was almost as if I could sense Luce's presence at my shoulder.

Australian Customs and Quarantine officials in Sydney yesterday detained the skipper of a boat recently returned from the Sydney to Lord Howe Island yacht race, after a search of the vessel uncovered a quantity of rare native bird eggs on board. A spokesman for the Australian Customs Service revealed that the search had followed a tip-off, but declined to identify the nationality of the suspect. He said that the illegal international trade in wildlife was estimated by Interpol to be worth $10 billion annually, and was surpassed in value only by drugs and weapons.

This surely was what I had been searching for. Birds' eggs were exactly the reason why Luce and the team were on Lord Howe Island—the grey ternlet's eggs, to be precise. I did remember that much from what Luce had told me. They were carrying out research into its breeding habits, so you could say that she had died on account of the sex life of a small, rather delicate seabird, listed as a vulnerable species in Schedule 2 of the New South Wales *Threatened Species Conservation Act*. About the only other thing I could remember about the bird was that the sexes were practically indistinguishable, with no plumage variation during the breeding season, which, as I suggested to Luce, might have been one reason they were a vulnerable species.

And now here was someone recently returned from Lord Howe and accused of smuggling rare birds' eggs. Had Luce discovered what was going on? Had Curtis and Owen been somehow involved? I scanned the papers for the following days, but could find no further reference to the case. Eventually I gave up and walked back to the hotel, head spinning. The race yachts had arrived at the island on the twenty-seventh of September, I remembered, just five days before Luce's accident. She had gone to the party that was held for them on the twenty-eighth, and they had helped in the search for her.

I returned to my room and began going through the police report again, working at it far into the night, until I finally stopped at around four and fell into a troubled sleep.

The next morning I phoned Anna. She said she'd given Luce's diary to the computer whiz who serviced the equipment at the nursing home, but hadn't got a result yet. I told her I had something to discuss with her and we arranged to meet that lunchtime. When I got there she took us to the deserted library room, where she'd arranged a tray of sandwiches.

She saw how agitated I was. 'What's wrong, Josh? Have the police been in touch? Mr Corcoran?'

'No, nothing like that. I've been doing a bit more digging, and I think I've come across something. Look.' I showed her the print I'd taken of the newspaper article, and she made the connection straight away.

'I couldn't find any other newspaper reports about the boat, but you see the timing.'

'Yes, of course. Luce would probably have come across this man at the party they had. What are you thinking?'

'Well . . .' I rubbed my face, trying to put together the chain of logic that had seemed so compelling the previous night. 'It seems to me that the smuggler would have had someone helping him on the island, someone who knew the right places and had collected the rare eggs beforehand.'

'Right.'

'It struck me, going through the police report again, how often the Kelso family crops up. Marcus and the team stayed on their property, went to the party at their house, and were ferried around the island by one of the sons, Bob Kelso, listed as a fisherman. The other son, Harry, runs adventure hiking trips over the mountains at the south end of the island for visitors. You can check out his website.' I showed her some pages I'd printed off. One had a picture of Harry Kelso and a group of grinning, windswept kids roped together against a panoramic backdrop of rugged scenery.

'I think that's taken on Mount Gower, near the cliffs where Luce fell.' I turned the pages of the police report I'd brought until I came to the photographs of the site of the accident.

'Did you look at the index that lists the sources of these pictures?' I asked.

'How do you mean?'

'There are the ones taken from sea level, blurry views up the cliff, using a telephoto lens by the look of them, from a boat pitching in the swell. Detective Maddox took those, from Bob Kelso's boat. Then there are the others, closer shots of the area where Luce is assumed to have fallen, much sharper but still difficult to interpret. Curtis, the team's photographer, took those.'

'So what?'

'Maddox never went up to the accident scene. He wouldn't have been able to climb up there. Think about it—the investigating police officer never got within a hundred metres of the accident scene. He just had to take Owen and Curtis's word for everything.'

I pointed to one of the views from sea level. 'The place where Luce disappeared was to the right of this buttress—you can see its shadow. She was out of sight of Curtis and Owen. Up above you can see the forest coming right to the edge of the cliff. It wouldn't have been impossible for someone else to have abseiled down from there to where Luce was.

Someone who knew Mount Gower well, for instance.'

'Harry Kelso?'

'I'm just speculating. But suppose the Kelso boys were doing a bit of illegal trafficking on the side, and Luce overheard them talking to the yachtie at the party, say.'

Anna shook her head. 'She wouldn't have kept quiet about it, that's for sure. She'd have been horrified. She'd have told Marcus.'

'Maybe it wasn't as clear-cut as that. Perhaps she only had suspicions and was trying to get proof—remember how she seemed to withdraw in those last days.'

'And Curtis and Owen were involved?'

'That's possible, I suppose.' I thought of how they were both always short of cash. 'Look, this is pure speculation. It probably wasn't like that at all.'

'Maybe the diary will tell us something, if we can get into it.'

'Yes. The other possibility is to speak to some of the other people who were there at that time. I'm thinking of Sophie Kalajzich, for instance, the girl who cleaned the house they rented and became friendly with Luce. She was on a short-term contract over there, and could be back on the mainland now. There's a Sydney address given in the statement.'

I got the number from directory inquiries, and tried it. An answering machine responded, its message giving me the number of Sophie's mobile. I finally got through to her, saying we were old friends of Luce, and she agreed to see us. She was a model now, doing a job at a photographic studio in Newtown, she said, and we could meet her there and talk between sessions.

The address was a converted industrial building, grubby brick walls hemming a narrow laneway. Inside, past a flashy little logo, the old structure had been given a veneer of white minimalism. From the entrance lobby we could see through to a dazzlingly lit studio space in which two girls were posing in swimwear. Through another opening, seated models were having their hair and make-up worked over. I saw the expression of bemusement on Anna's face as she took it all in, as if we'd wandered in on a freak show.

A woman came past us, heading for the make-up room, and I said, 'Excuse me?'

She stopped and turned to me, disconcertingly pretty, but not quite real, a life-size china doll. The industrial brick and steel of the surroundings made the butterfly-bright fabrics and the tanned flesh and the impossible hair seem blatant and somehow embarrassing, even to me.

'We're meeting Sophie Kalajzich,' I said. 'Would you know where she is?'

'That's her.' The woman indicated the model in the yellow bikini. 'I think they've nearly finished. Take a seat.'

I thanked her and we did as she said. There were magazines scattered on a low table beside us. Anna picked one up, touching her hair self-consciously. I was watching Sophie being posed by her photographer across a striped deckchair. She was very thin. Another kind of phasmid.

Eventually she finished and wrapped herself in a robe and came towards us. We introduced ourselves, and she said she could only give us ten minutes before she'd have to get changed for the next shoot. 'This isn't some legal thing, is it?' she asked cautiously.

'Legal?'

'You know, insurance or something. Only I don't know anything about the accident really. I wasn't there.'

'Oh, no!' I smiled brightly. 'No, no, nothing like that. What it is, we're old friends of Luce, and I've been in London all the time since it happened.'

'London? Oh, you're the boyfriend, are you?' Her eyes lit up with interest.

'She mentioned me?'

'Only briefly. We were discussing men.' She grinned.

'Ah, well . . . anyway, when I got back we decided, Anna and I, to try to remember her on the fourth anniversary of her passing with a little book of memories, of people who knew her, especially in that last month. Something for her family to have, you know?'

Her very full lips turned down as if she'd tasted something unpleasant. 'Oh, right. That's really . . . sweet.'

'Yeah.' I gave her a sad smile. 'So if you have one or two memories of her, a shared laugh, a special thing you remember about her, that would be really great.'

'Um, well, let me see.' She put a perfectly shaped long nail to her chin and stared upward in thought. 'She loved her birds, the seagulls, you know? Said she wanted to be as free as them, high up in the air all the time, never coming down to land.'

I was writing dutifully. She came out with a few more fairly banal memories.

Then she said, 'She showed me your picture, standing on the edge of that cliff, you know? And one day I met her out walking, and she asked me to take a photo of her standing in the same sort of position, with the sky behind. I think she wanted to stick it onto your picture, so it would look like they'd been taken together.'

I stopped writing, a lump in my throat.

'Oh, sorry,' she cried. 'That's so tactless of me!' She reached out a hand to touch my arm.

'No . . . it's okay, Sophie. It just catches me sometimes, you know.'

'Yes, of course! I'm so sorry. I still have a little cry about her sometimes too.'

'Do you? It must have been terrible for you all when it happened.'

'Oh yes, everyone was devastated. And the boys! Being there when she fell! Watching her . . . They were a mess. They locked themselves away that night and got totally smashed. Well, you couldn't blame them.'

'No, of course not. And do you remember how Luce was herself in those last days before the accident? I mean, did she seem depressed or anything?'

'Not really, but I didn't see her after the party at the Kelsos' house.'

'Right. I just feel so guilty, not having been there. It helps talking to someone who was.'

'Oh.' She smiled sympathetically. 'I can imagine. She did seem a bit run-down physically, you know, like tired? She had a tummy bug, and saw the doctor a couple of times.'

Sophie had striking, attenuated features, and I guessed that Damien must have made a play at her. 'I suppose you got to know them all pretty well? Damien?'

She smiled. 'Oh, Damien was fun. Of course he only came for the last couple of weeks, but he livened things up.'

'I wondered if he might have been, well, comforting Lucy, after our break-up?'

'No, actually,' she grinned, 'he and I got together for a while. Then . . .' She ducked her head.

'What?'

'Oh, when the racing yachts came in, there was this really

dishy guy on one of them, and when they had the party I went off with him. Damien got pretty annoyed.'

'Luce was at that party, wasn't she?'

She thought. 'Ye-es, she must have been. Yes, I remember her talking to one of the yachties, an American I think.'

'Do you remember anything else about that evening?'

Another big smile, half-embarrassed. 'I was pretty pre-occupied—but I remember Lucy was very quiet, not drinking. I think she got upset with something the yachties said. But I pretty much had my hands full with . . . Do you know, I can't even remember his name now.'

'They were due to fly out on the Saturday. Didn't she say goodbye to you?'

'Not that I can remember. Anyway, they stayed on, didn't they? The weather turned foul.'

'So, did you see them again after that?'

'Ye-es. At least, I saw Damien. It was the night before the accident. He was pretty annoyed with me, but it wasn't just that. Something was wrong, something to do with their work. They were all pissed off.'

'And Lucy?'

'No, I'm sure I didn't see her. I think she was feeling ill again.'

'What, they told you that?'

'I suppose so.'

'And the next day, the day of the accident?'

'No, I didn't see her, but she must have felt better.'

'How do you mean?'

'Well, she went climbing with them, didn't she? I thought I might have seen her when I went to the house that day—that was my regular cleaning day—but she wasn't there, because she'd gone with them. It's terrible to think, isn't it—if she'd been a bit sicker she wouldn't have had that accident.'

'Yes, true enough. How about the Kelsos, were they nice people?'

She screwed up her nose. 'I was glad to leave, frankly. Muriel—Mrs Kelso—seemed all right at first, but she was a hard bitch if you were working for her. I didn't have much to do with Stanley, but he's an important man on the island and you wouldn't want to get on the wrong side of him.'

'How about the sons?'

'Not my type. Bob was okay, I suppose; didn't say much, spent all his time with his boat. I did think he might have had a bit of a crush on Luce, the way he looked at her sometimes. Harry . . . he tried it on with me a few times, until I finally got it into his head that I wasn't interested.'

'Bit pushy, was he?'

'Yeah, seemed to think I'd make myself available as part of my contract.'

'Was there some rumour that they were into something dodgy, smuggling or something?'

'Drugs? I never heard that.'

'Not drugs necessarily.'

But she didn't like this line of questions. She looked pointedly up at the clock and said she'd have to go.

'Sure. We really appreciate you talking to us, Sophie.'

'You're welcome. Who else have you spoken to?'

'Oh, you're the first we've tracked down, really. Who do you suggest?'

'Well, she was friends with Carmel Bisset, the National Parks ranger; they used to meet every day on account of their research project. And she knew Dick Passlow—that's the doctor—and his wife Pru. She was the island nurse.'

'Right.' I was making notes, playing the part of a grieving boyfriend. 'But they'd still be on Lord Howe, I suppose.'

'Not necessarily. I know the Passlows only had another year of their contract to run, though I suppose they could have extended it. Carmel would probably be in the same boat. They weren't permanent residents.'

'Sophie!' The call came from a harassed-looking young man who had burst out of the make-up room.

'Yes, coming. Sorry, I have to go.' We got to our feet and she added coyly, 'Do you still keep up with Damien?'

'Yes, saw him just the other day, actually.'

'Oh, well, you might give him my number, if you like.'

'I'm afraid he's married.'

She shrugged. 'All the same . . .'

Anna spoke for the first time. 'You should be careful with all that lipstick, you know.'

Sophie looked at her in surprise. 'What?'

'It's full of synthetic chemicals. Over your lifetime you'll swallow about four kilos of it.'

Sophie raised a carefully engineered eyebrow and stalked off.

Outside, as we stepped around the rubbish bins in the lane, I said, 'Four kilos?'

'Whatever. You enjoyed that, didn't you?'

'Did we learn anything?'

'Not much. The Kelsos don't sound like very nice people to stay with.'

'No. Well, you can do the talking next time.'

Dr Passlow was in the Sydney phone book, listed under a group practice in Leichhardt. Anna rang, saying that we wanted to speak to him on a private matter relating to the death of Lucy Corcoran. He agreed to see us at the end of the afternoon's surgery, at around five-thirty.

The waiting room was still crowded when we arrived, full of Italian women and their bambini suffering from what looked like an epidemic of spring sniffles. The confined, overheated space, full of coughing, sneezing, snot-encrusted infants, seemed to me like a pretty ideal breeding ground for viruses, and I thought we'd be lucky to get out unscathed. It was almost seven when we finally saw the doctor. He looked exhausted and didn't try to hide his disappointment that we were still there. In fact, as he quizzed us about what exactly we wanted, it seemed to me that he was rather worried about our appearance after all this time. He refused to elaborate on Luce's health or state of mind, and said he couldn't remember when he'd last seen her during the final week.

'Well, look,' he said finally, becoming more pompous as we became more probing, 'there's nothing I can tell you that wasn't said at the inquest. I really don't understand what you're after. You're not her relatives, are you? Is this just idle curiosity, or do you have some specific issue?'

'Yes,' I said. 'Can you think of anyone who might have had a reason to murder Lucy?'

He looked as if I'd punched him, his face going pale, mouth open. 'What? What are you talking about?'

'It's a simple question. Did she say anything to you to suggest she was afraid of anyone?'

The colour flooded back into his face again. 'No, certainly not. I'd have told the coroner if she had. Do you have some new information?'

'We just find it hard to accept that Lucy fell accidentally,' Anna cut in. 'She was a very expert climber.'

'Expert climbers are killed in accidents all the time. The coroner's investigation was very thorough. And now, years later, you find it hard to accept? Is that all?'

Anna shrugged. He shook his head in irritation and showed us to the door.

As we walked back through the waiting room a nurse stopped him with a query and I veered off to the desk where the receptionist was clearing up. 'Is Dr Passlow's wife around?' I asked, hoping he couldn't hear me.

'Wife?'

'Pru—the nurse.'

'Oh, Pru.' She smiled as if at some private joke. 'No, they divorced several years ago.'

'Don't know where I could find her, do you?'

'Sorry, no idea.'

Out on the street, Anna said, 'That was subtle. You almost had him calling the cops.'

I shrugged, becoming fed up with all this. 'I need a drink to kill some of the germs I must have picked up in there.' But Anna was reading a text message on her phone. It seemed the young bloke who looked after the computers at the nursing home had managed to unlock Luce's notebook. He didn't know what it all meant, he said, but he'd sent her the contents by email, so we walked along Norton Street until we found an internet café where Anna could access her account.

I waited outside on the pavement, breathing in the smell of pizza from the Italian restaurant next door. I felt tired and fed up after our prickly encounter with the doctor, and I just wanted to sit down with a bottle of red and a plate of spaghetti and forget about the whole thing. I noticed an empty table for two through the window, and when I saw Anna still hunched in front of her screen, shaking her head, I decided to take the bull by the horns. I opened the door and called to her, 'Anna, I'll see you in the restaurant next door.'

She frowned over her shoulder. 'Okay . . .'

I got the empty table and ordered a bottle of wine while I waited. By the time she joined me my first glass was drunk, and I felt slightly better. She was still frowning.

'Take a seat,' I said, pouring the wine. 'You look as if you need this. What's the matter?'

She slumped down and handed me half a dozen pages. 'That's the print-out.'

While she sipped at her wine I scanned the pages. On them were printed lines of letters and digits, row after row. A typical sequence of lines ran:

```
2509  1105  57J  WF  06663  04432  055
2509  1443  57J  WF  06712  05512  072
2609  0906  57J  WF  06584  04470  046
```

There were hundreds of lines like that, all following the same format with slight variations to the digits.

'Is it some sort of computer code?'

'No idea. My expert hasn't a clue.' Anna sounded flat. After going to so much trouble to get the notebook, this was obviously a major disappointment.

'You were expecting the names of the guilty parties,' I said. 'But I told you before, things like that only happen in books. This could be data on anything—tides, weather, bird migrations, buried treasure . . .'

'Buried treasure?'

'I'm joking.'

'Ha ha.'

'I'm sorry, but what could we realistically have expected?'

A harrowing account of the breakdown of a wonderful young woman after she was heartlessly ditched by a slimebag called Josh Ambler, I thought. I couldn't tell Anna how very relieved I was to see those meaningless data strings.

'So what now?' I saw the waiter approaching. 'Let's order.'

We picked the day's pasta special, then Anna said, 'I suppose you had lots of holidays when you were in London.'

'Sure, cheap flights everywhere—St Petersburg, Istanbul, New York. Lots of places. How about you?'

'I haven't had a holiday in three years.'

'Really? You must need a break.'

'That's what I was thinking. Some island getaway.'

'Aha,' I said, suddenly cautious. 'Sounds interesting. Would you go on your own?'

'It'd be more fun if I could persuade somebody else to come along. Even if I haven't got big lips and a yellow bikini.'

'You could always get that—the bikini, I mean.'

'And I might even do a bit of climbing, if I had a partner.'

'That's possible. No breaking and entering, though.'

'Agreed.'

'I don't think Damien would approve.'

'Well, I wasn't planning on inviting him.'

'You know, I always wondered about that night at the Hibernian Hotel. How did it turn out for you?'

She looked impassively at me. 'Josh, there are some questions a gentleman doesn't ask.'

When I got home after dropping Anna in Blacktown, Mary met me with a happy smile.

'Your friend Damien rang up half an hour ago. Such a charming young man. We had a good chat.'

'That's nice. I wonder why he didn't ring my mobile.'

'No, it was me he principally wanted to talk to.' Mary sounded quite flirtatious.

'Really? What about?'

'He and his wife wanted to invite us both to dinner, and he was worried I might not be able to take an evening off from the hotel.'

'Good point.'

'But I said it wasn't a problem. We're going tomorrow, is that all right with you?'

'Well, yes, fine.'

12

The next evening I realised I didn't know where Damien lived, and asked Mary if he'd given her his home address. She said yes and named a new apartment tower in The Rocks, overlooking Circular Quay. I whistled. 'Prime real estate.'

'It does sound rather grand, doesn't it? On the twenty-eighth floor.'

We drove down there, and I found a parking meter not far from the address. It was a spare, elegant tower with tiers of curved balconies disappearing up into the night sky. At the glass doors I rang the number Damien had provided and his voice gave a tinny but affable welcome. He buzzed us in, and the door clicked open. Inside we gazed up in awe at the scale of the lobby, three storeys of space with bridges and balconies supported on slender creamy concrete columns, more like the foyer of a theatre or art gallery than a block of flats. A glass swimming pool was cantilevered out above our heads, so that we could look up at the pale belly of a figure stroking through the green water, and on another level, beyond a small herd of Barcelona chairs, other residents worked resolutely on treadmills and exercise bikes.

We found the lifts and went up to the twenty-eighth floor, where Damien was waiting for us, freshly showered and scented. He gave Mary a hug and we shook hands, and he led the way across the lobby to his open front door. Inside we passed through a hallway and into his living room. The furniture was stylish muted browns and creams, and the wall beyond was floor to ceiling glass, through which the lights of other towers glittered against the dark.

'Pretty stunning apartment, Damien,' I said.

'Seidler,' he murmured, unable to suppress the little smile of pride. 'One of his last.' He cocked his head to a side door. 'Darling?'

Lauren appeared. She was pretty stunning too, a svelte brunette with shrewd eyes and an ironic smile. She kissed us in turn, saying how wonderful it was to meet us finally, Damien having told her so much about us. Mary was clearly captivated. She handed over some chocolates and asked if the evening was meant to celebrate something, perhaps the new flat.

Lauren said, 'Oh no, we've been here six months now.' Then she turned to Damien and said, 'Shall I?'

He smiled, shrugged, uncharacteristically sheepish, and she said to us, 'There is something to celebrate, though. I'm pregnant—we've just found out.' She gave a laugh. 'We haven't told anyone yet. You're the first.' She went to him, and he put a protective arm around her shoulders, grinning broadly.

'That's wonderful,' I said. 'Just as well we brought champagne.' I shook Damien's hand again and handed him the bottle.

'I suppose I shouldn't,' Lauren giggled. 'I'll give up after tonight.' She looked flushed and excited, and it was impossible not to be touched. 'I'm sorry, I was going to be so cool about this and not say a word, but the first people we meet I blurt it out. We've been trying for a while.'

Mary said, 'When is it due?'

'The beginning of May.' We sat on beautiful Italian leather while Damien brought flutes of champagne, and we drank a toast to the baby. Mary was full of questions. Would Lauren give up work? Certainly not. Were there conveniently available grandparents for baby minding? Lauren raised an incredulous eyebrow and spoke of a nanny agency. She offered to show Mary the rest of the flat, and Damien and I took our glasses out onto the balcony.

We were about a hundred metres off the ground, a couple of pitches up Frenchmans Cap, and gravity yawed at me through the glass balcony front. We were in a canyon of towers, between which we could make out a section of the Harbour Bridge, the lights of a harbour ferry. These peaks glittered with light, and were inhabited not by grey ternlets but by migrating tourists and mum-and-dad investors. Damien leaned on the rail and waved at another couple on a balcony facing us across the dark void. They waved back.

'How was Suzi?' he asked.

'About as expected, I guess. Don't worry, I behaved.'

He smiled, then reached into his pocket for his wallet, and plucked out a business card, which he handed across to me. 'Friend of mine,' he said. 'Merchant bank.' He grinned. 'Thought that would appeal to you. Looking for bright guys like you. If you're interested, give him a ring. He's a good bloke. You'll like him.'

I tapped the card with a finger. 'Hm, thanks, Damien.' I pocketed it and said, 'I met an old girlfriend of yours the other day.'

'Really? Who was that?'

'Sophie Kalajzich.'

He couldn't place her at first, then I saw it register. 'You saw Sophie Kalajzich?'

'Yep. She's a model now, remembers you fondly—actually asked me to give you her number, but I guess you won't be needing that.'

He studied me carefully. 'Why did you want to speak to her?'

'I had a bit of a brainstorm, mad idea probably. Looking back over the old newspaper cuttings about Luce's accident, I came across a report that one of those yachts that called in to Lord Howe while you were there had been involved in smuggling rare birds' eggs.'

His face froze for a brief moment, then he very slowly shook his head. 'Birds' eggs.'

'Yes. Quite a coincidence, I thought. So I wondered if someone on the island had been helping this smuggler, and I thought about the Kelsos, who seemed to be involved in everything. Sophie worked for them for six months, so I thought she might have an idea.'

'And did she?'

'No.'

Damien just stared at me for a bit, then said, 'Josh, you've obviously got too much time on your hands. You need something to occupy your mind again.'

I grinned. 'Yeah, you're probably right.'

And he probably was, but I couldn't get this odd coincidence out of my mind, and the following day I decided there was only one sensible way to move forward. I rang Kings Cross police station, and eventually got put through to Glenn Maddox, now a detective sergeant. I could tell he was intrigued when I introduced myself, and he suggested we meet in a café in Victoria Road, not far away. I recognised him from a photo in the press clippings Anna had copied for me. He was short and wiry, aged about fifty, with the air of someone who'd seen everything but was still game for one or two more rounds. His face was lined, with the trace of a scar on his left cheek, eyes steady, grizzled hair going grey around the ears, and his crumpled suit looked as if it had spent too long slouched in courtrooms and seedy bars. It had a bulge under the left arm that I guessed was his gun. He was in fact exactly how I might have imagined an experienced cop from Homicide to be.

We shook hands and he said, 'So, you're the boyfriend.'

'That's right. I just got back, trying to catch up, and I only just learned that you tried to contact me at the time. I'm afraid my father had the wrong address for me in London.'

'Well, it didn't seem relevant to my inquiries. Should it have been?'

'No.'

'So how can I help you?'

'A friend of mine had collected newspaper clippings about the accident, and when I was reading them I happened to notice another item on one of the pages.' I took my photocopy of the article from my bag and showed it to him.

He read it. 'So?'

'Well . . .' I was beginning to feel a bit stupid, playing the amateur sleuth, doing exactly what I'd accused Anna of. 'Luce and the others were studying rare birds and their eggs on Lord Howe, and this boat had just returned from there. It seemed a pretty big coincidence. I wondered if Luce might have . . . got wind of what they were doing.'

'And the smugglers decided to shut her up by pushing her off the cliff?' The deadpan way he said it made the notion sound all the more ludicrous, an episode from some adventure of the Famous Five.

'Something like that.'

He sipped his cappuccino, getting chocolate foam on his upper lip. He licked it, then said, 'Yes, I noticed that report too. The boat had been at Lord Howe when Lucy was there,

149

and it's even possible she met them. Unfortunately the eggs that were found on board didn't come from there—they were endangered cockatoo eggs, Major Mitchell and gang-gang cockatoos that aren't found on Lord Howe Island. They'd been bought from a dealer in Sydney by an American crew member on board the yacht. The tip-off probably came from a rival dealer. The American was fined twenty thousand dollars, the dealer got three months.'

'Oh.' At least I didn't feel quite so stupid, seeing he'd also been interested enough to investigate. 'So there was no connection to Luce's disappearance?'

'Not that I could see. You're trying to find some other explanation for the accident?'

'Just trying to come to terms with it, I guess.'

'Is that a copy of my report to the coroner in your bag, by any chance?'

I coloured. 'Yes, it is actually.'

'Sounds like you're taking this pretty seriously. Let me guess, you're even wondering if she isn't dead at all, that maybe the yachties took her off the island somehow and spirited her away.'

I gaped at him. 'How did you know that?' It was barely more than a fantasy that I'd allowed to take shape somewhere at the back of my mind, creeping out in the bleakest hours of the dark night to tantalise and comfort me.

'You said just now "Luce's disappearance", not her death.'

'Did I?' Just like Anna.

'Missing persons are like that. No body, no way to be absolutely certain what happened. People hang on to hope long after I know there is none. And you're feeling guilty, right? You weren't there. You never said goodbye.'

'Yes, yes.' Just like Mum, I thought. One day I left her

sleeping in the hospital bed, and the next she wasn't there any more. She'd vanished. And I couldn't even cry properly because all I felt was bitter guilt. I should have done more. I could have been a better son for her.

'Believe me, I've seen every kind of pain and grief. I've experienced a good many of them myself, too. And I know that there's only one person who can help you.'

'Really? Who's that?' I thought he was going to recommend a psychiatrist or a private detective or something.

He held me with that steady gaze and said, 'The Lord Jesus Christ.'

'Oh . . .' I was stunned into silence for a moment, then muttered, 'Um, I don't think I'm quite ready for that.'

'Well, when you are, you contact me.' He took a card from his pocket and passed it to me. There was a man's name and phone number beside a cross. 'I'll introduce you to this man, or you can get in touch with him direct. He will lead you to the Lord, and you won't look back. Trust me, I know.'

I had been about to tell him about Owen's confession to Anna, but now I stared dumbly at the card and said nothing.

'And I'll give you something else to put in that bag of yours, son. Something that'll help you a lot more than my report to the coroner.' He reached into his jacket, to the bulge that I'd noticed, and drew out not his service Glock but a copy of the New Testament, which he handed to me.

'Thank you,' I muttered, not quite sure what to do, but his phone rang and he listened for a moment, then got to his feet.

'I have to go now, but you remember—get in touch with me any time.'

I shook his hand, and then on impulse added, 'I'm thinking of going to Lord Howe for a visit.'

He stared at me, still gripping my hand, then said, 'Pay your last respects, yes, maybe not a bad idea. Say hello from me to the young copper over there if you see him, Grant Campbell.'

He turned and walked away.

13

I didn't do much more climbing with Luce and her friends after Frenchmans Cap. Instead she and I found safer ways to fulfil ourselves, moving into a flat together when we returned to Sydney. We were very happy that summer, she spending the days working in the Conservation Biology Centre, me earning money washing dishes in the restaurant next door while trying to get on with my MBA thesis on risk management.

She liked to tease me about risk management, as if my choice of subject betrayed some aspect of my personality. I don't mean that she was being critical of me—that summer we each believed the other perfect—so much as hinting that I was in need of some realignment, a process largely achieved on Frenchmans Cap. It was something to do with accepting the intractable nature of things, of experiencing the exhilaration of dangerous reality, of letting go and falling yet still climbing out.

I saw things a little differently. It seemed to me that climbing perfectly illustrated the centrality of risk management in life. It was an extreme metaphor of everyday experience, in which risk was always present to some degree, but capable of being managed—superbly in her case, clumsily in mine.

Risk management became sexy in financial circles after the big scandals of the nineties—Baring Brothers, Metallgesellschaft, Orange County, Sumitomo—demonstrated the degree to which the growth of financial derivatives could expose institutions to enormous losses. The ease with which a single trader could lose over a billion dollars and bring down the oldest private bank in London was very scary, and led a lot of people to become interested in how such risks could be managed. My research area was on the computational side, examining case studies using variants of the Black–Scholes–Merton model and Monte Carlo simulations. I tried to explain all this to Luce, but she found it unreal and, I suspect, rather silly. She was amused, though, when I told her that Nick Leeson might have got away with it, had it not been for the Kobe earthquake, which caused a sudden drop in Japanese equities. She seemed to think there was some sort of natural justice in that. After Frenchmans Cap I had a finer appreciation of sudden drops and natural justice, and could see what she meant.

But by the following June, my master's almost completed, things weren't going so well for Luce and me. I blame myself entirely now, although at the time I found all kinds of reasons and rationalisations for my discontent. I was becoming restless, feeling unreasonably restricted and tied down. Perhaps it was a character flaw on my part, something more intractable than even the experience on Frenchmans Cap could cure. One telling symptom of my malaise was a creeping sense of that feeling that Groucho Marx identified when he said that he didn't want to belong to any club that would have him as a member. It's more common than we like to admit, that feeling, but made invisible because we don't seem to have a name for it. We need to borrow one, as we did with *schadenfreude*, literally *harm-joy*. Perhaps *selbsthassfreude*, self-hate-joy. I began to think that there must be something wrong with Luce, something inadequate and unworthy, simply because she loved me.

One weekend Luce went back to see her father in Orange. I didn't go, and after finishing at the restaurant on the Saturday night I called in at a student party we'd been invited to. There was a girl there, quite a pretty little thing, who took a great fancy to me. I couldn't shake her off, and didn't really want to. I slept with her that night.

The next day I tried to tell myself it was a trivial thing and didn't matter. I chased the girl away and told her I didn't want to see her again, and tried to put the whole thing out of my mind. But when Luce came back and I watched her unpack her bag, talking about her trip, I felt sick with shame. Of course she wouldn't see it as trivial, no more than I would have done in her place. I wondered how long it would take for her to find out, and thought I should tell her first, but I couldn't. I wasn't brave enough. I had a poisonous secret now, and hated myself for it. Every time she came into the room, every time she looked at me, I scanned her face for the knowledge. It became a void between us, a thousand-foot drop that I couldn't cross.

Then I got an email from a friend who'd been a year ahead of me at uni. Gary McCall was a New Zealander who, like me, had been steered into quantitative finance by our tutor. Now he was in London, working for the BBK Bank. They were running an innovative new in-house program for their staff, he said, rotating them through a number of the bank's departments in both London and Frankfurt to get a thorough practical grounding in risk management strategies. He was very enthusiastic; the program was highly regarded and the bank was recruiting. He had been specifically asked by his boss, Lionel Stamp, if he knew of any more like him who might be interested in coming over. Without telling Luce, I said I was definitely interested, and received an application form by return.

So I decided that I had to leave. I had always assumed that I would have a spell working abroad after I'd finished uni, but now this vague ambition became focused into a compulsion. I had to leave Australia, I told Luce; my career demanded it. She had to finish her honours year, culminating in the field trip to Lord Howe Island. And after that she had been accepted for a master's in Marcus's Conservation Biology Centre. We discussed alternatives, her following me to London after she'd done the field trip, or me delaying my departure to go with them to Lord Howe, but nothing was resolved, and there was an emptiness between us when it finally came time for me to leave.

Anna phoned me the next morning to say that she'd tracked down Pru Passlow, the doctor's ex-wife. My first reaction was to tell her to forget it, and I described my meeting with Detective Sergeant Maddox, whose thoroughness had begun to make me doubt our ability to discover anything new. But Anna had already arranged to meet Ms Passlow, who was now a lecturer in the Faculty of Nursing at the university, and who had said we could catch her at the university library that morning.

I picked Anna up at Central and drove her to the campus. It felt very strange going back into the library, the first time since that sweet, intense time over four years before when I had been immersed in my master's, and in Luce. So redolent was that familiar library smell that my pulse began to race and the arteries in my throat began to swell, as if I might catch sight of her at any moment.

We tracked Pru Passlow down by Dewey decimal, at 610.73 among the stacks. She seemed a brisk, capable woman, with bright, sharp eyes. We sat around a table and kept our voices low, in deference to the readers in the adjoining carrels.

'So what's your interest?' she asked. 'Are you writing a book or something?'

'No, nothing like that,' Anna said. 'We were close friends of Lucy's, but we weren't with her at Lord Howe. Josh has been in England all this time, and now he's back, he wanted to speak to some of the people who were there.'

'I've never been able to get it out of my mind,' I said.

'Ah, closure,' Pru Passlow nodded. 'Yes, I'm still haunted by it. Never finding her made it seem worse. When was the last time you saw her?' She directed this at me.

'Um, August the eleventh, about three weeks before she went to Lord Howe. I left for London, and she saw me off at the airport. Actually, we wanted to ask you the same question.'

'Why is that?'

Ms Passlow had obviously found the Socratic method a good teaching technique—answer a question with another question. That's Socrates the philosopher, of course; Socrates the dog also uses the method, but he only ever has one question: 'Can I have something to eat?'

'Well, from what people have told us, she seemed to be depressed and unwell in those last weeks. We wondered if that could have contributed to her accident.'

'You've spoken to my ex, have you? What did he tell you?'

'Not a lot.'

She gave a little smile. 'And how well did you know Luce, Josh?'

Luce, not Lucy. I shifted uncomfortably in my seat, and wondered why she kept asking these questions. 'Pretty well. No, very well. We were close.'

'I see. I did wonder if there was someone . . .'

'So when did you last see her?'

'It would save you a lot of time if you just asked the coroner's office for their report on the inquest, don't you think?'

'We've read it.'

'Well then.'

She still seemed incapable of giving a straight answer.

'You said you last saw Luce on the evening of September the twenty-eighth, at the party at the Kelsos' for the yacht crews.'

'Yes I did, didn't I?'

'That must have been a big party.'

'Social event of the year.'

'Did you get much of a chance to speak to Luce then?'

'Not really. I just noticed she was there.'

Anna suddenly said, 'What was making her sick?'

The abruptness of the question threw the other woman for a moment. 'You read my husband's diagnosis, didn't you? Gastroenteritis.'

'Why are you being so evasive, Pru?' Anna said. It was a belligerent question, but spoken gently. Then she added, 'She was pregnant, wasn't she?'

Pru Passlow just stared back at her, unblinking.

I looked from one to the other. 'Pregnant?'

'Must have occurred to you,' Anna said, though whether to me or Pru, I wasn't sure.

Finally Pru broke eye contact with Anna and gave a shrug. 'You said it.'

'Why didn't you tell the coroner?'

'Luce asked me to keep it to myself, although I did tell my husband. He was very embarrassed. Asked me to keep quiet about it.'

My head was buzzing, and I had difficulty concentrating on what they were saying.

Anna said, 'Embarrassed about what?'

'His misdiagnosis. And the fact that Luce came to me, not him.'

'I still don't understand.'

Pru took a deep breath. 'Dick was in love with her. Horribly, grovellingly, embarrassingly so. Things were pretty bad between him and me at that stage—we went to Lord Howe originally to patch things up after I'd had a stupid affair. We thought it would bring us back together again, the two of us on an idyllic island, but it turned out to be a very bad idea. By the time Luce came along we couldn't stand the sight of each other. We hadn't slept together for six months. And, of course, he couldn't look at any of the women on the island, not in a place like that—everybody would have known about it within ten minutes. We were just about at breaking point, ready to throw it in and return to the mainland, then this beautiful, intelligent, sympathetic girl stepped off the plane.'

'Morning sickness?' I hissed. 'Are you sure?' I felt like the man who was mugged in the library and had to whisper for help.

Pru turned and looked carefully at me. I understood her caution now.

'She came to see me late in the afternoon of that Thursday, before the party, when she knew Dick wouldn't be at the hospital. She asked me to test her, so I did. It was positive. She didn't say much more other than to ask me to tell no one.'

'Didn't she say how late her period was?' Anna said.

'No. And I didn't ask about the father. She didn't want to talk.'

'How soon does morning sickness happen, after conception?' I whispered.

'Usually between two and ten weeks.'

'Did your husband . . .' For once Anna seemed to have difficulty finishing a sentence.

'Have sex with her? I honestly don't know. He was certainly badly shaken up when I told him about the positive test. That was a couple of days after the accident, when it was becoming clear that she hadn't survived.'

'Did you ask him?'

'Yes, but he didn't say anything. He just burst into tears. I debated what to do, but in the end I decided I should respect Luce's wishes.'

We sat in silence for a long moment, then Anna said, 'What really happened to Luce, Pru?'

Pru frowned, as if not sure what to make of that. 'What the coroner said, presumably. Why? Do you know something different?'

'We're not sure. Can you think of any other explanation for Luce's disappearance?'

'No, of course not.'

'Was anybody angry with her?'

'What are you getting at? Are you suggesting somebody pushed her? The two boys with her that day?'

'Is that possible? Or somebody else?'

Pru shook her head in disbelief. 'I'm sorry, I haven't the faintest idea. They seemed like nice boys. Have you spoken to them?'

'They're both dead, Pru. They were killed in a climbing accident in New Zealand about a month ago. They left a message, you see, that was ambiguous.'

Pru looked shocked. 'My God, so many accidents . . . I suppose theirs was an accident?'

'As far as we know.' I gave her one of Mary's cards and wrote my mobile number on the back. 'Please give us a ring if you think of anything else.'

Anna said not a word as we tramped back to the car. We got in and I said, 'Leichhardt?' and she just nodded. I said, 'Did you suspect it all along, or was it just a sudden brainwave?'

She looked at me as if I was a bit slow, and turned away. I had a powerful urge to kick her out and drive somewhere quiet and just scream or weep or jump into the ocean. But there'd be time for that. I buckled up and started the engine.

We were in luck. Dr Passlow had a Saturday morning surgery, for the older ragazzi and their dads by the look of it. I asked the receptionist for a piece of paper and an envelope, and wrote a short note for the doctor. 'Would you mind giving him this as soon as you can, please? It is rather urgent.'

After ten minutes he appeared, ushering an old man to the desk. He looked impatient as he took the note, ripped it open, read, and then turned very pale. He scanned around the room until he saw us, then gave a brief jerk of his head for us to follow him to his room.

'What did she tell you?' The muscles of his mouth bunched around the words as if they were sour.

But I'd had enough of being questioned. 'Why don't you just tell us.'

'I had no reason to suspect pregnancy. She didn't hint at the possibility to me. The symptoms were compatible with gastroenteritis, which was going around at the time.'

'Can you estimate how far gone she was?'

'No, I've no idea.'

Anna took over. 'Why did you tell your wife to hide it?'

'For Luce's sake. She'd specifically asked Pru to say nothing.'

'You were in love with Luce, weren't you?'

He dipped his head. 'That's none of your business.'

'Did you try to have sex with her?'

He winced, then said, 'No.' It didn't sound convincing, but it was an ambiguous question. Had he had sex, or had he tried?

I said, 'I've been in touch with the detective who drew up the report for the coroner. Maybe we should tell him about this.'

Passlow shook his head hopelessly. 'Please don't do that. It has no bearing on anything.'

'How can you be sure?'

'Well, you're the amateur detectives!' he shot back suddenly, switching to bluster. 'Work it out. If anything suspicious happened to Lucy then those two on the cliff with her must have been involved, right? And I don't believe that for an instant. They . . . they were good friends. They'd never have hurt her.'

He had picked up something about Curtis and Owen, I thought.

'Look, if you want reassurance, go to the island. Speak to the ranger, Carmel Bisset, or Bob Kelso. They were her friends too. She may have confided in them.'

Anna was reluctant to let it go at that. 'So you still maintain that the last time you saw Luce was at the party on the Thursday evening?'

He nodded sadly. 'I barely saw her there. She was avoiding me, I think. I never saw her again.'

'What about Damien Stokes? Remember him? He complained of having a tummy bug in that last week, too. Did he come to see you?'

'Stokes?'

I described him. 'Black hair, beard, my height, science/law student. He arrived halfway through their month on the island.'

'Oh yes, I remember. Pru took a fancy to him, as I remember.'

'That'd be right,' Anna muttered.

The doctor had got to his feet and was searching through a row of large desk diaries in his bookshelves until he found the year. He turned to late September, scanning the pages. 'Yes, I saw him on the Tuesday, but not because of a stomach upset. He came to see me that evening to dress a scrape on his knee he'd got while climbing with the rest of them that day. Nothing serious.'

'May I?' I asked, and reached for the book in his hand. He released it reluctantly. I checked the pages for that last week. Damien's was the only name from the university group that was mentioned. 'Thanks.'

When we got back into the car, Anna said, 'Passlow's right. We're going to have to go to the island.'

I felt queasy. 'I think we should consider this a bit more, Anna. I'm not sure it'll do any good going there. In fact it could do a lot of harm.'

'I need you there, Josh.'

'Why?'

'I was never one for solo climbing.'

14

Nor was I. One of Luce's heroes was an American climber, Lynn Hill, whom she had met once when Lynn visited Australia. Lynn was the first person to free climb, without artificial aids, the Nose route up El Capitan at Yosemite, an almost impossible thousand-metre ascent, in just twenty-three hours, much of it in darkness. Luce had shown me photographs of the epic climb, to me unimaginable. I remembered that as I was poking about in the boxes I'd left with Mary four years before, pulling out my old climbing shoes from one, my helmet and chalk bag from another. They looked worn and tired, someone else's possessions, not mine. How had Luce ever come to love that other person, that other me I could hardly recognise now?

Even my nylon rope looked worn out. I put the stuff down with a flutter of anxiety. I was different in other ways now, out of shape and out of practice, hands soft from office work. I couldn't see myself scaling the cliffs below Mount Gower any more. Not without Luce. But this was for Luce, Anna insisted; one last climb for Luce.

My phone rang. I returned abruptly to the present, recognising Damien's voice.

'Josh, hi. How's it going?'

'Good, thanks. You? Lauren okay?'

'Fighting fit. You been to see my friend yet?'

The merchant banker. I'd forgotten about it. 'Um, no, not yet, Damien. Been a bit tied up. Maybe when I get back.'

'Back?'

'Yes. Anna and I are going away for a short trip. To Lord Howe.'

'What?' I heard his breathing, heavy against the mouthpiece. 'What exactly do you hope to achieve there?'

'I don't know. Talk to some of the locals. Listen, that last week on the island, the week of the accident, you mentioned that you were pretty much out of it in the days after the party, not feeling well.'

'Yes?'

'So you didn't go climbing on the Friday, the day following the party?'

'I . . . I can't remember now. Is that what I said? Why are you interested?'

'Just trying to place everybody at the scene.'

'Jesus, Josh, listen to yourself. Who do you think you are, Ed McBain? Where are you going to stay?'

'We booked on the internet. It's one of the Kelsos' cottages.'

'Well . . . I really don't see the point, but if it helps you get over this, good luck.'

'Thanks.'

He rang off. I hadn't mentioned our big discovery. The thought of him knowing—of anyone knowing—that Luce had been pregnant when she died just made me feel sick.

I didn't tell Mary either, but I did have to discuss our trip with her. She thought it was a good idea, but I didn't let her see the climbing gear I'd packed. That evening I roamed around the hotel, apprehensively checking the locks and light bulbs, as if I might not be coming back.

15

Luce had told me something about Lord Howe Island. It was the remains of an ancient volcano, the only island in the Pacific that the Polynesians missed as they hopped across the ocean. When HMS *Supply* came upon it in 1788, it was one of the last places left on earth on which no human foot had ever trod, a true Eden burgeoning with unique species. The sailors managed to eat a good few of them to extinction as well as introduce some feral predators, and the arrival of the black rat, *Rattus rattus*, from a grounded ship later didn't help, but still, a great deal of its natural state had survived and was now being nurtured and restored.

For my benefit, hoping to tickle my interest, Luce spoke of the island's economic history too; of how the early settlers survived by selling fresh meat and vegetables to passing American whaling ships; of how they were almost wiped out by the collapse of the whaling industry in the 1870s, and were saved by the discovery of the kentia palm, uniquely adapted to a cooler climate and so ideally suited to the Victorian drawing rooms of the northern hemisphere; of how the black rat took a fancy to kentia seeds as well as everything else, and had to be hunted on a bounty system, a rat's tail being worth one penny in 1920, rising to sixpence by 1928.

She tried hard, but I was determined not to be interested. I was going to London. What could I possibly want with a place whose whole history could be told in a couple of paragraphs? Now, belatedly, I was on my way.

We met up at Central and took the train together out to the airport. I thought Anna looked younger, with her backpack and holiday gear, and there was a blush of colour in her cheeks. I still had that hollow apprehensive feeling in my stomach you get before a journey or a climb, and we talked with a forced cheerfulness. Neither of us referred to Pru Passlow's revelation.

An hour out from Sydney, as I watched the shadows of puffy clouds glide across the rippled surface of the ocean far below the little plane, I told her I bet I could guess what she was thinking.

'Oh yes?'

'Islands,' I said. 'In books. *Robinson Crusoe, Treasure Island, The Lord of the Flies* . . .'

'*And Then There Were None*,' she replied. '*The Executioners, The Skull Beneath the Skin* . . .'

'Er, *The Magus, Lost* . . .' That was about the lot as far as I was concerned, but she had plenty more, all mysteries of course.

'*The Singing Sands, Evil Under the Sun, Five on a Treasure Island, The Lighthouse* . . .'

'You win,' I conceded. 'Is there a common theme?'

'Oh yes; the presence of evil in the Great Good Place. It's the very first story of all, the serpent in the Garden of Eden.' She cast me a sideways look, and I wondered if that's how she saw me now, Luce's serpent.

'*Rattus rattus*,' I muttered. 'Do we have a plan? I imagine all your island detectives had some kind of plan.'

'To have a close look at the place of the accident, and to check out the Kelsos.'

'Do we tell them we were friends of Luce's?'

'We may have to later, but let's wait until we've had a chance to look around. There's no reason they should know who we are.'

'Right, stealth—good thinking.'

I turned back to the window. The view was unchanged and the hollow feeling returned to my stomach; such a vast ocean to absorb one tiny human being. One and a bit tiny human beings.

As we banked in, we got a fine view of the island, a dark crescent in the gleaming ocean, embracing a long narrow lagoon contained by the most southerly coral reef on the planet. The sun glinted off tin roofs among foliage in the low-lying land in the centre of the island, flanked by the two high peaks of Mount Lidgbird and Mount Gower to the south, and by lower hills to the north. The airstrip lay in a narrow sandy waist in the middle, and as we began our approach the pilot warned us to expect a bumpy landing. We descended, losing speed, and the plane was buffeted by surface winds channelling around the mountains. Our wheels touched the runway with a squeal, then lifted again as a gust threw the plane sideways. It corrected, skewing around, then dropped abruptly onto the deck, bounced and skidded to a halt. Everyone clapped.

We clambered out and made our way to a small building to claim our bags. There were drivers standing there holding up signs, and while we waited I idly read their messages, all displaying names of hotels, except one. I blinked with surprise at that one, which said JOSH & ANNA. The man who was holding the sign across his chest was staring directly at me, and I was immediately sure that he knew exactly who I was. I touched

Anna's arm and said, 'We're expected,' and nodded at the man. Anna looked, and he stared back at her, unsmiling. He was in his early thirties, perhaps, weathered and tough.

He came towards us as the trolley with our bags arrived, and held out his hand. 'Bob Kelso.' He didn't seem to need confirmation of who we were.

We loaded the bags into the back of his truck, and climbed into the front beside him. I said, 'You seem to know who we are, Bob.'

'Recognised your name on our guest list, Josh. Luce spoke about you. She had your picture in her wallet.' He spoke with a soft, deliberate slowness, eyes slightly narrowed as if more used to focusing on distant waves than people. 'We were friends.'

I felt a small jag of jealousy. Luce, not Lucy; they'd been friends. He'd seen inside her wallet. And he'd shared her last month on earth.

'So what brings you over here?'

'I was away in England when it happened, and I just got back. I bumped into Anna, and we thought it would be good to visit the place where Luce died. Closure, you know.'

He didn't say anything. Perhaps he disliked that word as much as I did. I thought it best not to start asking him questions at this point, and Anna seemed to feel the same. As we drove off Bob pointed out landmarks. On our left we could see the wide sweep of the beach and lagoon, with a rim of white breakers along the line of the distant reef. To our right the road was lined by thick groves of trees among which we caught glimpses of white timber houses, and after a kilometre or so we turned into a driveway which led through the trees—kentia palms, I noticed, but full-size, much larger than the indoor plants I'd seen before—to a clearing surrounded by verandaed cottages. He pulled to a stop and led us inside one of them. It was a pleasant, self-contained cabin, two bedrooms with a lounge and kitchen bar, simple timber furniture, polished floorboards and shutters on the windows.

'Perfect,' I said.

'There's information leaflets on the desk over there,' Bob pointed. 'Where you can eat, things you can do, nature trails, beaches, stuff like that. But seeing as you're friends of Luce, I'd like to show you around.'

'That would be great, if you can spare the time, Bob. You must have been one of the last people to see Luce. We'd appreciate the chance to talk to you about it, if you don't mind.'

He gave his slow nod. 'I have a boat. We could go out tomorrow, see the place where it happened, if you like.'

'Yes, we'd like that.'

'Fine. Why don't you have a look around yourselves, and I'll come back at six. We can have a beer before dinner. Mum's invited you to the house to eat with us.'

'Sounds great.'

As he drove away I turned to Anna. 'So much for stealth.'

The place had a relaxed holiday feel about it, and I would have been happy to stroll around for an hour or two, buy a bottle of wine and put my feet up, but Anna thought we should act quickly before everyone on the island had been told to watch out for us. I thought they probably already had, but I went along with her plan anyway, which was to catch the ranger unprepared, if she was still there.

We walked down the road to the end of Lagoon Beach, where there was a store and visitors' centre at the heart of what passed for the town. There we got directions to the ranger's office, which we found in an old cottage further along the street. There was a light on inside, and a young woman with sandy hair, dressed in khaki shorts and shirt, was bent over a desk. She lifted her head with a smile. 'Hello. Can I help you?'

I looked at the nametag on her shirt. 'Carmel? I'm Josh and this is Anna. We were friends of Lucy Corcoran at university.'

'Oh, really? I'm very pleased to meet you.' She shook hands vigorously, and there was a warmth to her smile that suggested she'd be fun to have around. But then the smile faded. 'Were you friends of Curtis and Owen, too? We heard about the accident, of course.'

'Yes, we were. We all used to go climbing together.'

'That's terrible. Three of you . . .'

'We're just here on a short holiday, and we wanted to say hello to the people Luce met. You got to know her quite well during that month she was here, didn't you?'

'I did, yes, but . . . I'd love to have a good long chat to you, but you've caught me at the worst time. A friend's offered to shout me a trip back to the mainland for some leave, and I'm about to dash to catch the plane. In fact I was just about to close the office.' She checked her watch.

'Maybe just a couple of minutes, Carmel? We've come all this way.'

'Of course. Sorry, I feel so rude. Do you want to sit down?'

We sat around the office table and accepted the cups of water she offered us.

'How did you two come to meet?' I asked.

'Oh, it was part of the protocol. Dr Fenn had to have approval for his research program from the Island Board, which consulted with us here at National Parks and Wildlife. Part of the agreement was that his team would log each day's activities with my office. Luce was the person who liaised with me, so we soon got to know each other. She was brilliant . . .' Carmel paused, looking wistfully at her knees. 'We got on well. We shared the same values.'

'Maybe you could take us through that month they were here. It would really help us come to terms with Luce's death to hear it from you.'

'I met with them here the day they arrived, and we confirmed their program. They were going to start on Roach Island . . .' She got up and pointed it out on a big wall map. 'It's part of the Admiralty group just off the coast to the north, up here. There's a grey ternlet colony on the cliffs of Roach Island, and they were planning to spend the first two weeks there, until the fourth climber, Damien, arrived, when they would move down to the much bigger cliffs below Mount Gower, right down at the southern tip. When you leave here you could take the trail up to Malabar Hill, where you can get a good view of the Admiralty Islands. You'd really have to see the Mount Gower cliffs from the ocean side. Maybe Bob Kelso could take you.'

'Yes, he's already said he will.'

'You've seen him, have you?'

'He met us at the airport.'

'Oh good.'

'How did Luce seem when they first arrived?'

'Seem? Well, excited I suppose, about being here and getting started on the project. They all were.'

'And later, when Damien arrived?'

She frowned, thinking. 'They'd got into a routine by then, but they seemed pretty happy with things. They'd kept to their program, and finished the first phase as planned.'

'You got to meet the others, Owen and Curtis?'

'Oh yes. They were really nice boys, good fun, and Damien too.'

'How about Dr Fenn?'

'Yes, we got on all right. He could be a bit intimidating, but I'd got to know him on his previous visits.'

'So there were no quarrels, fights, that you were aware of?'

'No. Why do you ask that?'

'We heard that Luce became withdrawn and depressed towards the end of the trip. Were you aware of it?'

'She had a bit of a tummy bug,' she said, pondering. 'But she didn't say anything to me about feeling down. Damien would know better.' She looked at her watch again. 'I'm afraid I have to get changed.'

I said hurriedly, 'Could we see Luce's daily log reports, Carmel? We have so little record of her, it would be good to see some of her work.'

She frowned, her eyes straying to the filing cabinet. 'Oh, I'm not sure where they'd be now.' She got up and began searching through the drawers. 'No, I think they must have gone to Sydney . . . Oh, hang on.' She pulled out a file, checked its title and handed it to me. I flicked through the pages. Each day had a new page, on a standard National Parks and Wildlife form, filled in by hand. I turned to the first one, and a familiar string of numbers caught my eye:

1030 57J WF 05935 14723 023

Beneath was a paragraph describing observations of grey ternlets.

'What's that?' I pointed to the numbers.

'It's a map reference.'

'It doesn't look like one.'

'It's a UTM reading—Universal Transverse Mercator?' I looked blank. 'It's different from the old longitude and latitude way of fixing a position. The UTM system divides the surface

173

of the world into grid rectangles—we're in grid zone 57J. Then each zone is subdivided into hundred-kilometre squares; we're in WF, see?'

'Right.'

'The next ten numbers are the eastings and northings of the position, and the final three numbers are the height above Australian datum. The numbers at the beginning are the time; so, at ten-thirty on that morning, Luce logged a reading from the GPS equipment she carried. They were on Roach Island, twenty-three metres above sea level, and the reading tells us exactly where they were, to the nearest metre.'

'Neat. I didn't get any further than degrees and minutes at school.'

'The GPS equipment can convert from one system to the other. They happened to use UTM.'

'And they had to report every move to you?'

'It was part of the deal. Lord Howe has World Heritage listing, and the surrounding waters are protected as a marine park, so anyone landing on the offshore islands has to get approval from the board, which can take months. Dr Fenn had his research program approved long before they came.'

I turned the pages through September, and came at last to the twenty-eighth, the day after the yachts arrived. The handwriting was different. I noticed that the signature at the bottom was Owen's and the date next to the signature was the twenty-ninth, the following day, whose page had also been completed by Owen, on that day; the thirtieth had a note that bad weather had prevented work; the first of October was again written by Owen, and the second, the day of the accident, was blank.

'Luce stopped doing the reports in that last week,' I pointed out. 'Why was that?'

She shrugged. 'I don't know. As I said, she was feeling a bit unwell. Maybe that's why he took over. I can't really remember.'

Anna asked again about Luce's state of mind and about the party on the Thursday night, and while they talked I went through those final pages again, studying the number strings, the terse reports. Apart from Luce's electronic diary, they formed the only contemporary record of her last days, and I desperately scanned them for some clue, some hint of that final drama. But there was nothing, not even a single mention of Luce's name.

'Now I really must go.'

'Of course. Have a good trip. Who did you say is treating you to the trip?'

'Mr Kelso,' she said. 'He's very supportive of our work. It came up at the last minute—he'd booked a flight that he couldn't use, and he offered it to me. I'll be away for a couple of weeks.'

'Then we probably won't see you again. Thanks anyway for talking to us.'

16

'Could we have been the cause of Carmel's sudden holiday?' I asked Anna. 'Or am I being paranoid?'

'It wasn't as if she had any answers.'

'No, but we had no time to work out what the right questions were. Ten minutes later and we'd have missed her altogether, thanks to Mr Kelso.'

We had decided to take Carmel's advice to walk up to Malabar Hill, and were following the road that led over to Neds Beach on the eastern side of the island. Ahead of us a man was walking, and as he turned off the road we recognised him as Bob. When we reached the place where he had been we saw that he had gone down a path leading to an old timber house with a tin roof. There was no sign of him, and I assumed he must have gone inside. There was a white picket fence around the house, and a child's tricycle by the gate.

At Neds Beach, a wide arc of pale sand, we found a small crowd standing in the sea in swimsuits, and as we got closer we could see the water boiling around them. After a moment we discovered why—one of them was throwing something into the water from a bucket, feeding a huge shoal of fish. We watched for a while as the people shrieked and pointed, the pitch of their cries rising when someone noticed a small shark's fin cruising through the turmoil.

From the beach we found the sign for the trail up Malabar Ridge to the point. As we climbed above the trees, wide panoramas opened up along the coastline and back over the settlement towards the louring humps of the two big mountains to the south. A steady north-easterly breeze whipped our faces as we hiked up to the peak of Malabar Hill and gazed out from the cliff top to the islands lying a kilometre offshore. Hundreds of white gulls wheeled around us, dancing in the up-draught. They had bright scarlet beaks and improbable scarlet streamers in their tail feathers, and they were performing extraordinary aerobatics in front of us, great sweeping backward somersaults and plummeting dives, like hyperactive circus stars. We could make out clouds of seabirds over Roach Island too, the largest of the Admiralty Islands, and for a few moments I imagined that I could see Luce out there, recording her observations in the glow of the late afternoon sun. We watched the red disc drop to touch the ocean, an odd thing for us who live on the east coast, then turned for the hike back. The twilight was deepening when we reached Neds Beach again, where nature put on another performance for us—the return of the muttonbirds from their day out on the ocean, skimming in fast and low like demented Kamikaze, almost clipping the heads of the people gathered to watch, then wheeling and dropping to their burrows around the shore.

It was after six when we reached the cabin, and Bob was already there on the deck, feet up, can in hand. We had picked up a couple of bottles of wine and a six-pack on our way back, and I put these in the fridge along with those he'd brought. I decided I could let my fellow detective keep the clear head. She'd disappeared for a shower when I stepped out onto the veranda, and I sat with Bob and we chatted about the footy. Though I hadn't really been keeping up, I could remember enough about the Sydney teams to make conversation. But all the time I had the feeling that the real subject was me, what

I was made of, what I knew, what I was doing there. Sprawled out on the chair, behind lowered eyelids and over the rim of his cold tinny, he assessed me. Was I a fisherman? he asked. He'd been out that afternoon and caught a couple of trevally for dinner. Maybe the next day we could drop a line from his boat. Was I a climber? A nature-lover? He suggested I join a group going up to the top of Mount Gower with his brother as guide. I wondered if he'd had a look in our bags and seen the climbing gear. We avoided the one subject we were both really interested in—Luce's accident. Then again, maybe he really did want to know my opinion of the Rabbitohs' chances. All I managed to extract from him was that neither he nor his brother was married and they lived in the main house with their parents, with whom we would be dining that night.

Anna joined us, refreshed, and I fetched more drinks. It was a pleasant, cool night, with no mosquitos or flies, the breeze rustling the tops of the palms. Then we heard the sudden piercing cry of a baby. It stopped, then was followed by another, further away, then a third. The sound was so plaintive it made my hair stand on end. Bob saw the look on our faces and grinned. 'Muttonbirds. You get used to it.'

We later followed him along the path that wound through the groves of palms towards his parents' sprawling timber-framed house, where Stanley Kelso met us at the front steps. A stockier, more heavily built version of his son, he was blunt and pugnacious, obviously a man used to getting his own way. He must have been fifteen centimetres shorter than me, but he straightened his back and pushed out his barrel chest when he took my hand in a hard grip. He offered us drinks and got straight to the point. 'Lucy's death was a tragedy for us all. We got to know her and we liked her, so any friend of hers is welcome in this house.'

We thanked him, and he went on, 'And those two colleagues of hers, Curtis and Owen, they've gone now too in much the same way. It beggars belief. I'm very sorry. You're not climbers as well are you?'

'As a matter of fact we are. In fact—'

But he cut me off. 'A very dangerous pastime, obviously. At least you won't be doing anything like that when you're here.'

Bob said, 'I did suggest that they might like to go with one of Harry's groups to Mount Gower, if they've got the time.'

'Well, that's safe enough, as long as you follow his instructions. You'll no doubt want to see the places where Lucy worked. Bob tells me he's taking you out on his boat tomorrow if the wind doesn't get up too much. He'll be able to show you the bird colonies she was studying, on Roach Island and below Mount Gower, where the accident happened.'

'Yes, we're grateful,' I said. 'But as a matter of fact we do plan to do a bit of climbing, up to the place where Lucy fell.'

Stanley Kelso's head rocked back on his shoulders as he glared at me. 'Out of the question.'

'We're both experienced climbers, and we've brought our equipment . . .'

He was shaking his head firmly. 'No, no, no. Lucy's was the first fatal accident we've had on the island in years. I was very doubtful about what they had planned at the time—there are no mountain rescue services within five hundred kilometres of here. I blame myself now for letting myself be persuaded. There's no chance that we're going to allow anyone to repeat the exercise.'

I made to argue, but he raised his hand to silence me. 'No. We agreed in the end to their proposal because Lucy and the others were doing important scientific conservation work, but we have no intention of encouraging mountaineering thrill-seekers here.'

'We just want to pay our last respects at the actual place, Mr Kelso,' I said. 'I understand that it was the island's administrative board that approved their program. Perhaps if we put in a proposal?'

'Won't make any difference. In any case, the board doesn't meet for another month. I suggest you take some flowers with you tomorrow, and Bob will get you as close to the place where she fell as he can.'

Bob had been watching this exchange with a trace of wry amusement in his eyes, as if his father and I had been having the sort of tussle he'd been used to losing for years. He turned his head towards the door as his brother Harry came in. He was fresh out of the shower after a day leading a group through the rainforest in the southern uplands. He had the same brown outdoor complexion as his brother, but he seemed leaner and tougher. His dark hair was cut very short, and I thought he looked as if he might have been in the army.

His father said, 'We were just explaining to Josh and Anna that there's no possibility of them climbing up the cliffs where Lucy fell, Harry.'

'You're climbers too, are you?' He looked me over as if assessing me. 'No, Dad's right. We've had a bit of rain recently and the cliffs are running with water. If you take a boat down there you'll see a few good waterfalls. The view from the sea is fine anyway, if you've got binoculars.'

'Exactly.' Stanley shook his head to dismiss the topic.

Harry said, 'You had any dealings with Marcus lately?'

He said it almost as if they were old mates, and I looked at him in surprise. 'Yes, we saw him recently.'

'How's he doing these days?'

Muriel Kelso bustled in at that point, a very different character from her husband, and the atmosphere in the room immediately brightened. Her welcome was irresistibly warm, her face, haloed by fine silver curls, glowing as she hugged Anna and then, slightly to my embarrassment, myself. 'My dears, how wonderful to see you both here. Are you comfortable in the cottage?'

It was almost as if she'd personally invited us to stay there, instead of Anna booking it on the internet. Her charm seduced us all, and even Stanley became more mellow. She was sure that our stay would help heal the wound of the loss of our dear friends, and she insisted that her family would move heaven and earth to make it so. She only wished she'd been able to persuade Lucy's dear father to come and do the same. But I remembered Sophie Kalajzich's assessment of her, and could see the tough old bird beneath the charm.

'Who were you talking about when I interrupted?' she asked.

'Marcus,' Harry said. 'I wondered how his leg was doing. We heard he'd been sick again.'

This was news to me, and I was surprised they were still in touch. 'He did look a bit frail when we saw him, but he didn't mention being sick.'

'Poor man,' Muriel said. 'A brilliant mind. I believe the accident affected him deeply.'

'Did you know him well?' I asked.

'Well, yes, he'd been coming here for, what, eight or nine years before the accident. He'd become like one of the family really.'

Stanley grunted, and from the look on his face I guessed he didn't quite share his wife's enthusiasm.

* * *

I found it hard to get to sleep that night. It wasn't the food that kept me awake, for Muriel had cooked her son's trevally as perfectly as she'd managed everything else. Nor was it the wine we'd consumed, which was excellent and plentiful enough to have knocked me out. It might have had something to do with that muttonbird, still giving its baby cries, heart-rending in the night.

There was something I'd intended to do earlier, and had been deflected by Bob's presence when we'd returned. I'd wanted to look again at the sheets of paper with the codes from Luce's diary, while the log records I'd studied in Carmel's office were still fresh in my mind. I got them out of my bag and sat up in bed to study them.

The first thing I noticed was that they all had an extra four numbers at the beginning of each string, which I soon realised was the date. Given that, and Carmel's lucid explanation, the whole sequence became intelligible. It was the final entries that interested me, and here I did notice something odd, for there was a single entry for Thursday the twenty-eighth of September, the day on which Owen had taken over the reporting. It was the very last line in Luce's diary, and it ran:

2809 1325 57J WE 23674 85849 149

I stared at it for a while, struck not only by the date, but also by how different it looked from all the other lines. Here, for example, was the previous reading, taken on the Wednesday:

2709 1508 57J WF 06588 04470 103

That was similar to all of the entries from the previous two weeks, when they'd moved from Roach Island down to the southern cliffs. For a start, the two groups of five digits—the eastings and northings readings—were quite different. Even more significant, I thought, the WF symbol on every other reading on the list had become WE in that final entry. Could that have been a simple typo? I tried to remember what Carmel had said about the WF, and recalled that it identified the hundred-kilometre squares into which the UTM zone 57J was subdivided. If it wasn't an error, the final entry must have been taken in a completely different grid square from all the rest. Wherever it was, it was big, for the final three digits showed that they were 149 metres above sea level.

I sat there staring at the numbers for a long time until they became a blur. I felt sure that Julian, Dick, Anne, George and Timmy the dog would have instantly understood this vital clue, slamming down their ginger beers and rushing off to tell Uncle Quentin. But I hadn't the faintest idea what to make of it.

17

I woke to the smells of toast and fresh coffee. Anna had been up since dawn, she told me, and I noticed a small bunch of flowers lying on the kitchen worktop. Muriel Kelso had given them to her, apparently, to take to the accident scene. In the light of a new day it seemed a thoughtful gesture, and I wondered if I'd misread the Kelsos, put off by Stanley's domineering manner. Soon Bob tapped on the cabin door and gave our gear a quick squint—a backpack with a bottle of water and windcheaters, but no climbing equipment. We followed him down to the beach and along to the jetty where his boat was moored. It looked as if it was designed to take small groups out fishing or sightseeing, with a covered wheelhouse at the front and bench seating around the middle and stern.

Bob steered us out into the calm waters of the lagoon, turning the boat south to run parallel to the long beach, several kilometres of deserted golden sand. We passed the end of the airstrip and continued towards the foothills of the first of the two southern mountains, Mount Lidgbird. Here the reef closed in against the shore, and Bob turned us towards the passage between the lines of foaming surf that would take us out into open water. The swell out there was quite heavy after the calm of the lagoon, and we pitched and yawed as we got clear of the reef and turned south again beneath the increasingly formidable basalt cliffs of the mountains.

I know next to nothing about boats, and I was interested

to watch Bob and ask him how things worked—especially the GPS navigation equipment next to the wheel. He was pleased to demonstrate it, pointing out the features on the glowing map of the island on the screen and our position on it.

'So, these figures show our position in degrees?' I asked.

'That's right, degrees decimal. You can switch the readout to degrees, minutes and seconds if you want . . .' he showed me, 'or to UTM.'

'Neat. What about the reverse? Can you put in a map reference and it'll show you where it is?'

'Yeah.' He pointed ahead to a steep valley between the two mountains and handed me binoculars to look for waterfalls. I went back to join Anna and spoke quietly to her.

'I need a couple of minutes alone in the wheelhouse. If we get the chance, see if you can keep him occupied out here.'

'What are you doing?'

'Not sure yet. Are you all right?' She looked grey.

'This heaving up and down . . . I feel a bit sick.'

'Concentrate on the mountains. Look out for waterfalls. See? Over there.' There were several silver threads of water cascading down the immense black cliffs.

I stayed with her as we moved under the shadow of Mount Gower, its dark flank looming overhead as we approached the point of South Head. The sombre blackness of the basalt cliffs was oppressive, and as Bob throttled back the engine and turned the boat closer to the shore I realised that this must be the place.

He joined us and pointed to an area halfway up the sheer wall, where white birds flitted in and out of the shadows. 'That's where they were working. I put them ashore on that narrow beach over there.'

I scanned the cliffs with my camera, then with the binoculars, hoping to see some sign of the protection they might have used to anchor themselves up there, but it was too dark and too high up to make out any details, and the image swayed with the movement of the boat. The idea of working unsecured in such a place seemed unthinkable, and I blurted out, 'I can't believe she wouldn't have had a rope.'

He shrugged. 'Yeah.'

'Where did she come down?'

He pointed to a spot where waves broke against the base of the cliff, sending spume high up the rock face. 'Reckon that was it. Don't want to get any closer. The currents are treacherous down this southern tip of the island.'

Anna gave a little sob and reached into the bag for the flowers. She was looking very pale. She leaned over the side and dropped the blooms over. They drifted away, tiny white petals against the dark water. Then she suddenly gave a retch and ducked her head, being sick.

As Bob went to her, I backed away towards the wheel-house and began fiddling with the GPS controls. One thing I had managed to do the previous night was memorise the coordinates of Luce's last entry, but first I had to convert the instrument to UTM readings.

'What're you up to?'

I stiffened at Bob's voice at my shoulder. 'Oh, sorry, just seeing if I can work this thing. How is she?'

'She'll feel better in a minute.'

I nodded, looked up and froze. 'Holy shit!'

Ahead of us, glowing in the haze that obscured the southern horizon, I had seen for the first time what looked like the spire of a drowned cathedral rising out of the ocean depths.

When Lieutenant Henry Lidgbird Ball, captain of HMS *Supply* and then aged thirty, discovered Lord Howe Island, he was careful to do the right thing. He named it after Admiral Lord Richard 'Black Dick' Howe, First Lord of the Admiralty. Then he named its highest peak after Rear Admiral John Leveson-Gower, also an Admiralty Lord. The cluster of offshore islands to the north he called the Admiralty Islands, and even named a small island at the edge of the lagoon after his ship's master, David Blackburn. He gave the second highest peak, rather coyly perhaps, his own middle name. But his surname he reserved for an extraordinary spike of rock lying off to the south. When I first saw it through the boat's windshield I guessed it might be a kilometre away and perhaps eighty or a hundred metres high. Bob corrected me—it was twenty-three kilometres off and rose an astonishing five hundred and fifty-one metres, the tallest sea stack in the world, a third higher than Frenchmans Cap and one and a half times the height of the Empire State Building—my measures of terrifying altitude since my night on the mountain with Luce. There is a portrait of Henry Ball in the National Library of Australia, one of those little black-and-white Georgian silhouettes, with a rather dandyish quiff of hair standing up on his forehead and what might be either an arrogant or determined set to his lips and the push of his chin. I like to imagine his crew running to the rail as they caught sight of the amazing volcanic fang rearing out of the ocean in that remote place and crying, 'Bleedin' heck, what's that?' and Henry, studying this vision of Nature Sublime through his telescope, replying, 'Gentlemen, *that* is Balls Pyramid.'

It shook me, I have to admit. Not just the thing itself, but also the absolute certainty that I knew its UTM coordinates. Later in the trip, in calmer water, Anna managed to distract Bob for a couple of minutes while I checked it out on his GPS set, but I already knew I was right.

'Can we go and see it?' I asked.

Bob shook his head dubiously. 'Sea's a bit rough out there, Josh.'

'But it's amazing. Can we at least try?'

He didn't seem to want to make an issue of it, and said he'd detour that way.

I went to sit with Anna at the back, plastered with sun cream, as we bounced across the choppy sea, circling out towards the south. I felt a bit mean, for all she wanted was to get back onto dry land, but that couldn't be helped. As our angle of view slowly shifted we saw that from its flank Balls Pyramid resembled a tall triangular sail, while from end-on it appeared to be a slender spire; so thin in fact that in one place the wind had punched a hole clean through. This ragged tooth was all that was left of a huge volcanic crater rim, and beneath the waves it continued down to the ocean floor, two thousand metres beneath us.

The sea wasn't too rough, and once he'd resigned himself to taking us out there, Bob became determined to prove just how inaccessible it was. To begin with, there were the tips of lesser peaks around it, barely breaking the surface, that made it dangerous to approach. Then there was the impossibility of making a landing, there being nowhere a boat could safely moor against the vertical sides. And finally, the thing was too exposed, too sheer, its rock too eroded and crumbly, to safely climb.

'So it's never been climbed?' I asked, thinking that would make it even more irresistible to Luce and her friends.

'It was climbed in the 1960s,' Bob conceded, 'and once or twice since, but it's so dangerous that it's banned now. It's a bird reserve.'

We watched vast flocks of gulls floating in the air around its high flanks, and I said, 'Luce would have loved this place, Bob. Did you ever bring her out here?'

He ducked his head away as a wave hit us, and adjusted his steering. 'Nah. She saw it all right, though, from South Head. Couldn't very well miss it, could she?'

I thought he was lying. As I took pictures he pointed out some of the features that the first climbers had christened along the steep ridge that ran up to the summit from the south—the twin spires of Winklestein's Steeple, the Black Tower and the Cheval Ridge, so named because it was so narrow, with sheer drops on either side, that it had to be traversed as if sitting on a horse, with a leg down each side. I felt sure he'd told Luce the same story.

We could also clearly see the huge breakers crashing against its base.

'So how did they get ashore?'

'Their boat stood off while one of them jumped in and swam to the rock with a line, then pulled their gear and the others over. But there are sharks, huge sharks, and the waves and currents are bad around here, mate, real bad. Chances are you'd be swept away or bashed against the rocks before you could get out of the water.'

I could see the difficulties all too clearly, but as we turned back towards Lord Howe I was even more convinced that Luce had stood on that thing. Why was I so sure? There was the map reference in her diary, of course, but it was more than that—I'd felt her presence there. That sounds absurdly fanciful, like Owen seeing her on the mountain before he fell, and Marcus on his terrace, and as we grew further and further away from the Pyramid I tried to convince myself to be rational. But each time I glanced back at it, glowing solitary in the morning sun, the sensation came back, creeping up my spine.

The wind picked up as we approached Lord Howe, the waves got bigger, and Anna was sick again. Then we were running up the eastern side of the island, Bob pointing out the landmarks among the cliffs and rocky bays. For Anna's sake, and having spent an extra couple of hours on the detour to the south, we agreed to forgo the fishing, and Bob circled the Admiralty Islands, showing us the wave-cut tunnel through the middle of Roach Island. Seabirds swooped around us, dazzlingly blue, and it was only when they climbed away that we realised they were pure white, coloured by the light reflected off the blue waters. We followed the line of the northern cliffs and circled around North Head to approach a northern passage through the reef. Ahead of us we could see people on the jetty.

We clambered ashore, unsteady, and thanked Bob. I asked how much we owed him, but he wouldn't take any money. Instead we bought him lunch at the café, and he suggested we borrow a couple of bikes from the house and spend the afternoon exploring.

When he'd gone, Anna, a little colour returning to her cheeks, looked at me and said, 'So, what's the mystery?'

'What do you mean?'

'You were up to something. What?'

I felt suddenly reluctant to tell her. I was uneasy about how she might react, and anyway, sitting there at a café table surrounded by people, my imaginings just seemed utterly fanciful.

'What did you want in the wheelhouse?' she demanded.

'He had a GPS set in there,' I said reluctantly. 'I just wanted to check something.'

'Without him knowing. What was it?'

So I told her about that last, erratic reading from the diary, and of the significance of WE as against WF. She knew less about maps than I did, and I had to explain it all twice.

'But you thought you could put the numbers into Bob's navigation system and it would tell you where the place was?'

'That's right. I thought the WE might have been a mistake, but it wasn't. When I entered the numbers with WF, I came up with a point in the middle of the ocean.'

'But with WE?'

'Yes, I got a landfall, but not on Lord Howe.'

'Where then?'

'Near the southern tip of Balls Pyramid.'

'And that wasn't the same map reading that Owen entered in Carmel's log?'

'I can't be sure of that. I didn't have time to copy down his entries. But they told the inquest they'd been working on the Mount Gower cliffs all that week—there was no mention of Balls Pyramid. And if they did go out there Bob must have taken them in his boat, but he denied it, didn't he? And he claimed no one had set foot on it for years.'

Anna rubbed her forehead, thinking. 'Maybe they were just *talking* about Balls Pyramid, and Luce looked it up on her equipment and jotted down the coordinates.'

'Yeah, I might have gone with that if she hadn't also put down the time and the altitude, just like the other entries. One twenty-five in the afternoon, and one hundred and forty-nine metres up. I think I saw the place as we sailed round. Bob called it Gannet Green, a shelf with a bit of vegetation on it.' I showed her the pictures on the screen of my camera. They were a bit tipsy with the motion of the boat, but you could see it all right.

She shook her head. 'I don't know, Josh. The implications . . .'

'Yes. One little number, and if you interpret it that way, it means that everything that Curtis, Owen, Damien, Marcus and Bob said about that final week is in doubt.'

'Why would they have done it?'

'Because it's there. Let's say they'd finished their officially sanctioned project early, at the end of the previous week, so they decide to go out to have a look at this amazing place. Maybe there are birds out there that you don't find anywhere else. It's certainly the most fantastic rock climb I've ever heard of. But it's forbidden to land there and there's no chance the board will consider a scientific study without a proper submission, and that could take months. So they decide to do it on the quiet, only something goes wrong. Luce has an accident, maybe she's swept away getting from the boat to the shore. They'll be in deep shit if they say what happened, Bob especially, so they change the place of the accident to where they should have been, where their daily reports said they were.'

'How would they have persuaded Bob to take them out there, to let them land?'

'I don't know. Money? No. Maybe because he was soft on Luce, and she persuaded him.'

We were silent for a long time. It sounded almost plausible, but there were details that bothered me. I decided to give the great detective time to mull it over.

'Anyway, if there's a grain of truth in it, we'll have to be very careful. I don't think it's a story that anybody is going to want to hear. So I propose we do as Bob suggested and go for a cycle, and pretend that everything's just fine.'

She nodded agreement. 'You're right. And really, if it did happen like that, there's nothing to be gained from opening it all up again.'

'Right.' Except that, if it did happen like that, then those five blokes had deliberately conspired to direct the rescue effort twenty kilometres away from where it should have been focused.

We walked back to the cabin and Anna had a shower and I a couple of beers—our respective ways of recalibrating ourselves to the world. Then we went out to the driveway in front of the house, where half a dozen bikes were stacked against the veranda rail, with helmets piled on the edge of the deck. We selected our mounts, I helped adjust the height of Anna's seat, and then we wobbled off up the driveway to the road. We turned south, back along the way Bob had first brought us from the airstrip, which we came to after ten minutes. The headwind caught us as we turned onto the long stretch of road that ran parallel to the runway, and we laughed as we battled at barely jogging speed, straining against the wind.

At the far end the road curved around the end of the airstrip to head back towards the lagoon shore. Dead ahead there was a sand dune, and parked on it a small white four-wheel drive bearing the crest of the New South Wales Police. We pulled off the road and walked our bikes up to it. There was a track through the dunes here, leading down to the sandy sweep of Blinky Beach, the island's surfing beach. A lone figure was far out among the breakers, and we sat on the tufted grass watching as he caught a wave and coasted in. He looked as if he got a lot of practice.

He spotted us, and slung his board under his arm and padded up the beach towards us.

'G'day. Grant Campbell,' he said as we got to our feet. 'Looking for me?'

'Not specially, Grant,' I said, and introduced us. 'We're friends of Lucy Corcoran, remember her? Who had the accident four years ago?'

'Course I remember.' He eyed us steadily.

'Guess you don't get much crime here.'

'Nope.' Grant seemed even more laconic than Bob, and equally aware of our presence on the island.

'I was talking to Glenn Maddox in Sydney recently. He's a sergeant now.'

'Oh yeah? The big guy.'

I assumed he was being ironic. Maddox was shorter than any of us. 'I told him I was thinking of coming out here. He said to say hello.'

'Did he manage to convert you?' He grinned. 'How come you were talking to him?'

'Just wanted to check if there'd been any developments.'

'Developments? Like what?'

I shrugged. 'I've been overseas for four years. I just wondered if anything new had come up. Anyway, Sergeant Maddox seemed to think us coming here would be a good idea. Help us come to terms with it.'

'And has it?'

'Well, this is only our second day. You were involved with the rescue effort, weren't you, after she fell?'

'Yeah.'

'Were you happy about how it was done?'

'How d'you mean?'

'Well, did you get all the resources you needed?'

'We had the navy and the air force. By Monday evening we had twenty boats and aircraft out there.'

'Were you involved in directing the search?'

'Me and others.'

'Would you mind taking us through what happened?'

He sat beside us on the dune, the sand sticking to his black wetsuit, and picked up a piece of driftwood to draw a crescent in the sand. 'Lord Howe. Bob got a message from them at two that afternoon that Lucy had fallen and was in the water.' He poked the stick at the bottom of the crescent. 'He contacted me, then got in his boat and headed down there. I found as many people as I could with boats and sent them down after him. Towards three they reported that there was no sign of her.

'They reckoned there was something like a three-knot current down there, running due west, so by then she might have been carried anything up to five kilometres out to sea.' He drew a line across the foot of the crescent. 'There were several of us in my office by this stage, and we identified a search area and directed everyone out there except for a couple to keep searching the waters around the cliffs, just in case. By this time some of the yachties from the Sydney to Lord Howe race had heard about it, and they began heading out too. We notified AusSAR, the national search and rescue people in Canberra, and they alerted the navy and air force. The RAAF Maritime Patrol Group is based at Edinburgh in South Australia, so it would take their Orions over four hours to reach us, by which time it'd be dark, but they sent one over anyway with thermal imaging equipment, and then another came towards dawn the next day. HMAS *Newcastle* was exercising in the area and was directed our way, and its helicopter flew over around five. Meanwhile a small fixed-wing set out from Port Macquarie, but didn't make it before dusk.

'The boats stayed out till midnight, using lights, though we knew the chances of them spotting anything were slim. They set out again at dawn, by which time the *Newcastle* and the second Orion had arrived.' He shrugged. 'What can I say? The experts had taken over by then, plotting the currents, defining the search area. They were using radar altimeter measurements from satellites. It's like plotting pressures on a weather map—the ocean currents were rotating in a huge anticlockwise flow around a high spot way to the south. Mate, they were taking her far, far away from land. We knew she was a goner, even if she'd somehow survived that fall. I'm sorry. I don't reckon there was anything else we could have done.'

'No, I'm sure there wasn't, Grant. Thanks.' I took a deep breath. If my suspicion was right, the whole effort in those critical first hours on the Monday afternoon before sunset had been wasted, displaced twenty kilometres north of where they should have been looking. It made me sick to think about it. No wonder Owen had felt guilty. I wanted to ride back into town and find Bob and choke the truth out of him, but I guessed he'd just deny everything, as Damien would too.

We thanked the cop, and mounted our bikes again and pressed on down the road. There was a steep climb past the golf course, and the physical effort helped work out a little of the frustration I felt. We stopped at a sign to Lovers Bay, and sat on the hillside looking out over the ocean. The sight of that vast sea chilled my heart, and I immediately began pouring out the anger I felt. Anna listened in silence while I ranted on about them searching the wrong sector. Then, when I ran out of steam, she said simply, 'No, it couldn't have happened like that.'

'How do you mean?'

'If they were on Balls Pyramid when they radioed for help at two that afternoon, how would they have got back to the southern cliffs in time to meet the rescue boats?'

I was stunned. Of course she was right. I wasn't thinking clearly. 'How did it work, then?'

'I'm not sure. It would depend on whether Bob and his boat were there with them when it happened. If he was, they'd have searched for a while themselves, until they were convinced they weren't going to find her. How long would that take? Hours, surely, if they weren't prepared to call for help.

Then they'd have returned to the southern cliffs, dropped the climbers, and Bob and Marcus would have headed back to the jetty to wait for the radio call from Curtis. If Bob wasn't with them, it would have taken even longer—he'd have had to go out to them, then search and so on as before.'

'You're right! And then there's Damien. Was he really sick in bed, or was he with them, refusing to have anything to do with it and demanding to be taken back? However you look at it, she must have gone in hours before they gave the warning—maybe first thing that morning.'

'Why that morning, Josh? I told you right at the beginning, didn't I? We only have their word for any of this. We haven't found anyone else who saw Luce after Thursday night. Why did Owen take over filling in Carmel's log?'

The timing—that's what had been bothering me all along. Why did they delay their return to Sydney?

I said, 'There's something else I thought of, to support the idea that they weren't on the southern cliffs when she fell.'

'What's that?'

'If they were there, and they were doing their research project, why wasn't her electronic diary lost with her? Why didn't she have it on her, the way she had all the previous month, recording their positions? It was found in her room, and now we know that her last entry was for the Thursday.'

If there's a psychic equivalent of vertigo, I felt it then, the giddy sense of having nothing solid beneath you. 'Would they have really done that—just not told anyone about the accident for *days*?'

Anna didn't reply at first, then she whispered, 'Accident? How do we know that? How do we know she fell into the sea? Maybe it took them days just to cook up that story.'

18

We cycled back and parked our bikes where we'd found them. Anna returned to the cabin, but I heard the sound of someone working in the garden behind a hedge, and when I looked over I saw Muriel Kelso among rows of lettuce and potatoes. She had a wide straw hat on her head, a hoe in her hand and a determined look on her face.

'Oh, hello, Josh. How was your ride?'

'Good. We met Grant Campbell out at Blinky Beach.'

'Ah yes, his favourite spot.' She laughed. 'Surfing was he? He wanted to be a professional, but not many people can make a living out of it, so he did the next best thing and took old Billy's job when he retired. That's life, isn't it? Making accommodation. Oh, and I have something to show you.'

She peeled off her gardening gloves and led me to the back door of the house and into the kitchen. 'You're probably thirsty after your ride. Would you like some homemade lemonade?'

'Thanks.'

She poured me a glass from an enormous fridge in the corner and told me to sit while she fetched whatever it was. Photographs as it turned out, taken at the party for the sailors from the yacht race. And there she was, Luce, looking pretty good, maybe a trace of shadow around the eyes, but still our Luce, smile fixed in the flash. I studied them all carefully, getting Muriel to identify the locals and the yachties. There were two pictures with Luce, one standing with Damien and the other with Marcus, an ironic smile on his face and a rotund man with a scowl on his other side.

'American, I think,' Muriel said. 'Or Canadian. From one of the boats. Can't remember his name. Quite taken with Lucy, as I remember.' The idea was grotesque. I felt her eyes studying me as she said that. 'I thought you might like to see these, but I wasn't sure . . .'

'No, I'm glad you did, Muriel, thanks.' But my voice sounded odd.

'It's hard to know. After my sister died I couldn't bear to see pictures of her. Guilt, you see. She was living on the mainland, and I should have gone over earlier, but I put it off, and finally I was too late. The guilt stopped me grieving as I should. I think it's like that with a lot of people. We should have done more, or less, or differently, and now it's too late and we blame ourselves and can't bear to think about it.'

I nodded, eyes fixed on Luce's picture. 'That's right. I understand exactly what you mean.'

'But that's so sad, isn't it, being unable to remember someone for such a reason? It's very important to forgive yourself, Josh.' She laid a hand on my sleeve. 'Just remember how wonderful it was that she shared her life with you, if only for a brief time.'

'Yeah. Looks like a good party. Did you see Lucy the next day?'

She thought. 'I'm not sure. I think I remember waving to them all as they set off with Bob the following morning.'

'And after that, over the weekend?'

'I really can't remember, Josh.' She looked at me curiously. 'Why?'

I shrugged. 'Thanks for letting me see these. I'll tell Anna; she may want to have a look.'

'Take them and show her.'

At the door she put her hand on my arm again. 'You're not worried that she may have taken her own life, are you, Josh?'

I froze, staring at the floor. 'Er . . . it's a possibility I've wondered about.'

'I'm sure she didn't. She would have left a note, wouldn't she?'

'I don't know.'

'Yes, I'm sure she would—for her father, if no one else. She was a very considerate girl.'

Anna was sitting on a sofa in a bathrobe with a towel around her head. She was staring blankly at a book in her hands. I noticed it was upside down.

'Good book?'

She gave a shiver and put it aside. 'Just thinking.'

I handed her the photos and sat down beside her. As she went through them I told her the names that Muriel had given me. I'd recognised one or two of them, wealthy Sydney businessmen. There was one of Damien and Pru Passlow, both laughing wildly. When she'd gone through them all, Anna returned to the picture of Luce with Damien.

'They don't look as if they've fallen out, do they? They look just like good friends at a party.'

'Yeah.'

'I've been thinking about your theory. If it's true, none of them—Bob, Damien, Marcus—will admit it, will they? We'd need to have evidence of some kind to make them, and there's really only one place where it could be.'

I turned away. I didn't want to hear this.

'The last place we know for sure where Luce was,' she persisted. 'Balls Pyramid.'

I shook my head. 'We'd never find anything out there now.'

'We won't know until we try.'

I looked at her in disbelief. 'Are you crazy? That is a seriously dangerous place, Anna. You saw it. They'd never agree to us going there.'

'No, I'm sure they wouldn't.'

'Oh no. Look, maybe—maybe if we told Grant Campbell, he might do something, organise a search out there.'

'When his best mate, good old Bob, tells him we're mad? Of course he won't, and neither will anyone else.'

'Sergeant Maddox?'

'Not without something more substantial than an obscure map reference that might mean anything or nothing.'

'I wish I'd had more time to note the readings that Owen entered into Carmel's log. I mean, we're assuming that he put down false readings, but suppose he didn't? If he had a map reference for Balls Pyramid in there somewhere, then we would have evidence, wouldn't we?'

It was clutching at straws, but I wanted to deflect Anna. She had a gleam in her eye that I'd sometimes noticed in the old days, and which had briefly been rekindled in Orange. Next thing she'd have us stealing a boat and heading out across the open sea with ropes and magnifying glasses and lashings of ginger beer.

'Shouldn't be that difficult,' she said.

'What?'

'To have another look around Carmel's office. There could be other stuff there about what they were doing.'

'What, break in?' I saw the look on her face. 'Bloody hell, Anna, larceny's gone to your head. Remember what happened the last time.'

'We got what we wanted, Josh. Without it we wouldn't have come this far. But this time you can go in, and I'll keep watch.'

'I'll think about it.'

'Or I'll go alone.'

I sighed. 'All right. On one condition—that they don't have a burglar alarm. I'm not going through that again.'

'Fair enough.'

We went out that evening to eat at a restaurant not far from Carmel's office. The street was deserted as we walked back, and I ducked into the shadows and had a look around the outside of the bungalow. There were no warning stickers, no alarm boxes, no indicator lights.

We returned to our cabin and waited till midnight, then crept out, wearing the darkest clothes we had. When we reached the place, Anna waited in the shadow of a tree across the street while I padded down the drive beside the bungalow. I wasn't sure how she could help, but it was reassuring to know she was out there. At the back of the building I selected the window next to the rear door, wrapped my jacket around my elbow and slammed it through the pane. The noise was shocking, and I stood motionless for a long time waiting for some reaction—lights, dogs, voices. There was nothing. Not a thing. Just the sighing of the wind in the palms.

I reached into the hole and slipped the latch and climbed in, my feet crunching on the broken glass inside. Anna, ever resourceful, had given me a tiny flashlight with which I picked my way through to the front office, where I closed the venetian blinds. Even so, I didn't dare risk turning on the lights, and used the pencil beam to grope across to the filing cabinet. It was locked.

There was a board fixed to the wall nearby, with keys hanging from hooks. None of them looked small enough. One caught my eye, and I lifted it off its hook and examined it; then, with a buzz of guilty excitement, I slipped it into my pocket. I turned to the desk and found the keys to the filing cabinets in the top drawer.

The tension was getting to me now and my hand was shaking so much I could hardly fiddle the key in. How did thieves do it? Did terror give way to boredom, just another job? I found the file easily enough, flicked it open and shone the light on the final pages. WFs, all WFs; no Balls Pyramid readings there. Then I heard the crunch of a heel on broken glass. I almost cried aloud. With heart hammering, I fumbled the file back into its hanger and slid the drawer shut. Then the light snapped on, and I found myself blinking, dazzled, at the face of Constable Grant Campbell.

'What d'you think you're doin', mate?' he drawled.

'I . . . Goodness, Grant, hi! You gave me a hell of a fright. Well, jeez, you won't believe this.' I grinned wildly at him and he didn't smile back. 'Well, you see . . . I was in here the other day, talking to Carmel, right? And she let me see the reports that Lucy did for her, on their research project. Well, she said she'd need some identification, so I gave her my driver's licence, and she photocopied it on the machine over there. Only, we were chatting, and she forgot to give it back. I only realised tonight, and I remembered she said she was going away, and I thought I was stuffed. So, hell, I'd had a few wines, and I thought I'd better just come down here and get it back.' I whipped out my wallet and pulled out my licence and waved it at him. 'Sorry about the window. I'll pay for the damage, of course.'

'Why didn't you contact me? I could have arranged something.' His eyes were scanning around the room, looking for signs of disturbance.

'Sure, yes, that's what I should have done, of course. Sorry. I feel kind of stupid.'

'I'll need to take a statement.'

'Fine, fine. Well, it was like I just said . . .'

'Not here. At the station.'

'Oh, right. Is it far?'

He gave me a grim little smile that I didn't understand. Then he took one last look around and ushered me out by the front door. Across the road I saw Anna shrink back into the shadows, and prayed she wouldn't try some stupid ploy to rescue me.

The police station was the bungalow next door. It was also where Grant lived. He'd heard the breaking glass while he was lying in bed reading *Surfing Life*. We sat in the office at the front and I dictated a statement, which he typed on his computer then printed off for me to sign. He also told me to turn out my pockets, but took no notice of Carmel's key. I offered him a fifty-dollar note to give Carmel for her window.

'Will that be enough, do you think? Maybe a hundred?'

'Fifty should do. I'll get Frank to fix it before you leave if he's not busy. I'll let you know what it comes to.'

'Thanks, I appreciate that, Grant.'

'Anything else you want to tell me?'

I shook my head.

'I'm letting you off with a caution. I won't call in your accomplice across the street. It might be awkward if you hadn't agreed on your story before you set out and she told me something different.'

I mumbled something incoherent.

'Just be thankful you're friends of Lucy's, mate. Now have a nice holiday and behave yourself.'

Anna caught up with me as I turned the corner. 'Wasn't that Grant Campbell?'

'Yeah. He caught me red-handed.' I told her the story, getting to the end as we climbed the steps onto our veranda.

'Oh well, no real harm done.'

'Not until Carmel comes back and tells him she never asked for my driver's licence.'

'It sounds like he'd worked that out for himself, Josh.'

I fingered the key in my pocket, telling myself to say nothing, but the feeling was like vertigo, the inevitability of falling. 'I did get something from Carmel's office . . .' I drew it out and showed her.

'Her car key?'

I pointed to the logo. 'I don't think Yamaha make cars, do they? But they do make outboard motors. I guess she has a boat.'

19

We decided to go that night, mainly because delaying would have driven us crazy, like waiting for a battle or the electric chair. We stowed what we thought we'd need in a couple of backpacks and aimed to get away before the fishermen came down to the beach. Since neither of us was a sailor, the thought of what we planned to do terrified me, especially the possibility of drowning on the reef or in the open sea, or being taken by sharks. I was starting to hope that we wouldn't be able to find Carmel's boat, when around three-thirty we did. The little aluminium dinghy was drawn up on the sand with a group of others, a National Parks and Wildlife Service crest helpfully painted on its side. We hauled it down to the water and piled in. The motor started without difficulty, though I had no idea how much fuel it had. We told ourselves we'd be back that evening and no one would be any the wiser.

I aimed south down the lagoon, following the shoreline, on low revs to keep the noise to a minimum. Towards the western horizon a big moon, almost full, shone through broken cloud, coating the black water with a glittery sheen. The dark bulk of the land on our left side grew higher as we approached the foothills of Mount Lidgbird. Somewhere along here Bob had turned to head out through the passage in the reef, and I was desperately wishing I'd paid more attention. He'd pointed out some feature on the shore with an ironic smile—Lovers

Bay, that was it, with some Norfolk pines on the hill behind. I could just make them out now in the moonlight. Looking out to the west, I thought the sea seemed blacker, unmarked by the phosphorescent surf breaking on the reef on either side. I told Anna what I was doing, and got her to hang over the bow to watch for rocks as I turned the boat and headed straight for the moon, like a beacon. The swell gradually increased, and as we made headway out into the open sea I opened up the throttle, waiting till I felt sure we must be clear of the reef before turning the bow to the south. I felt cautious relief; we had passed the first big hurdle. Maybe this was going to be possible after all. Then the moon dipped below the horizon and the dark became absolute, and I heard Anna being sick.

We bounced and pitched across the South Pacific for what seemed an age, unable to make out any sign of the great rock in the darkness. I was beginning to think we'd gone way past it when the first grey light crept out of the east, enough to make out the form of the enormous stack, towering out of the water directly in front of us. I slowed to a stop, and as the sky lightened and the swell lifted us up I was able to make out the low rocks to our right, in particular the one they called the Wheatsheaf, on account of its profile. I turned away from them, towards the east, and began a slow circling of Balls Pyramid as the sun's first rays clipped its peak and began a golden striptease down its flank.

'Awesome,' Anna muttered. She looked washed out, but gave me an encouraging smile. 'What do you reckon?'

We had circled around to the dark west side, into the space between the Pyramid and the Wheatsheaf, and it seemed to me that the only possible landing areas were at the southern end of the rock, where the south ridge plunged down into the sea. This was the end where Gannet Green was located, and there was a rock shelf at the tip where, if we managed to get onto it, we might organise ourselves for a climb. I steered back to the place on the calmer leeward side, holding the boat twenty metres or so offshore, and explained to Anna what I thought we should do. She nodded, face tight, clearly not happy about the idea of jumping into that dark heaving swell. I set about uncoiling our rope and sealing the backpacks inside the plastic bin liners we'd brought. I stripped down to my swimmers, wishing I had a wetsuit, put my clothes in another plastic bag and tied the two ends of the rope securely around my waist. At the last minute I decided to make up a fourth bag, transferring into it half of our food and water, the first aid kit, some of our clothes and a blanket we'd brought. That way I reckoned we'd increase our chances of arriving on the other side with at least some of our gear. Risk management, you see.

'Your helmet,' she said. 'Put your helmet on.'

We'd brought our hard hats with our other climbing gear, and she opened one of the bags and fished it out. Looking at the waves crashing against the rocky sides to the platform I thought it good advice, and wished I had knee and elbow pads too. I fixed the strap of my helmet and turned to say goodbye, and was startled when she grabbed me and planted a salty kiss on my mouth. 'Take care,' she said, in a tone that suggested these might be our last words.

'Yeah, no worries,' I muttered and jumped in.

The thought of sharks is a great accelerant in the water, I've found, and despite the heavy swell I crossed those twenty metres faster than in any pool. The sea was rising and falling half a dozen metres against the rocks, and it seemed to me I should try to time my approach so that it lifted me up to the top, where I'd have to grab the rock and clamber out of harm's way before the wave rose again to suck me back down. That was the theory. The first time I tried it I was just too late, and the crest of the wave crashed back on top of me as I tried to clutch at solid matter, tipping me backwards and tangling me in the rope. I had to swim back out, clear the rope, then try again. This time it worked; I reached high up to a ledge as the wave peaked, and hauled myself up the rock face. In a few seconds I was lying panting and shivering on the platform, waving at Anna.

When I'd recovered, I loosened the rope from my waist and tied its two ends together, so that we now had a rope loop from boat to shore. Anna tied the first bag to the rope and I began to pull it across the gap. By the third load we were getting into the rhythm, hauling away like old sea hands. The fourth and final bag went over the side and came bobbing towards me. But then it began to feel heavier than the others, dipping deep under the waves as if maybe it was leaking and filling with water. I dragged on the rope as hard as I could until I saw the bag's dark form in the water below me, then a wave crashed over it and the rope went abruptly slack, almost toppling me back onto the rock. I hauled it in, the fourth bag gone.

There was nothing I could do. We worked the knot in the rope back to Anna, and she unfastened it and tied one end to the boat, while I pulled the other ashore and secured it around a jutting rock.

'Okay!' I shouted. She stood for a moment in the bow of the pitching boat, in her swimsuit and helmet, then threw herself into the sea. I lost sight of her for one minute, then another, and was beginning to panic when her head broke through a wave and she came soaring in towards me on its crest. It slammed her against the rock, but she managed to perform a remarkably athletic recovery, scrambling up to my waiting hand.

When she was safe we stood for a moment, laughing with relief, then stared up at the spine of rock rising above us. Our teeth were chattering, we were bruised and scraped, but we'd made it. 'That's the main thing,' I yelled. 'We're over safe and sound.' In the euphoria of that moment we forgot about the boat, now being swept around the point on the end of its line. I got a sharp reminder when the taut rope suddenly caught my leg and yanked me against the rock. I yelped, pulled my leg free and turned around, just in time to see the boat disappear behind an outcrop. We ran to the edge of the platform and looked down. It had vanished. We pulled on the rope, which now ran directly into the waves beneath us, and hauled out a good length before it suddenly jerked tight. We tugged and heaved, but couldn't free it. In disbelief we gazed down at the empty foaming water, then at each other. Carmel's boat had sunk, crushed against the rock beneath our feet. I dropped to my knees, refusing to accept that this had really happened. Didn't boats have flotation panels or something? Behind me I heard Anna moan through the sound of the crashing waves, 'Oh my God!' I slumped back on the cold rock and we stared at each other, our euphoria at getting there in one piece abruptly gone.

Finally the freezing wind forced us into action. Severely chastened, we pulled on our clothes and began to get ourselves organised. My climbing shoes felt stiff and old, like me. It was a long time since Frenchmans Cap, longer still since I'd broken them in on the climbing wall. I stared up at that intimidating ridge rearing high above us against the morning sky and felt an overwhelming sense of dismay. Technically it didn't look as hard as Frenchmans Cap, with plenty of cracks and ledges on the fractured and eroded surface, but this was completely unknown territory. With our backpacks and climbing belts firmly strapped, Anna led the first pitch. We climbed slowly and carefully, not wanting to take risks with no help available, and my legs and arms were soon aching. Along the way we found hammered into the rock several ancient bolts that looked old enough to have been placed by the first climbers forty years before.

I led the final pitch that took us onto Gannet Green, a steep unstable-looking slope with scattered patches of wind-scoured grass, and I made my way across to a stunted clump of melaleuca shrubs and collapsed against the rock face with a groan. Anna had more energy, and began to explore the shelf. She returned after twenty minutes, shaking her head. There was no sign that Luce or the others had been there.

'What now?' I said.

'Do you think they'll come looking for us today?'

'Shouldn't think so. They're not likely to notice we've gone.' That had been our intention, after all. We couldn't see Lord Howe from this end of the Pyramid, but there had been no sign of a boat all morning. My throat felt parched and I reached into my pack to check our diminished supplies. We had one small bottle of water each. With the loss of that fourth bag, our food store, scrounged from the kitchen as we were leaving, was now just as inadequate—a few crackers, a lump of cheese and an apple. The adrenaline and lack of sleep were getting to me, and I felt dazed.

Anna was scanning the ridge above our heads, and she suddenly frowned, pointing. 'What's that?'

I eased stiffly to my feet and looked. Something glinted in the sun. 'No idea.'

'I'll take a look.' She scrambled up the broken rock, sending small fragments skittering down behind her. All around, seabirds squealed in protest at our intrusion.

'Come and see,' she called over her shoulder.

I groaned as my legs flexed to push me up. Every muscle ached. I was definitely not fit. When I reached her she pointed to a stainless steel ring-bolt embedded in the rock. It looked very recent, different from the rusted mild steel aids we'd noted on the way up. You could see the lip of the epoxy resin that had been used to glue it in place.

'It's theirs, isn't it?' She was looking up the rock face. 'They must have gone further. Come on.'

'Do you think we should?' I looked behind me. The water already looked far below.

'Not much point hanging around here.' She sounded like my old gym teacher, annoyingly positive. She was holding up a lot better than I was. 'Might as well use the time we've got,' she went on. 'If we were picked up now we'd have achieved nothing anyway.'

We found another ring-bolt further up the ridge, then nothing more, and I just concentrated on each new step. We were giddyingly high now, with wide views across the ocean, though Lord Howe was still masked by the bulk of the peaks ahead. Huge numbers of birds wheeled and dived around us, filling the air with their forlorn cries. At one point we spotted a fishing boat some distance off to the north-east, but too far to try to attract its attention. As the afternoon wore on my pace became slower and slower. I had to keep stopping to rest my swollen fingers and aching knees, and my movements had become clumsy with fatigue. Finally I looked up and saw Winklestein's Steeple towering impossibly high above us. I called up to Anna, waiting at the top of the next pitch, that I was buggered and couldn't go on.

'There's a sort of cave up here, Josh. Just get this far and we can rest.'

I struggled up, inch by inch, until I could make out the dark hollow beneath a jutting overhang. I heaved myself over the lip and lay there groaning on the ledge, while Anna crawled in past me and fixed a couple of anchor wedges to tie us in. The cave was deep and broad enough for us to lie down, its floor covered with rubble, which Anna began to clear away. Then she stopped and muttered, 'Oh God.'

'What's wrong?' I turned to look and saw a piece of webbing in her hand. She tugged it clear of the stones and I saw that it was the strap of a climbing harness, and with it came a cluster of climbing aids—wedges and snaplink carabiners. Anna handed them to me, and I held the webbing up to the light. It was a faded red, just like Luce's. Anna had crawled deeper into the recess, and now she pulled out a coil of nylon rope and a helmet. We stared at each other.

'Well,' Anna said slowly, 'she didn't jump or get pushed, or she'd still have been wearing this stuff.'

I nodded. Even when sleeping she'd have kept the harness on to attach herself to an anchor. 'She must have gone on free solo,' I said.

There are various styles of rock climbing. The one that I was most familiar with is what is called aid climbing, in which you use bolts already in the rock or the gear you carry to support you and help you climb. An alternative is free climbing, in which climbers use only their bodies to progress up the rock, but still carry ropes and passive protection to save them if they fall. But there is another style, called free soloing, in which they go up without any hardware at all. It is the purest form of climbing, and some would say the most sublime. It is certainly the most dangerous, for if the climber slips there is nothing to save them. I watched Luce free soloing once, my body rigid with anxiety the whole time, expecting her to drop at any moment. Afterwards she spoke of a sense of liberation, and of confronting her destiny. I thought it was utter madness.

The thing about free solo climbing is that it's so dangerous it should only be done on routes the climber knows and that are well within their capabilities. This place was completely alien territory. Luce couldn't have had any idea what lay ahead. Without back-up or equipment, she could have found herself trapped in impossible situations, forced into hair-raising manoeuvres without any form of support. I felt my skin crawl, imagining it.

'Why would she do such a crazy thing?' For both of us, drained and almost defeated by the effort of getting this far, it seemed incomprehensible. Unable to come to terms with it, we turned away and busied ourselves with our meagre supplies.

We had what passed for a meal with barely a mouthful of water. We were on the east side of the ridge, watching the long evening shadow of the Pyramid stretch out across the green water three hundred metres below us. There was a nor'-easterly breeze that was becoming fresher by the minute, and we had no blanket or sleeping bags.

'It's going to be cold,' I said and we squeezed closer together. 'They'll come looking for us in the morning.'

'Yes,' she agreed, nodding her head firmly, but we both knew that wasn't likely. The Kelsos would probably assume we just wanted a bit of privacy, and with Carmel away her boat might not be missed for weeks.

The shadow spread out across the ocean and finally faded into a darkening void. In the gloaming we tried to make our little cave more comfortable, sweeping debris aside, and in the process disturbed some brown centipedes that scuttled away into the far recesses. I knew that every living thing on

Balls Pyramid, as on Lord Howe, had arrived either by floating through the air or on the sea, and I wondered how these little creatures had found their way to such a remote corner and how they survived. Now fate had placed them and us on the same small ledge of rock. Later, in the dark, as Anna and I clung together against the cold, we discovered they had distinct ideas about sharing their patch with us, as they attacked us with vicious bites. Soon we were scratching miserably at painful swellings on our wrists and ankles. Despite my exhaustion, it was a long time before I drifted off into a fitful sleep.

20

We were wakened by the first glow of the sun directly in front of us. Anna jerked out a leg and kicked me on the knee.

'Sorry,' she mumbled, and we disentangled ourselves and sat up, yawning and scratching, to watch the golden disc rise free of the horizon into a hazy sky. The wind had died away and only the occasional seabird disturbed the silence.

'How do you feel?' I asked.

'All right, considering. How about you?'

I shrugged. 'Stiff, sore.'

'A bit of exercise'll fix that. Let's see your hands.' She peered at them; the previous day's swelling had reduced and she said they'd do. I found myself admiring her sturdiness; the dogged persistence that had irritated me yesterday now seemed rather admirable. I smiled at her and she said, 'What?'

'Nothing.'

'We have to go on, you know—to the top if necessary.'

'Yes, I know.'

She hesitated, then said, 'This isn't too difficult, just bloody hard work. Luce could have climbed it in her sleep. I was wondering if it was about speed, leaving her gear behind. She'd have been able to move much faster.'

'True.' But what would have been the point in that? It seemed more likely to me that she'd just stopped caring about safety.

I thought about that a good deal as I led the way off the centipedes' ledge. My muscles were stiff and aching in strange places, my hands thick and clumsy and sore. I began traversing the flank of Winklestein's twin spires, making for the horizontal Cheval Ridge beyond. The height, three hundred and fifty metres of sheer cliff below us, worried me, and I was being very careful about where I looked and what I allowed my mind to think. But at least there were plenty of cracks and bumps and other reasonable hand- and footholds on the weathered basalt, and I was making cautious progress until I came to a slab of smooth rock with no purchase on it at all. There was a promising crack on the far side, and I thought I could just reach it at maximum stretch. I tried, extending myself as far as possible, but couldn't quite make it, and suddenly found myself flattened against a smooth rock face with only my right hand and foot properly engaged, a position I couldn't hold for long. Terrified of developing sewing machine leg, I forced myself to spring the few centimetres across to the crack, in which I safely jammed my left fingers and toes. But now I saw that there was another smooth stretch ahead, and that I was in the same unstable position as before, with nothing for my right hand and foot to cling to. I was further from protection now, and vividly remembered those anchors pulling out on Frenchmans Cap. Heart pounding, I knew I only had a moment to get out of this, but couldn't see how. Then a memory came into my mind, of a manoeuvre I'd seen Luce perform on that same climb in Tasmania. It was called a barn door, and involved turning your back to the rock face and swinging out, as if on a hinge, to grab whatever lay beyond with your free hand and foot. I could hardly believe it when I saw Luce do it, and knew I'd never have the nerve to try if I gave it any thought. So I didn't think, I just swung, flinging my right arm and leg desperately out into space and around to slam against the rock.

My fingertips and toes found something there, some minimal grip, though barely enough to support any weight. But the other problem was that, in twisting myself over, my rope had wrapped itself around my neck. I was now lying flat across a near-vertical surface, in danger of sliding off at any moment. If my anchors held I'd be strangled, if not I'd plunge three hundred and fifty metres into the drink.

'Anna,' I croaked. 'Anna . . .'

I heard nothing but the cry of gulls and sigh of the wind.

'Anna, help. I need you.'

Some loose stones clattered down from above, bouncing off my helmet. I was frozen, unable to look upwards. I felt the strength ebbing from my fingers, and gazed out at the bright air, waiting for it to happen. Then Anna came abseiling down beside me, at what I thought was a rather leisurely pace.

'Having fun?' she said. She clipped a rope onto my harness, then unfastened the one around my neck. 'Come on, you're wasting time.'

'You saved my life.'

'Don't forget it.'

We were now faced with a vertical climb of about a hundred metres up the Black Tower, also called the Pillar of Porteus, an obstacle that took us until the early afternoon to pass. Ahead of us we saw the long Cheval Ridge leading to the base of the summit pinnacle, and beyond it we caught our first glimpse back to Lord Howe Island, looking very distant, with long white clouds trailing across the peak of Mount Gower. The sun was warm, and we lay on a grassy patch and stretched out to recover our strength. It was in that position that I heard the distant putter of an engine.

I wasn't sure at first, and when I struggled to my feet the sound faded away. Apart from the area masked by the summit pinnacle, I had a 360-degree view all round over the ocean, but I could see nothing. I stood motionless, trying to blank out the cries of birds.

'What is it?'

'Shhh . . . I thought I heard a boat.'

I concentrated, and suddenly heard it again. It seemed to be coming from behind me—from the south, where we'd landed. Although we were surrounded by sheer drops, the view of the immediate area around the south end was hidden by the hump of Winklestein's Steeple. Then, as I stared downward, a boat emerged around the point and into view. 'There!' I cried. 'I think it's Bob's boat. He's looking for us.'

It seemed so small, a tiny white speck. We were like people on the observation deck of the tallest skyscraper, looking down at the ant-like activity far below. We began shouting and waving our arms, hoping he might be scanning the peaks with his binoculars. Our throats were so dry that we quickly became hoarse, and then the boat slid out of sight beneath the lee of the eastern cliffs. We hoped it would do another circuit around the Pyramid, but perhaps it already had, for the next sighting we got was of it heading out across the sparkling sea, back to Lord Howe.

'Oh fuck.' I sagged.

'Come on.' Anna was pulling her backpack on again. 'One last effort.'

We had discovered no further signs of Luce that morning, and I had pretty much given up hope of finding any answers to our quest. The summit pinnacle was a formidable cylinder of rock, like an ancient watchtower with a domed cap. To get to its base we inched across the Cheval Ridge, feet dangling over five hundred metres of space on each side. Halfway across I paused to ease the strain in my arms, and looked down, first one side, then the other. Far below, beyond spinning seabirds, I saw the foam of breakers. I felt the suck of vertigo dragging on my feet and stomach. My head felt hot and swollen inside the helmet and I became dizzy.

'Josh!'

I dragged my eyes away from the void and saw Luce on the ridge ahead of me. I cried out her name.

'Josh? It's me! Come on!' I blinked. It was Anna, of course.

'Yeah . . . coming.' My throat was so parched I could barely speak, but I focused on the rock in front of me and began to move forward again.

I really can't remember that last climb, only the feeling of relief when we finally crawled onto the summit, a dozen square metres in extent, covered with tufted grass. How had it got up there? The sheer bloody-minded persistence of living matter seemed astonishing. I lay down with a groan, and as if at a signal the sunlight faded and died, and a cold gust whipped across the quivering grass.

There was a small cairn of loose stones that the first climbers had piled together on the crown. Anna crawled towards it and began dragging it apart. She pulled out an old rum bottle, and handed me the messages that former climbers had left inside. The last one ended with a confident . . . *and now attempting to descend the North Ridge*. I hoped they'd made it. But there was nothing from Luce.

'Nothing at all?' I said. I don't know what I'd expected, but the futility of what we'd done filled me with despair.

Anna gave a little yelp. I thought she'd been bitten by something, Ball's Last Insult. But it wasn't that. She'd turned over another stone and pulled out a small candy-striped bag. I knew it well—I'd followed it with my eyes many times, bouncing around on Luce's shapely rump. It was her chalk bag.

I got up and walked unsteadily to Anna and looked over her shoulder as she prised the thing open and drew out a slip of paper. She read it and then handed it to me. There were tears brimming in her eyes.

I recognised the handwriting, but not the quotation.

> *For with earth do we see earth,*
> *with water water,*
> *with air bright air,*
> *with fire consuming fire,*
> *with Love do we see Love,*
> *Death with dread Death.*

I wasn't sure what the poem meant, but it seemed pretty obvious what Luce had intended. I just stood there for a long time without speaking, without really thinking, just surrendering to the earth, the water, and the bright air, to love and death.

A spatter of rain slapped my cheek. I turned and saw a grey mass of cloud advancing on us across the ocean from the south. Anna was sitting at my feet, hands tucked up into her armpits, absorbed in some private meditation of her own.

'I think we're in for a storm,' I said.

She looked up at me, eyes puffy with tears, then out to sea. To the north Lord Howe was rapidly disappearing into grey cloud, the sun was gone and the wind was picking up, cold and harsh. She roused herself and I helped her to her feet, scooping Luce's chalk bag into my pack.

'Sure there's nothing else?'

She shook her head, and I piled the rocks back into the semblance of a cairn.

We abseiled down the pinnacle a great deal faster than we'd gone up, then worked our way back along the Cheval Ridge, the wind now ripping alarmingly at us on our exposed perch. By the time we reached the Black Tower the southerly change had reached full force, scouring us with driving rain. Refreshing at first, it rapidly chilled us through and we decided we'd better find somewhere to shelter. We chose what seemed the least exposed flank and I began to lower myself down, cautiously now. I knew that more climbers are killed abseiling downwards than climbing up, and the rock was streaming with water. About twenty metres down I came to an overhang, beneath which was a relatively dry ledge. I called up to tell Anna, and a few minutes later we were both down there, huddled against the wind and gusting rain. I tried with limited success to rig up a water collection scoop with my nylon coat, and after a while managed to get us a drink and begin to fill our water bottles. Soaked and freezing, I sank back against the unyielding rock, feeling that this was certainly the most miserable situation I'd ever found myself in. I sneezed and shivered and began to laugh.

'What's funny?' Anna said, through teeth clenched against the cold.

'I was just thinking that my specialty was risk management.'

She gave a snort. 'That was with the bank, was it?'

'Yes.'

'I don't like banks.'

'Nobody does.'

'But you left Luce to go and work for one.'

There was no real answer to that. Put so bluntly, it seemed preposterous.

'Yes. I did a stupid thing.' I'd never spoken about this to anyone, but what did it matter now, marooned on a crag in the middle of the ocean? 'I slept with someone else, one weekend when Luce was away. It didn't mean anything and I didn't think it mattered, but it did. I couldn't stand the thought of her finding out. So I left.'

It was more complicated of course—my restlessness, my doubts about us. But I felt a tremendous relief to tell someone this simple, shameful fact at last. The wind howled around us, and Anna said nothing for a while.

'She was a first-year student of Marcus's.'

I thought I'd misheard. 'What?'

She repeated it, and I said, 'You knew? I didn't think anyone knew. How . . .?'

'Marcus told us.'

'Us?'

'Well, Damien certainly, probably Curtis and Owen.'

'My God . . . And Luce?'

'I don't know. I didn't say anything. She never mentioned it.'

I was astounded. 'How did Marcus know? He wasn't even there.'

'He arranged it, Josh. He never forgave you for having Luce fall in love with you. He got the girl to do it.'

I think if I hadn't been tied in I'd have slipped off the rock at that point. I thought of everything that had flowed from that betrayal, leading ultimately to Luce's death. If I hadn't left so abruptly, if I'd waited till the end of the academic year, say, and come to Lord Howe with Luce, and climbed with her on that fateful day . . .

As if she was listening to my thoughts, she said, 'I had the impression that Marcus wanted to get rid of you. That he didn't want you coming here with Luce.'

'I feel terrible, Anna. So ashamed.'

'That's why we're here, isn't it?' She put a cold hand around mine and squeezed it tight.

'Me, maybe. But you've got nothing to be ashamed of.'

'Haven't I?' She hesitated.

'Of course not. You were always her truest friend.'

'Maybe not. She was very upset after you left for London, and finally came to tell me that she'd decided to withdraw from the course and take a year's leave of absence, to go over to be with you. I persuaded her not to.'

'Oh . . .' I wiped water out of my eyes. 'Well, that was sensible advice. She was so close to finishing her degree.'

'No, it wasn't that. I was jealous of you two. I was just the same as Marcus. I wanted to climb with her over here. I was being very selfish, and because of that she died.'

'But you didn't come.'

'No. I met someone—a man.' Another surprise. It wasn't that Anna wasn't attractive, but she had always seemed rather diffident around men, and her occasional dates and encounters never seemed to come to anything. 'He wanted me to stay with him. It would have been difficult anyway coming over here so close to my end-of-year exams. I thought he was wonderful. When Luce and the others came over here I moved in with him and I felt I'd never been so happy. Then we got the terrible news. He helped me a lot, getting through the first shock—but I was inconsolable. I couldn't think about anything else, and with the inquest and everything . . . I was obsessive, I suppose, pretty impossible to be around. Anyway, one day he told me that when we met he'd just split up with this other girl, and now he was going back to her. I didn't eat for a week, and then one day I was standing at a bus stop, and I saw this truck coming and I just walked out in front of it. It wasn't a big decision or anything—I just did it. The poor driver . . . He almost managed to stop, but I was sent flying. I spent five weeks in hospital getting patched up, then two months as an in-patient in a private psychiatric clinic in Waverley.'

'Oh, Anna . . .' I put my arm around her shoulder and pulled her close.

A blast of cold wet air, more vicious than the rest, slapped us so hard it sucked our breath away. 'Oh!' Anna gasped, gripping me tight. 'This is terrible.'

'Yeah, marginally worse than working at the Walter Murchison Memorial Nursing Home, I should imagine.'

She dug me in the ribs with her free hand, then said, 'So, go on then, tell me about your bank.'

'It's very boring. You wouldn't be interested.'

'Try me. I think we've got all day.'

So I began to tell her about credit derivatives and risk management. It seemed quite surreal in such a setting, and as I spoke I found it hard to believe that I had once found that stuff incredibly interesting. It was all so remote now, so utterly devoid of real meaning. Yet in the city, where the real world rarely set foot any more, it had seemed close to the vital essence, the purpose of life. It was sexy. I was doing what every young man wants, to be involved in something clever and important that hardly anyone knows about.

It became sexy, as I said before, after the Barings Bank and other disasters.

In the post-Barings wisdom, the essential principles of risk management require a separation of powers within an organisation between the front-of-house traders and dealers, who are greedy for contracts and commissions, and senior management, with its more sober perspective on risk. Between these two groups should sit the RMU, the Risk Management Unit, assessing the dangers of promised deals and ensuring that the policies of the board are implemented on the shop floor. No longer would it be possible for a rogue trader to approve his own deals, as Nick Leeson had at Barings, getting deeper and deeper into trouble without senior management having a clue what was going on.

That was the theory, but of course policies and strategies, no matter how rational, depend upon inadequate human beings like ourselves to carry them out. We have our weaknesses. We have an undue respect for people with grand reputations, especially if they appoint us to much-sought-after positions; we develop an attachment, then a dependence, on the absurdly generous rewards they offer us; and we feel proud loyalties which cloud our view of those outside our circle, who increasingly appear stupid and obtuse.

We didn't gamble recklessly on the Nikkei like Leeson at Barings, nor drown in commodity options like Hamanaka at Sumitomo. Our failure was more innocent, I liked to think, like sewing machine legs, or tidal waves, just one of those things that happen. Imagine a chemical engineering company in the north of England—let's call it Sunderland Petchem— with a track record of supplying equipment to the North Sea oil fields. They have done business with BBK Bank before, and are regarded as a soundly managed small company. But now contracts in the North Sea are on the decline, and they have been forced to look further afield, to the booming oil business in Venezuela. There they have possibly secured a major contract, subject to final details. This project is much larger than any they have previously undertaken, and would require a major injection of capital for expansion. BBK's loans staff are highly enthusiastic, having reached agreement on lending rates which would be extremely rewarding for the bank, not to mention the bonuses of the negotiating staff. However, the RMU is worried; Sunderland is inexperienced in this part of the world, and with this size of project our analysis rates the risks as rather high. Our boss, Lionel Stamp, calls a team meeting to discuss what we should do.

Lionel was an impressive fellow. In his mid-thirties, energetic, imaginative, with a startling memory, his reputation was outstanding. When I first met him I was most struck by his floppy hair and languid English accent, which I thought rather ludicrous, but I soon got over that when I realised how sharp he was. Now he hadn't got to lead the central RMU of an organisation like BBK by being negative and obstructive. On the contrary, his mentor, Sir George Henderson, had picked him because he could not only sniff out possible problems, but also provide ingenious remedies. In the case of Sunderland, the problem basically was to reduce the levels of risk to BBK if something went wrong with the Venezuela contract. The straightforward way to do this would be to sell on part of our Sunderland loan to other lenders in the secondary loan market, or to investors in the asset-backed securities market. Either way, BBK would reduce its exposure on the deal to a more acceptable level. The trouble with this approach was that we would be legally obliged to tell Sunderland what we were doing, and obtain their agreement. In effect we would be telling them that we didn't have complete confidence in them, upsetting not only our client, but also perhaps the whole Venezuela deal if word got out.

The answer was synthetic CDOs. Through the use of credit derivatives, these could imitate the operations of conventional collateralised debt obligations without requiring us to make public what we were doing. Synthetic CDOs were a favourite weapon in Lionel's armoury, and he had refined them to an exquisite degree. He became quite evangelical as we discussed the intimate details of how it should be done, the array of subordinated and senior mezzanine tranches, the choice of first-loss investor, the ramp-ups and replenishments in the collateral pool. All very exciting, the more so for being clandestine and potentially dangerous.

There was a snag. It was referred to as a *moral hazard problem*, a term we liked, I think, because it made us sound like philosophers or priests, rather than loan sharks. The moral hazard problem lay in the fact that, since our dealings were not public and transparent, the CDO investors onto whom we were passing some of the Sunderland loans would only know as much about the risk involved as we were prepared to tell them. The riskier they thought the loan, the more they would charge us for it and the more our profit on the whole deal would be eroded, so there was a temptation for us to massage the information a little. Of course, if things went wrong and our secondary lenders suspected us of hiding the true risk, then BBK's name would stink. To Lionel, this, like all moral problems, was just another risk management issue. It was clearly important that the board of BBK in general, and Sir George Henderson—the director charged with oversight of the RMU—in particular, be shielded from some of the trickier details so that, if worst came to worst, they could honestly deny all knowledge of any moral hedging. This, of course, is a risk management technique perfected by our political leaders in recent years.

For a while things went very well in Venezuela, so much so that BBK offered Sunderland further and larger loans, quietly offsetting them with more synthetic CDOs. Then one spring day, four years after I had answered that fateful email from Gary McCall urging me to come to London, things went abruptly wrong in Venezuela. It was a political rather than an engineering problem, but its financial consequences were just as devastating. Sunderland Petchem, massively overstretched, collapsed, and BBK was faced with huge unpaid debts, which it promptly passed on to a cascading series of CDO investors. As the Sunderland story became public, its history painstakingly revealed by investigative reporters, the investors became more and more belligerent and the BBK Board increasingly defensive. There were whispers of legal action, fraud and criminal charges.

Once again, Lionel recognised this as a risk management problem, the logic of which he explained to Gary and myself over a rather tense lunch at an excellent little restaurant over-looking the river. The bank was wounded, Lionel explained, and surgery would have to be performed before gangrene set in. There were really only two options. Option one entailed the removal of the whole RMU, including its board supervisor. Criminal charges would be brought against Lionel, Gary and myself, and very possibly Sir George. There would be a nasty public trial in which, to demonstrate the bank's innocence and resolve, our names would be dragged through the mud before we were given exemplary prison terms. Option two was the discreet route. It would be quietly explained to the secondary lenders that the bank would cover their losses after the discovery that two of its staff (reckless antipodean colonials, naturally) had bypassed internal controls and procedures.

The board was in a bloodthirsty mood, Lionel explained, and currently favoured option one. But he had carried out a very detailed worst-case scenario analysis calculating all the possible eventualities of both courses of action, and he was confident that cooler heads could persuade board members to go for option two. That, of course, would depend on Gary and myself making a full confession of sole responsibility for the debacle, making token reparations to the bank (basically everything we owned), signing a binding confidentiality agreement, and returning to the far side of the world, never to be seen again.

But what would happen to you, Lionel, we asked, and Sir George? Solemnly, and without a hint of shame, he explained the irresistible logic by which it would be necessary for the bank to demonstrate the limited nature of the breach by rewarding those who had isolated it.

We really had no choice. Within a couple of weeks Gary and I were boarding a plane at Heathrow, all risks neatly managed, moral hazards expunged.

'So you didn't even make any money out of it?' Anna said.

'That's right. Then on the plane, just before we reached Bangkok, Gary mentioned that Lionel had been screwing my girlfriend all along. He thought I must have known.'

Anna said nothing for a while, then murmured, 'Yes, I don't really think you were cut out for risk management.'

In the fading light I watched small gulls hurled backwards through the air in front of us by the force of the wind.

21

About the only thing that could be said for our ledge was that it was free of centipedes, probably because it was too inhospitable even for them. Soaked through and frozen, I passed the night in a semi-comatose state in which hellish winds swept in and out of nightmares steeped in guilt.

Just before dawn I jerked awake with the certain knowledge that Anna had died during the night. I felt for her hand and it was stone cold. I thought, oh, so this is the end. I didn't want to try to go on without her, and I was filled with the same sense of calm I'd experienced when I realised I was going to fall on Frenchmans Cap and nothing could be done. I didn't feel afraid. I reached for the clip attaching our rope to the anchors. My fingers were clumsy with cold as I worked to release it so we would plunge down into the ocean, as Luce had surely done.

Then the corpse stirred and mumbled something about scrambled eggs. I had actually just managed to unfasten the clip, and any movement would have sent us slithering over the edge. I refastened it quickly, and we clung together as the first glimmer of light grew in the sky.

With dawn we untangled ourselves and speculated about raiding seabird nests, but the thought of a raw gull's egg was only marginally more appealing than that of a raw gull. While I was groping around in my pack to see if there was one last cracker hiding in the lining, I came upon Luce's chalk bag.

I had a look inside, but all I found was the remains of a large black insect curled in the chalk dust. It didn't look edible.

The important thing, Anna said, was to get back down to the southern tip of the Pyramid, where we might hope to attract the attention of a passing boat. And surely, we agreed, they would have to send out boats today. We said this forcibly, to cover up the fact that there was no reason why anyone should think to look for us out here. So when the rain died away we unhooked ourselves and stretched our aching limbs, and started abseiling and traversing down the cliffs in short, cautious stages.

In the late morning, as we reached Winklestein's Steeple, the weather closed in again and we were forced to take shelter in the centipede cave. This time we weren't in a mood for compromise, and swept and beat the little bastards back to the deepest recess. The weather was so foul and the visibility so limited that we could see no signs of a rescue boat out on the stormy water. Later, when the rain eased a little, we continued further down the ridge until we found a sheltered ledge free of wildlife. Then the rain began to pour down again and we tied ourselves in for our third night on the Pyramid.

The following morning dawned with a brilliant calm, the first rays of the sun sparkling on clear water, white birds swooping across the swell, as if the storm and our struggle down the rain-lashed mountain had been no more than a bad dream. We continued on down, step by step, pitch by pitch, until we stood on the rock platform at the southern tip on which we had first landed. And there, as if according to some prearranged schedule, we heard the purr of an engine, and Bob's boat circled into view, just fifty metres offshore. We waved and shouted, and the boat came to a stop. It stayed out there, bobbing in the swell, and we made out the figure in the wheelhouse, looking at us through binoculars.

There was something rather eerie about the way he just waited out there, and finally I said to Anna that I would swim over. I was worried about the weight and drag of the rope across that distance, but unless he came closer there wasn't much I could do. At least the sea was relatively calm, and if the worst happened I'd just have to untie the rope and let it go. So I stripped off and dived in. As I thrashed through the water I became aware of the engine noise increasing, and saw that he was heading towards me. Then he was alongside and hauling me aboard.

I lay in the bottom, spluttering, while he freed the rope from my waist and waved to Anna, who had tied our bags to her end of the rope, and now jumped in. I pulled myself up onto the seat and watched, shivering, as Bob hauled her across. And as I watched him, strong and capable, a nasty thought came into my mind. He had rescued us, yes, but what now? Whatever had happened to Luce on Balls Pyramid, he'd been a part of it, and it seemed to me entirely possible that he might prefer that we, too, should disappear into the ocean. I looked around, wondering if there was anything that I might use as a weapon, but I could see nothing apart from some fishing rods, an esky, a bucket and some lengths of rope. As a fisherman I assumed he would be carrying a knife. I tried desperately to think.

Now he was helping Anna over the side, and then pulling the plastic bags with our clothes and gear on board. I decided suddenly that this was the time to act, and I took a couple of paces over to the controls and pulled the key out of the switch. Immediately the motor coughed and cut out.

Bob turned to face me. 'What're you doing, mate?'

'Are you carrying a knife, Bob?'

'Yeah, sure.'

'Take it out of your pocket and place it on the seat over there.'

'What?'

On the other side of the boat, Anna, gasping and wiping wet hair off her face, stared at me in surprise.

'Put the knife down and step away, or I'll throw this key overboard.'

He squinted at me as if wondering what kind of beast he'd fished out of the sea. I must have looked demented—bruised and scraped and swollen all over, the light of madness in my eyes.

'What's that, Josh?'

'Do what I say!'

'All right.' He felt in his trouser pocket and brought out a large clasp knife, which he carefully laid down where I'd indicated.

'Step back.'

He did so, and I darted forward and grabbed the knife.

'What happened to Carmel's boat, mate?'

'The currents smashed it on the rocks,' I said.

'Ah, well, reckon the same's goin' to happen to us if you don't let me start that engine.' He spoke slowly, as if he didn't want to alarm me, or perhaps because he thought my brain wasn't quite right.

'Then you'd better tell us the truth, Bob. We found a note Luce left, on the Pyramid.'

'A note? What did it say?'

'Just tell us what happened. Then I'll give you the key.'

He frowned, then spread his hands. 'Okay, I'll tell you, but I reckon I need to start the engine.'

I followed his gaze and saw that we were being drawn into the foaming swell that bordered the rocks. 'All right.' I replaced the key in the ignition and joined Anna on the seat as he went to the controls. We pulled on our clothes while Bob got the boat going and steered it out into open water. When we were a safe distance away from the rocks he throttled back and came to sit opposite us.

'You'll be getting quite a reception when you get back. They've had search parties out looking for you all weekend. They reckoned you must have gone up Mount Gower on your own like you'd said, and got lost or hurt on the slopes, but my hunch was you were out here, specially when I couldn't find Carmel's boat.'

'And you know why, don't you, Bob? Luce was out here, wasn't she? You brought her.'

He nodded reluctantly. 'Yes.'

'You'd better tell us everything, the whole truth.'

'Mm. You hungry?'

'God, yes!' Anna burst in.

'I've brought some sandwiches and coffee. Here.'

I eyed him warily as he got up and brought a backpack from the wheelhouse. Anna ripped open the top of a plastic container and began stuffing a sandwich into her mouth. Bob poured coffee from a flask into a cup and handed it to me. 'There's cold beer and drinks in the esky, but I reckon you need to warm up.'

I took the cup gratefully. The coffee smelled wonderful. I felt as if I'd been shivering for days.

'They finished their work on the cliffs below Mount Gower,' Bob began, in that same slow drawl, as if we had all the time in the world, 'and they still had a bit of time left, and Marcus wanted to have a look at Balls Pyramid. It's the only place where the Kermadec petrel breeds, and he said he was thinking of doing a field study there the following year. Of course, being climbers the others were keen to see it too, although I told them it was out of the question to land there. Marcus said, no problem, he only wanted to take a look at the birds from the boat.

'So I agreed to bring them out here, that was on the Thursday. It was a fine day, and I took them slowly round, stopping to let them look up there with their binoculars. There was a fair bit of whispering going on among them, as if they were discussing something private, but I didn't take too much notice. Then, when we got to the south end, Marcus asked if I could take them in closer. I did it, and next thing, while I was concentrating on the water ahead, with Marcus standing at my side distracting me, those two blokes, Owen and Curtis, put on wetsuits and dived overboard. They made it over to the Pyramid and climbed up onto the rocks over there. They had a line, and were towing gear. Turned out they had a radio, too, so Marcus could talk to them. They'd planned the whole thing. Marcus apologised and said they just wanted to have a quiet look at the place. They were all very excited about it, Luce especially. She and Damien followed the other two over there.'

'So Damien was with them that day, the Thursday?'

'Sure, and the other days too.'

'You went back again?'

Bob nodded, looking unhappy. 'They spent most of Thursday over there, but they weren't satisfied. They wanted to come back on the Friday, the day before they were due to leave. And Curtis and Owen wanted to stay overnight on the Pyramid, to observe the birds. I didn't like it, but in the end I agreed.'

'Why?'

He shrugged. 'Marcus made me a good offer for the hire of the boat. They seemed to know what they were doing. I thought it would be okay. Big mistake.'

He hung his head. I thought the bit about Curtis and Owen staying there overnight sounded strange, and wondered if he was lying, but I let him continue.

'What happened?'

'We went out the next morning, weather fine as before, but there was something wrong between them. They didn't seem happy, not talking, Luce especially. I thought they were just hung-over after the party the night before. Anyway, they went ashore, and I anchored and we kept in touch with them by radio. Then around three in the afternoon something happened. They were up on Gannet Green, I'd been watching them with the binoculars. I had a line over the side and I got a bite. I was pulling it in—a nice big yellowfin—when Marcus began shouting into the radio. When I asked him what was wrong he just shook his head, angry. I landed the fish and he began arguing on the radio with someone. I couldn't really hear because he turned his back to me, so I looked up at the others on the rock. I could see the three men, staring upwards, but I couldn't make out Luce. Then two of them—Owen and Curtis—began climbing up the ridge above Gannet Green. I watched them through the glasses and then I spotted Luce, high above them and climbing fast.

'I asked Marcus what was going on. He wouldn't say at first, but eventually he told me that they'd had some kind of a quarrel, and Luce had stormed off.'

Anna and I exchanged a glance. This didn't sound right, not like Luce at all.

'Apparently Marcus had sent Owen and Curtis after her to calm her down and get her to come back, but they lost her. She was much quicker than they were, and it seemed she didn't want to come down. Time went by, no progress, and I started to get worried, the afternoon wearing on. They were high up and it was going to take them a while to get back to the boat, and I wasn't going to risk trying to pick them up in the dark. I told Marcus, and he radioed for them to return. He was mad, and said it would teach Luce a lesson to have to spend the night out on the Pyramid on her own. I didn't like that idea at all, but what could I do?'

There was something about the way he was telling the story that didn't quite jell with the impression I'd previously formed of him. He was too passive somehow, playing for sympathy. The sun was warm on our faces, and I asked if I could have a beer. I felt I needed one. He opened up the esky for me and went on with his story.

'So they returned to the boat, just made it as the light was fading. I was trying to keep an eye on the cliffs, but I didn't get another sight of Luce. We returned to Lord Howe, nobody saying a word.

'When we woke up the next morning a gale was blowing. The forecast was bad. We waited from hour to hour for the weather to ease. The flight from the mainland was delayed, and Marcus decided to postpone their return for forty-eight hours. The storm didn't die down, though—if anything it got worse. In the afternoon I tried to take the boat out, but I couldn't get beyond the reef, the seas were too big. Maybe we should have called for help then, but we'd already told people that Luce was safe with us, lying down in her room.

'The next day, Sunday, the weather was better, and we set out first thing for the Pyramid. Of course, we hoped to see Lucy waiting for us at the south end, just like I hoped to see you two down there on Saturday when I came looking for you.

But there was no sign of her. We circled the rock several times and couldn't see a bloody thing. Then the three blokes swam over and started searching on foot. By late afternoon they'd found nothing, and we called them back.

'We were in a panic now, I can tell you. What should we do? By the time we got back to Lord Howe we'd convinced ourselves that she was a goner, and the main thing now was to cover our backs. I'm not proud of myself, but I have to tell you, if I was put in that situation again, I reckon I'd probably do the same thing. We decided on what we'd do the next day—spend the morning at Balls Pyramid for one last search, then go to plan B. And that's what we did. At midday we called off the search and I took them to the Mount Gower cliffs where we'd been telling Carmel we were. They knew there was a patch of dangerous loose rock some way up, and the plan was to fake an accident there, where it would be difficult for people to take a close look. That's when Damien got cold feet. He said he didn't want anything to do with it, and insisted on being taken back. So I landed Owen and Curtis at the foot of the cliff and took Marcus and Damien back to the jetty. At two Curtis radioed Marcus, and I raised the alarm with Grant Campbell. Of course, it was all far too late by then.'

'And you sent them off to the wrong place,' Anna said bitterly. 'Didn't you think she could still have been alive on the Pyramid?'

'I did go back there several times during the search, but there was nothing. So . . . what did she say, in the note?'

'What does it fucking matter?' I said, hearing my voice crack. 'She died.' I glared at Bob. His air of penitent regret was irritating me. 'So what had happened on that Friday, Bob? What was the argument about? Why did she run?'

'I don't know, Josh,' he said, too smoothly. 'They wouldn't

tell me. They just said something about a professional dis-agreement, as if I didn't need to know.'

'And you didn't insist? They'd put you in the position of being an accessory to *murder*, and you didn't insist on knowing why?'

'It wasn't murder, Josh,' he said in that soft sad voice. 'The way I saw it, they'd had a row, and she went off to calm down and think things through on her own. But her timing was bad—it was too late in the day, and a storm was on its way. It was just bad luck, for all of us.'

'Not for all of you,' I corrected him savagely. 'Only for her. The rest of you wriggled out of it.'

He turned away and made to get the boat moving, but I called angrily after him, 'Sit down, Bob! We haven't finished yet.'

He looked back over his shoulder at me, then shrugged and came and sat down again.

'Since you can't offer a reason for their quarrel, Bob, let me suggest one. It goes like this. You and your brother Harry have a racket going here, collecting rare bird eggs from nesting sites all over the island and selling them to smugglers and dealers, like the American who came visiting on that yacht while Luce and the others were here. Highly illegal, of course, but very lucrative. This must be the most perfect spot on earth to run such a business, but I suppose some exposed sites might be a bit hard to access without being seen. Like on Roach Island, say, with all those lovely endangered grey ternlet nests. But Curtis and Owen had the perfect opportunity to go there with impunity, and so you and Harry paid them to do a bit of collecting for you. And with them being such great climbers, you had the bright idea at the end of their stay to get them to do a bit of prospecting on Balls Pyramid too. Kermadec petrel, was it? Its only nesting site? Very desirable, no doubt.

The only trouble was that Luce got wind of it, at the party you threw for the yachties, I think it was. Did she overhear something? She got suspicious, anyway, and finally, on that second visit to Balls Pyramid, she caught Curtis and Owen in the act. When she confronted them they panicked. They had to stop her from telling Marcus what they were up to, or they'd be finished—not just kicked out of uni, but up for a jail term, along with you too, of course.

'Did they talk to you before you set off that day, about their concerns that Luce was on to them? And did you tell them what they had to do if it looked like she'd make trouble? Stage an accident out of sight of Damien and Marcus? But she was too quick for them, wasn't she? She outran them, but in the end it made no difference. You just left her out here until she was exhausted and had that accident anyway.'

He'd sat there impassively right through the whole of this, listening to my accusations, showing no surprise or outrage. And when I finished he took a deep breath, rubbed his chin thoughtfully and said, 'Yep, I reckon you could have something there, mate.'

His calm was rather scary, and I wondered how I'd miscalculated. Clearly he was going to have to try to do something pretty drastic about us now, and me holding his knife didn't seem to bother him.

Then he said, 'You've just got a couple of things back to front. First off, Harry and I don't deal in eggs. Believe me, in this place you'd be crazy to try anything like that. You'd be found out in no time, and with everybody's livelihood tied up with wildlife conservation one way or another, you'd be as popular as a dingo in a kindy. But I wouldn't be surprised if Curtis and Owen were involved in something like that, only they weren't working for me.'

'Who then?'

'Marcus.'

'What? That's ridiculous.'

'Couple of years previously, at the end of one of his visits, I went to see him about something. He was packing up to go, and I caught him unprepared. He was placing eggs in a special foam container in his suitcase. He looked crook when he realised I'd seen it, but then bluffed it out, telling me it was all part of the research project, aiming to start a breeding program back in Sydney. He even showed me how the case had a little heater to keep them alive. Later I asked Carmel, in a roundabout way, how wouldn't it be a good idea to have a breeding program for the rarer birds on the mainland, and she said it might, but there wasn't one, and anyway it would be very difficult to get permission to remove eggs from the island to get one started. I decided to keep quiet about it. After all, he was the expert, wasn't he? Mr Wildlife Conservation himself.

'That was back when Marcus had two good legs, and was leading the fieldwork himself and doing most of the climbing. But four years ago he'd have needed someone else to do the collecting for him.'

I was stunned. This all sounded horribly plausible. Curtis and Owen were both intensely loyal to Marcus, and it was hard to imagine them getting mixed up in something like this without his knowledge and approval. I looked at Anna, her mouth open, about as gobsmacked as me.

'I'll tell you something else,' Bob added. 'That American you mentioned? Marcus knew him from before. He told me he was an old buddy from when he'd been at university in California.' He stared at me. 'Sorry, mate, but if you reckon something bad happened up there that day, you'd better make your inquiries closer to home.'

'What about Damien?' I asked. 'Are you saying he was in on it too?'

'What do you think? I'd say so. Not Luce, though. Straight as a die, she was. My guess would be that it was his job to keep her distracted while the others got on with it.'

'Distracted?'

'Yeah. He was her climbing partner, wasn't he? Can we head back now?'

Anna and I sat in silence as the great pinnacle shrank away behind us.

As we approached Lord Howe, Bob turned to us again, and said, 'So, what do you want to do?'

'How do you mean?'

'Well, are you going to 'fess up to stealing Carmel's boat and landing illegally on Balls Pyramid and forcing dozens of people to spend their weekend searching for you?'

'What's the alternative?'

'The alternative is that we say you set off on foot, along the base of the cliffs, to try to reach the place Luce was supposed to have fallen, and got lost, or trapped by the tide. Maybe one of you fell and twisted an ankle and couldn't get back, and the other stayed.'

Anna and I looked at each other.

'Why would you agree to that, Bob?'

'Because they'll tear you apart if you tell them the truth, and I don't fancy the questions you'd have to answer as to why you thought it was so damn important to go out to the Pyramid. As far as I'm concerned, the less said about that place the better.'

'What about Carmel's boat?'

'I can sort something out, get her a new one.'

'We'd pay for it,' Anna said quickly. 'I'd insist on that.'

243

It was a moral hazard problem, I suppose, a rather neat one. Bob was offering us a way out of an embarrassing predicament by doing something rather similar to what he claimed he had had to do in relation to Luce, forcing us to admit in effect that we'd have done the same thing in his shoes. It didn't appeal to me one bit, but I still wasn't sure about his story, nor whether I trusted any of the Kelsos, and it seemed to me that, without solid evidence either way, we were pretty much in their hands.

I exchanged a look with Anna. 'All right?'

She shrugged. 'As a matter of fact I do have a swollen ankle.'

'Good,' Bob said, and turned the boat towards the opening in the reef.

They made it easy for us to live with our moral turpitude. Everyone was so pleased to see us safely back, falling over each other to look after us, hailing us as heroes and Bob as scarcely less than a saint. And when I thought about it later, lying in a hot bath with a large whisky in my fist, it seemed to me that in a way it was true—our ascent of Balls Pyramid had been fairly heroic, and Bob had saved our lives. But I also couldn't shake the feeling that somehow he'd been let off the hook. I thought that much of what he'd told us was probably true—Luce going missing on the Friday rather than the following Monday, for instance, would be a risky thing to invent, and seemed to fit with the fact that we hadn't found anyone else who'd seen her during that period—but was it the whole truth? Once he realised we knew he'd taken Luce to Balls Pyramid this story was about the best he could have come up with to exonerate himself. And I still found his accusation against Marcus hard to come to terms with. I swung between incredulity and sickening doubt. And if it were true, the one I felt most bitter about was not Marcus, wrecked in his Castlecrag cave, but his lieutenant, Damien—Damien the survivor, in his luxury flat, the father-to-be. I thought of how he'd helped us, tried to steer us away from this, of how solicitous he'd been to Suzi and how he'd groomed Mary.

The thought of Mary reminded me how long we'd been away, almost a week. When I got out of the bath I phoned her and she assured me that everything was well. I didn't tell her about our little misadventure.

That evening Muriel Kelso insisted that we eat with them. We had both been examined by the doctor and Anna's ankle X-rayed and bandaged, and though he pronounced us reasonably fit, suffering from mild exposure, Muriel still regarded us as invalids. I had been expecting her husband to give us a rough time, but I must say he was quite merciful, even benevolent in the face of our contrition. I laid it on pretty thick, how we'd totally underestimated the difficulties and should have listened to his wise counsel. 'You must be fed up with the whole bunch of us by now,' I finished.

'Oh now, that isn't true,' Muriel said. 'What happened to poor Lucy was simply a tragedy, nobody's fault. And poor Curtis and Owen! No, we feel great sadness, of course, but we can't alter the past. We just have to live with it. And you say Marcus isn't well?'

I said, 'Not too well, I think. He seems to have left the university on bad terms, and become a bit of a hermit.'

'Oh dear. We knew that he never came back here again to continue his research project, of course, but I don't see how they could blame him for what happened. And what about Damien? I hear he's a successful lawyer now.'

She said this with a certain intensity behind her bright smile, I thought. How had she heard about him?

'Yes,' Anna said shortly.

'And some lucky girl has finally managed to pin him down, I believe?' She was watching Anna keenly for her reaction.

'Lucky woman,' Anna said dryly.

Muriel smiled to herself, and Stanley changed the subject to more innocuous territory. I was intrigued by Muriel's interest in Damien, and later, when Stanley excused himself to make some phone calls, and Bob went out to get another bottle of wine, I brought it up again.

'It sounds as if you got the measure of Damien while he was here, Muriel.'

'Oh well, by the time you get to my age you've seen most human types. I recognised his straight away. The way he looked at the girls. It's a handicap, really—makes life exciting, of course, for both him and them, but I do hope he's settled down now.'

I heard Bob returning and said quickly, 'Did he try something on with Lucy, Muriel? That night of the party, perhaps?'

'Oh.' She looked at me for a moment, then gave her head a little shake. 'I gave you my advice, didn't I, Josh? Let it go. The past is gone. Whatever she or anyone else may have said or done, she was always true to herself.'

What the hell was that supposed to mean? What had Luce said or done that Muriel knew and didn't want to pass on to me? I wanted to ask her more, but Bob had returned and the conversation switched to the cost of diesel.

22

The following day we flew back to Sydney. After a night of deep sleep I'd woken with a general sense of suspended reality, as if I hadn't quite surfaced from an intense dream. This feeling continued as the little plane rose up into the bright air above the island and banked to the south-west, giving me one last panoramic view. I could make out the white threads of surf along the line of the reef, the shadow of a cloud passing over one of the Admiralty Islands, a tiny boat lying off Neds Beach. And then, as we climbed higher, I caught sight of Balls Pyramid away to the south, stark and solitary. Had we really stood on top of that, Anna and I, just a couple of days before?

I glanced at her sitting beside me, reading an article in the in-flight magazine about adventure holidays in Tibet, and I smiled to myself, feeling a glow of affection for her. I imagined her going back to the Walter Murchison Memorial Nursing Home, readjusting to the grubby realities of ordinary life, and I suddenly realised how much I would miss her constant presence when we got back. She closed the magazine with a sigh, and dug a book out of her pack—a murder mystery, naturally.

The surge of people at Sydney airport roused me from my dreamy state like a slap in the face. We fought our way through the crowds to the entrance to the rail station and caught a train into Central. Anna had a twenty-minute wait for a connection to Blacktown, and I bought us coffees and sat with her, reluctant to leave. I guessed that she was feeling something similar. She'd said hardly a word that morning and now she stared at her hands, still raw and swollen from the climbing, and shook her head.

'It's hard to believe,' she murmured.

'Yes, like a dream.'

She looked at me with a frown. 'We haven't talked about what we're going to do now, Josh.'

A strident voice chanted something incomprehensible over the loudspeakers and the people at the next table jumped to their feet and hurried away.

'No, we haven't, have we?' I think we had both been doing our best to avoid it. Perhaps we hoped that a return to the reality of our home turf would put what we'd learned into some kind of perspective, so that we could separate fact from fantasy.

'Damien is going to have to be confronted,' I said.

'I suppose so.' Anna sounded as tired as I felt. 'Do you think he'll deny everything?'

'Luce's climbing gear is still out there on Balls Pyramid. The police would find it if they tried to check our story.'

Her frown became deeper, wrinkling those black eyebrows together. 'It would destroy his career if we made public what Bob told us, wouldn't it?'

'Very likely he'd go to jail. Marcus too. Maybe Bob. It'd be a big scandal.'

We sat in silence, then I said, 'I can talk to him on my own if you like. He might say more if there aren't any other witnesses around.'

She looked at me, uncertain, a bit worried. 'You wouldn't . . .?'

'What?' I laughed. 'Stick matches up his nails? Don't worry, I'd just talk to him.'

'Right. You'd be careful, wouldn't you?'

'Course.' I looked up at the clock. 'Your train'll be in soon.'

She finished her coffee and got to her feet, made to pick up her pack, then changed her mind and suddenly flung her arms around me. 'Thanks for everything, Josh,' she whispered.

'Hey, we made a great team, didn't we?'

She nodded and broke away. I watched her hoist her pack onto her shoulder and wave goodbye. She mouthed some final message, but it was drowned out by another announcement on the loudspeaker.

Mary broke off her baking to give me a big hug, too, Socrates circling us excitedly, tail thrashing. I was surprised by how good it felt to be back, to take in the familiar kitchen smells again, and some other deeper, more elusive scent, of old timber perhaps or ancient polish, that seemed to impregnate the whole house.

'And did you find what you were looking for, dear?'

I gave her the sanitised version I'd prepared, how we'd visited the place where Luce had had her accident, and spoken to the islanders involved, and how kind and helpful everyone had been.

'That's good,' she said, pushing her hair back from her forehead and leaving a smudge of flour. I sensed her relief. 'Now you've laid the past to rest, you can move on. I'm sure that's what Lucy would want.' I realised she must have been worrying about this.

'You're right. I've been thinking I should start looking at the job pages. I've been sponging off you for long enough.'

'Don't be silly. I'd be lost without my live-in handyman. The bulb blew in that high ceiling on the stair the other night, and I haven't been able to change it. But you're right—you should be thinking about your career. And Anna . . .' she added cautiously, 'she's happy after your trip?'

'Yes,' I said casually. 'As happy as she'll ever be. I think she just needs excuses to get away from that nursing home,' and I launched into a lurid description of the place.

Mary laughed. 'Well, we'll all end up there, or somewhere like it, in the long run.'

I unpacked my bag, and found that the sole of my right climbing shoe had split. I threw the pair away, deciding that my climbing days were over, then put a load in the washing machine, and phoned Damien.

'Ah, Josh, you're back?' He sounded wary. 'How did it go?'

'Good. I need to talk to you, Damien.'

'Of course.' He didn't sound surprised. I wondered if Bob Kelso had already phoned him. 'Lauren's going out tonight with her sisters. Why don't you come round? We can talk in peace.'

I spent the afternoon catching up on my chores, replacing the light bulb, finishing off the bit of paving I'd been repairing on the terrace, pruning some dead branches in the lilly pilly. And I did check the employment pages in the *Herald*. I looked at the banking and financial sections, and also contemplated a couple of academic positions, but I didn't get as far as applying. I thought I'd hold off contacting Damien's friend.

I got to his front door soon after eight. He buzzed me in and met me on the landing of the twenty-eighth floor as before, and took me into his flat.

'Drink? Scotch?'

'Thanks.' I watched him as he fixed them, thinking how amazingly well he'd done in such a short time. Surely he couldn't have been in practice much more than a year? Two at the most. Already I thought he was beginning to cultivate those little quirks that some lawyers like to affect—a flamboyant curl to the hair, a mild extravagance of dress—to make them distinctive, even a little eccentric. He had great survival qualities, I thought; ambitious, focused, intelligent and charming.

'Here.' He handed me the tumbler and sat down opposite me. 'Cheers.'

'Cheers.'

'So . . . your trip.'

'Has Bob Kelso spoken to you?'

'Indeed. He told me about your little adventure. Pretty impressive, actually. He said you got to the top of Balls Pyramid. Amazing. You must be in better shape than I thought. Anna too.' He grinned. 'Bob phoned me as soon as he'd put you on the plane back. The poor bloke was worried. It wasn't his fault. He just got caught up in something he wished he hadn't.'

I didn't say anything, watching his face, his body language.

'He said you found a note.'

'That's right.'

'Can I see it?'

'I haven't got it here.'

'Well, what did it say?'

'I'd rather hear your side of the story, Damien.'

He looked rather pained. 'You don't have to be like that, Josh. From what Bob said you'd pretty much worked it out anyway.'

'Go on.'

'About the eggs, right? It was true. Marcus had been collecting eggs for sale to dealers for some time apparently.' He saw the look on my face. 'I know! It sounds incredible, Marcus of all people. The thing was that, brilliant scientist as he no doubt was, he was pretty hopeless at getting research money. He was arrogant, he thought the review process demeaning, and he'd managed to offend or personally insult just about every one of his peers at one time or another. As a result he wasn't very successful with his grant applications. So he decided to supplement his research money by selling eggs. The way he put it to us, his birds were helping him save their necks by making a small contribution. He insisted the numbers were small, and made no difference to the breeding populations.'

'When did he explain this to you?'

'After we agreed to be part of his team. As he described it, it didn't seem like such a big deal. Marcus was the expert, and if he said it was okay, well, we thought it must be all right. It was a matter of loyalty as much as anything else.'

'Yes.' That did sound right. They were all very loyal to Marcus, their hip priest.

'Are you telling me that Luce was in on this?'

'No. I doubt whether she would have agreed to it, but Marcus never took the chance. He thought she was very special, you know. Full of the ideals that had driven him, and she trusted him implicitly. And that was the problem. She had no idea. Marcus asked me to be her climbing partner and help her do the scientific stuff and keep her out of harm's way, while the other two did the collecting. We thought it was all a bit of a lark.'

I felt that old nauseous reflux of jealousy. He had to stay close to her, distract her, amuse her.

'Why didn't Marcus just leave her out of the team?'

'He couldn't. She was mad keen to go, she was the brightest student, the best climber. He just couldn't.'

'But she found out what was going on?'

'I think she began to get a hint of something almost as soon as they arrived on the island. It's hard to keep secrets when you're all living together—a whisper, a nudge, a conversation that stops suddenly when you walk into the room. But she couldn't be sure, not until the yachts arrived. Marcus wasn't a very good actor. He got pretty anxious as the time got closer. There were some heated phone calls. The dealer was putting pressure on him. Marcus began to get very agitated during the party at the Kelsos' for the yacht crews when he saw Luce talking to the guy. He got me to butt in and try to get her away, but it wasn't easy. Apparently Luce had overheard him talking to Marcus about Kermadec petrel eggs, which was a bit of a giveaway, because they can only be found on Balls Pyramid, and our visit there was supposed to be a secret. She wanted to know what was going on, and I tried to fob her off. But I was a bit drunk and stupid, while she was sober and sharp as a needle. I don't know exactly what she imagined, but she stormed off. I'm not sure what happened after that, but the next morning she didn't say much, and watched everything we were doing like a hawk.'

'So what happened the next day?'

'Bob took us out to Balls Pyramid as planned, and we climbed up to Gannet Green. I was supposed to lead Luce round to the west flank, out of sight of Curtis and Owen, who were after a colony of petrels they'd spotted on the east. At first she seemed to go along with it, but then I turned to say something to her and she was gone. I scrambled back the way we'd come, and when I looked over the ridge I saw her, climbing down to where the other two were crouching among the melaleuca bushes. I called out, and they looked up and saw her. She started shouting at them . . . I couldn't hear what they were saying. There were gulls wheeling and screaming all around us, and the wind was whistling in the rocks. Then

Luce suddenly took off, racing up to the ridge, I don't know why. Curtis was on the radio, to Marcus I assume, and then he and Owen set off after her. I followed, but I couldn't keep up. Eventually I gave up and just waited until Curtis and Owen came back down. They said they'd lost her.'

'They didn't try to hurt her? You're sure that wasn't why she ran?'

'God, no, Josh. Nothing like that.'

We sat in silence for a while.

Disgust, I decided, was what had driven Luce off like that. Disgust with the friends who had so comprehensively deceived her; disgust with the teacher who had opened her eyes to the truth and then perverted it with his corruption and greed; disgust with her species that couldn't help destroying everything it touched, even on that lonely unspoilt place. And disgust, surely, with the lover who had left her with that little worm in her belly.

'Please,' Damien said at last, 'please don't make more of this than there is. In the final analysis it was a tragic accident. She stormed off, refused to come back down, and got caught by the weather on a dangerously exposed place.'

I suppose it was what I wanted to hear, the best that could be made of it.

'Of course, Curtis and Owen were stricken with guilt. That's why Owen said what he did to Anna.'

'Yes.'

'So . . .' He leaned forward in his seat, watching me carefully. 'The note.'

'It was a poem, of despair,' I said. But was it really?

'What, a suicide note?'

'Not in so many words.'

'Where did you find it?'

'At the summit.'

'You're kidding! She got to the top? That's eighteen hundred feet! Well, you know—you climbed it. But there were two of you. How would you describe it?'

'Tough,' I said. 'I really don't know how she managed it.' I didn't mention that she'd abandoned her climbing gear. It had been heroic really, the climb of her life, like Lynn Hill on El Capitan.

I took a swallow of my Scotch. It burned. 'I'll speak to Marcus.'

'Please don't,' Damien said quickly. 'Marcus is a mess right now. You've seen him, haven't you? He can't tell you anything more. *It was a tragic accident*, and everyone involved has paid dearly for it.'

Sitting in that beautiful apartment overlooking Circular Quay, sipping a ten-year-old malt, I felt that wasn't quite the way for Damien to put it. He saw the mistake register on my face and quickly added, 'Think of Curtis and Owen's families, for God's sake. Do you really want to brand those two as murderers? They were your friends.'

'I know.'

He leaned even closer across the gap towards me, as if wanting to physically bridge the rift between us. 'I do appreciate you coming here to talk about this, Josh, and letting me explain. We were mates once; I hope we still can be. I know you're a level-headed bloke. But it's worried me, having Anna involved. She's inclined to be a bit hysterical, when it comes to this subject. Did she tell you she went for me at the inquest? After one of the sessions, when Curtis said I wasn't at the scene when the accident happened, she flew at me, said I should have been there. She was a very disturbed young woman, believe me.'

'Why did you tell them you weren't there?'

He spread his hands. 'I panicked, basically. Just couldn't face the prospect of having to give an eyewitness account.' But it didn't sound like panic to me, more like risk management.

'Josh,' he said, 'please calm her down. She's got to get over this. I could get ten years for smuggling native wildlife and misleading the coroner, you know. *Ten years.*'

23

I returned to Potts Point feeling the need to unwind before going back to the hotel, and stopped at the pub around the corner. I felt exhausted after all that had happened recently, capped by that talk with Damien. Thinking about it, I remembered the feeling I'd had when I met him at Curtis and Owen's funeral, as if I'd been worked over by a pro. Basically he'd fed back to me a more acceptable version of the scenario I had put to Bob on the boat. He'd confirmed what I'd suspected, but little else. The only time he'd seemed at all hesitant was when talking about Luce's note. Perhaps I could have made more of that, but I wasn't quite sure how. I had a couple of schooners of New and began to feel a little better. Between the thump of the music from upstairs and the footy commentary on the big TV, it occurred to me that I should try to trace the source of that verse of Luce's. It certainly wasn't what I'd have been tempted to write as my parting shot to a cruel world.

I couldn't get any results for the first line on Google, so the next day I went out to the university library to see if I could track it down. It took me a couple of hours, but I found it eventually, a passage from the surviving fragments of a poem by an ancient Greek philosopher by the name of Empedocles, called *On Nature*, which made a kind of sense, although I couldn't remember Luce ever showing an interest in the classics. But Empedocles would certainly have interested her. Apparently he was the first to propose a detailed explanation of the origins of species, and of the mechanisms by which a couple form an embryo. He was also a radical pacifist and vegetarian, believing that animal slaughter was murder, meat-eating the equivalent of cannibalism, and animal sacrifice a blasphemy. It was he who originated the idea that the world was made up of four elements—earth, water, air and fire. He suggested that two opposing forces operated on these elements: one, which he called *philia*, or love, to bind them together, and the other, *neikos*, or strife, to break them apart. So the passage Luce quoted was really about the basic physics of the world:

> *For with earth do we see earth,*
> *with water water,*
> *with air bright air,*
> *with fire consuming fire,*
> *with Love do we see Love,*
> *Strife with dread Strife.*

But Luce had altered the last line, changing *Strife* to *Death*. Was that a mistake, or deliberate?

Empedocles was a mystic, too, with lots of ideas about the transmigration of souls and the cycle of reincarnation through various natural forms, and the more I read, the more I was reminded of Marcus Fenn's ramblings about Steiner. I also remembered him quoting Greek sources in that video of him at Oslo, and I thought he must have put Luce onto this.

I also discovered a rather disconcerting thing about Empedocles, concerning his death. It was said that he killed himself by climbing to the top of Mount Etna and throwing himself into the active crater, so that no one would find his body and people would think that he had been taken up to heaven as a god. When I read that I felt the hairs prickle

on the back of my neck. The legend went on to say that the
volcano coughed up one of his bronze sandals, revealing the
deception. Another version had it that the volcano erupted
when he jumped in, sending him flying up to the moon, where
he still wanders around, living on dew. I thought of the moon
guiding us out of the lagoon that night at Lord Howe.

More confused than enlightened by this research, I
returned to my room at the hotel. Luce's chalk bag was lying
on the desk, and I opened it and saw again the black insect
curled up inside. The sight of it took me back to the pinnacle
of Balls Pyramid, as the first fierce spots of rain had hit us.
I pulled the insect out and disentangled it as best I could,
and was surprised by its size—five inches, twelve centimetres,
long. Its shiny black shell was tinged with red, and of its six
legs, the rear pair were the biggest and most muscular. I had
never seen anything like it; it seemed rather primitive and
formidable, and I wondered what it was doing in Luce's bag.

So later that morning I took it to the Australian Museum
in the centre of the city, threading my way through a long
crocodile of ankle-biters in school uniforms queuing up the
steps and through the sandstone entrance. A helpful woman
at the inquiry desk told me to take the lift to an office on
an upper floor, where another woman, equally patient and
attentive, scrutinised my grubby little specimen. I felt faintly
ridiculous, like one of the schoolboys down below, showing
his very interesting find.

'Oh! I know what that is. Goodness. Was your grandfather
a sailor or something?'

I looked perplexed.

'I just thought . . . This is extinct, you see. Has been for
years. *Dryococelus australis*—the phantom phasmid.'

'Sorry?'

'The Lord Howe Island Land Lobster. It's a phasmid, a kind of stick insect. It was only ever found on Lord Howe Island, and it was killed off when rats got ashore from a grounded ship in 1918. We have quite a few specimens in our entomology collection. There's one on display in Insects, down on level two. So, how did you come by it?'

'Oh . . . long story. A friend found it. Bit like what you said, probably, left by some old relative.' Old Uncle Marcus perhaps. 'So it's been extinct for a while?'

'Oh yes. There's a small island near Lord Howe where they found the last remains, but no live specimens unfortunately.'

'That wouldn't have been Balls Pyramid, would it?'

She beamed at me, clever boy. 'That's right! Some people landed there in the sixties, and found a few dead phasmids.'

I found their specimen on level two, in a glass case labelled RARE AND CURIOUS. Apparently it was extinct on Lord Howe by 1935. In 1966 three dead ones were found by the first climbers on Balls Pyramid. How they'd got there was a mystery, for the phasmid was wingless.

I walked out of the museum, crossed the street to Hyde Park and sat on a bench in the sun. Young office workers were lying on the grass, eating sandwiches and sunning themselves. I was thinking of the sentence in Luce's draft final letter to me.

I feel ~~like the last phasmid.~~ so sad.

So she'd been thinking about the phasmid before she went out to Balls Pyramid on that final fatal day. Perhaps she had written the draft the day before, after they'd made their first landing there, maybe on the evening of the party. The more I thought about it, the more it seemed to me that the group would have been much more interested in investigating the phasmid on Balls Pyramid than yet more gulls' eggs. The rats had never reached the Pyramid, so no one could have been sure that these strange creatures hadn't survived out there. What could be more intriguing to a bunch of young zoologists than the possibility of rediscovering something thought extinct for seventy years? And yet Damien hadn't mentioned it.

If Luce found the dead phasmid on her final climb, did she keep it in her chalk bag with the note as another kind of veiled message? If so, it, like the poem, could surely only have been directed at Marcus. It upset me to think that her two final messages might have been intended for him. But what did they mean?

I was struggling with this when my phone played a little tune in my pocket. It was Anna, wondering if I'd spoken to Damien yet. I apologised for not getting back to her sooner, and told her about my talk with him.

'Mm . . .' I could imagine her eyebrows furrowed in concentration as she thought about it. 'It does sound right, doesn't it?'

'Maybe.'

'You're not sure? It's pretty close to what you thought, isn't it?'

'I suppose that's what bothers me. He already knew all about our trip—Bob had called him.'

'Oh. But still . . .'

Then I told her about the poem and the land lobster, and the way they seemed to refer back to Marcus.

'Damien was particularly keen that we shouldn't talk to Marcus again. Too upsetting for the poor bloke.'

'You want to go anyway?'

'Yes. He also wanted me to get you to back off. You're too hysterical, apparently.'

'Hysterical? Me?'

'Yes. He said you attacked him at the inquest.'

'Oh, that. It was a bad time for me, Josh. I told you.'

'Yes. So, you want to go out to Castlecrag tonight? We could grab a bite to eat first.'

I picked her up from her flat that evening at six, and we had a pizza on our way through town. There was a sudden shower and the traffic slowed and became more congested, headlights and wipers on. By the time we reached Castlecrag the light was fading beneath the heavy clouds. I turned off into the winding laneways of the Griffins' estate, and came to a stop outside the house in The Citadel.

It seemed to be in total darkness and I thought we were wasting our time, but then Anna noticed a glimmer of light from a small side window. I parked on the verge further down the street where it was slightly wider, and we hurried back through the rain towards the rugged stone bunker, brooding beneath its dripping canopy of foliage. I almost slipped in the pitch-dark defile of the entry pathway, treacherous with wet moss, then rapped the knocker on the heavy front door, which swung open of its own accord. A sigh seemed to come out of the house, like a gasp of its own breath, heavy with the odours of damp and mould and sour age, which made the hairs prickle on the back of my neck.

'Marcus?' I called out. 'Dr Fenn?'

There was no reply, and we stepped tentatively over the threshold and I ran my fingers across the cold wall feeling for a switch. I found it finally and switched the light on, a rather dim, low-watt bulb in a heavy shade. Directly beneath it we saw papers scattered across the floor, as if there had been a robbery. We stepped cautiously across them to the sitting room, with its obstacle course of heavy furniture. There didn't seem to be any obvious signs of disturbance here, but the building's breath was more pungent, a cocktail of strange odours—burnt sulphur, ammonia, bad eggs, the vapour of concentrated acid. They were the remembered smells of the school chemistry lab.

There was a glimmer of light ahead, through the doorway to the study. Inside I could see Marcus's throne, illuminated by the small table lamp.

'Marcus?'

We moved forward cautiously and more of the room came into view. It looked even more chaotic than before, with papers, books, mugs and plates scattered everywhere. As we stepped in a figure suddenly appeared at a door in the side wall, from an adjoining room I hadn't seen before. I jumped back, startled by the mask over mouth and nose, the goggles, the white coat and gloves.

'Hello?' A man's voice, muffled by the mask. Then he pulled off the gloves and tossed them aside, peeled off the mask and goggles, and we recognised Marcus, wearing a lab coat blotched with chemical stains and burns.

'Oh, Marcus. Sorry, we knocked and called out, but the front door was open. We thought there'd been a burglary or something.'

He looked at us in turn, frowning as if still preoccupied with whatever he'd been doing. 'Um? No. I was just working.' His voice sounded rough and croaky. 'Didn't hear you. What's up?'

'We wondered if we could have a word. We could come back if you're in the middle of something.'

'No, it's all right. Clear a pew, will you? Want a drink? There's some Scotch over there. Make mine a big one. Water?'

'Yes, thanks.'

He turned back into the side room, obviously the source of the smells, which were very strong here. I found three grubby tumblers, and while I poured we heard the sound of Marcus coughing, clearing his throat and spitting, then the rush of water from a tap. He reappeared with a brimming beaker in his free hand, manoeuvring awkwardly with his stick around the obstacles, and I wondered what kind of safety risk he must be, handling chemicals. I took the beaker and slopped a little water into Anna's and my drinks. Marcus pivoted himself down into his throne and shook his head at the water, gulping at the Scotch neat. The glow from the lamp at his elbow picked out his Adam's apple, working like a piston in his corded throat as he swallowed greedily. His eyes seemed enlarged in his skull, the lowered lids more hooded.

'What can I do for you?'

'It's the same thing as we came about last time,' I said. 'We've been to Lord Howe Island.'

His eyes snapped open. 'Have you now?'

'Yes. We know, Marcus.'

'Know? Know what?'

'About the eggs . . .'

He made a baffled face. 'Eggs?'

I shook my head impatiently. 'Yes, about you stealing rare eggs from the breeding grounds.'

He just stared at me, impassive, and I thought, well, if we're going to play poker.

'And about other things.'

I reached into my jacket pocket and brought out the phasmid, taped to a piece of card, and got up and put it in his lap without a word.

He blinked with shock when he realised what it was.

'Where did you get this?'

'It was in Luce's chalk bag, on Balls Pyramid.'

'You've been on Balls Pyramid?'

'Yes. And we've talked to Bob Kelso and Damien. They've told us everything.'

'Ah, then you do know.' He stared sadly at the remains of the insect. 'You do know.'

He sucked in a deep breath and said, 'You mustn't blame them. It was all my fault. They only wanted to protect me. If only I'd told my friends that there could be no eggs this time, or else told Luce about it, as I told the others. But I was ashamed, you see. Shame.' He gave a bitter smile. 'It was the very first thing Adam and Eve experienced after the Fall, remember? After they'd tasted of the fruit of knowledge. The original human emotion. I could tell the others about the eggs, and persuade them it was all right—I could even persuade myself—but I couldn't tell Luce. She was like my original self, long ago, before the compromises. Her faith in me was quite terrifying, you see. So she didn't understand, and that was how the tragedy happened.'

'Didn't understand what? That you were a crook?'

'Oh, Josh, really. The eggs were nothing. Those grey ternlets and Kermadec petrels are probably doomed anyway. They started their decline when we showed up on the scene, two hundred years ago. Don't you get it yet? Didn't Luce teach you anything? We are a curse, a plague upon the earth; we're too many, too greedy and too smart. And we don't want to die. We just don't want to die. Which was why Luce had to. That's what this was all about.'

Now he'd lost me. He saw the puzzlement on our faces and said, 'The phasmids.'

I shook my head, and he said, 'Didn't Damien tell you about the phasmids?'

'You wanted to sell them too,' I guessed.

He smiled. 'Well, they certainly were a very desirable commodity—the rarest insect, the rarest invertebrate indeed, on the planet. Worth a great deal of money. My friend on the yacht was beside himself when he heard about it. The irony is that it was Luce who told him. She was chatting to him at the party, thinking he was just a pleasant, ignorant American visitor, interested in our native wildlife, and she mentioned the phasmid, and how there was a chance it still survived on Balls Pyramid. He tackled me about it soon after, insistent, *very* insistent, that we check it out, and I let slip that we were doing just that. I'm afraid I didn't realise quite how ruthless a businessman he was. I had to do a lot of hard thinking, and was up half the night making preparations. And to make matters worse, Luce must have overheard something that evening, because she spoke to Damien later, and he was convinced she suspected that the rest of us were involved in something she didn't know about. Didn't he tell you all this?'

'Yes, yes,' I lied. 'But I want to hear it from you, Marcus. I think Damien spared us some of the philosophy. We want to hear it all.'

'Well, you'll have to fill up my glass.'

I got up to do that for him and he continued with a sigh.

'That first day on the Pyramid we were disappointed, but towards the end they did find insect droppings up among the melaleuca bushes on Gannet Green that seemed promising. The insects were nocturnal, so we decided to leave Curtis and Owen up there overnight to see if they could spot them with torches.

'The next morning Damien, Luce and I were having an early breakfast together when Curtis came on the radio to tell me that they had been successful—they'd found and photographed half a dozen live specimens. Damien started talking about coming back later with a properly approved project to remove some of them for a breeding program at the university, and reintroduce them to Lord Howe when the rats were eradicated. But I noticed that Luce didn't say much, watching my reaction carefully. I was sure that Damien had been right about her having suspicions, and I was in quite a bind. As soon as she left to get ready, I spoke to Damien and radioed Curtis to tell them what they had to do. They were very surprised, of course, but I insisted, and they had to agree.

'Bob took us back out to the Pyramid, and Luce and Damien went ashore and climbed up to Gannet Green with food and hot drinks for the other two. Something about the way they were behaving made Luce suspicious, and she noticed Damien passing Curtis a pack I'd given him. When Curtis said that she and Damien should return to the boat while they cleared up their things, she sensed that something was wrong. She asked them what was going on, and said she wanted to look in the pack. They refused, but she grabbed it. They tried to stop her opening it, but she was too quick for them and pulled out the container inside. Curtis grabbed it and in the confusion it fell to the ground and burst open.' He shrugged, took a sip of his drink and shuddered.

'What was in it?'

'Black rats,' he said softly. 'A large breeding pair. Harry Kelso had caught them in the traps he has set, and I persuaded him to let me have them. They jumped out and scuttled off into the rocks.'

We both stared at him, stunned, imagining the scene.

'But . . . *why?*' Anna finally managed to gasp.

But I thought I knew. 'Supply and demand,' I suggested.

He smiled, as at a satisfactory student. 'The merchant banker is correct. My dealer friend didn't just want *some* phasmids, he wanted *all* of the phasmids, the only ones. That was his demand, the last living phasmids on the planet. He wanted to corner the market. He didn't want someone coming back later and finding more. He made it plain that life would be very uncomfortable for me if I didn't oblige him. I really hadn't seen that side of him before.'

I tried to imagine Luce's reaction as she watched those rats scuttling off among the rocks, trying to come to terms with the extent of the others' treachery, Marcus's most of all.

'She wasn't running away from the others,' Anna said. 'She was trying to catch the rats.'

'Exactly. I was worried she'd have an accident, and I told them over the radio to try to reason with her, tell her the truth. But it was too late for that. Far too late.'

I felt sick, still finding it hard to absorb the extent of Marcus's fall from grace. 'So there's a breeding stock of phasmids somewhere in the States, is there?'

'No, no. I'd already told Curtis and Owen to kill the ones they'd captured. I told my friend that we'd had no success, that it was plain that there were no phasmids left alive. Which was now in fact true.'

Now we just gawped at him. The man was unbelievable. 'You killed them all? You exterminated a whole species? In God's name, why?'

'So you didn't really know the story. Well, no matter. I'll tell you, then you can judge.'

The rain was picking up again outside, pattering against the glass of the French windows.

'The Lord Howe phasmid was a very special creature. I'd been studying it for years.'

'How could you study it, if it was supposed to be extinct?' I objected.

'There were a number of records from the time when they were plentiful on the island, up until the arrival of the rats. People were clearly fascinated by them. They believed that the females could reproduce by parthenogenesis, cloning themselves without the aid of males. And they wrote of their longevity, how a favourite phasmid living tamely in a family garden, almost as a pet, would survive from generation to generation.

'I also got hold of phasmid remains. Harry had found some on his treks across the island and made them available to me. I carried out tests to establish their age, and found they were extraordinarily old. I could see a good evolutionary reason for this. Imagine you are a very well-adapted creature, living on a tiny island, remote from the rest of the world and with no predators. How should you reproduce? If you do it the normal way, frantically breeding every spring, you risk overpopulating and upsetting the balance of your habitat. One response would then be to evolve a shorter and shorter life cycle, so as to restrict your numbers by speeding up the natural process of death. Or you could go the other way—you could restrict your breeding to cover the minimal replacement of accidental deaths, and extend each individual's life span almost indefinitely. That's what the phasmids had done. Over the millennia, they had evolved their own immortality gene. As long as their habitat remained unchanged, they could live pretty well forever, but as soon as the black rats arrived, they were doomed. They simply couldn't breed their way out of extinction.'

I said, 'So your dealer wouldn't have been able to breed them?'

'Oh, that wasn't the problem. I'm sure he could have created conditions favourable to faster breeding. No, the problem was what would happen when he discovered that he had the world's sole supply of a creature with a built-in immortality gene. A rare insect is one thing, but this . . . Its value would have been beyond anything.

'Did Luce not tell you about Arne Naess's eight principles of deep ecology, the principles that must underlie any part that we may have in sustainable life on this planet?'

'I think she did mention . . .'

He shook his head. Bad student. 'The fifth principle states that the flourishing of both human and non-human life requires a substantial decrease of human population. As I said, we are a plague, and our population is out of control. And we don't want to die. Imagine the discovery of the immortality gene, and its transfer to the human genome. It would be a catastrophe, unimaginable . . .'

He let that sink in for a moment, then he murmured, 'That's why the phasmids had to die.' And then, almost a whisper, 'That's why Luce had to die.'

'What?'

'What if she killed the rats? What if she and the phasmids survived out there, and she was rescued? What if she came back and told the world? We simply couldn't risk it.'

'So . . .' I hesitated, knowing that we'd finally reached the cusp, the moment of truth, and that the next seconds would change our lives forever. 'So, what did you do?'

'On the fifth day, when the search had moved far out to sea, I sent Damien and Curtis out to the Pyramid in a Zodiac from my friend's yacht. Owen didn't have the stomach for it. I must say I didn't blame him. They found her eventually.'

'She was alive?'

He nodded. 'Weak, but alive.'

'What did they do?'

He gazed sombrely at me. 'I'm sorry, Josh.'

The room erupted in noise. Through a singing in my ears I heard Anna wailing, and another voice, my own, screaming, *You bastards! You fucking bastards! She was pregnant!* and Marcus's startled face as I lunged for him and tried to smash my fist into his face. We tumbled and fell, struggling, in a heap on the floor. At some point the singing in my ears faded, and I found myself sitting astride Marcus, his terrified face staring up at me. I got off him and staggered to my feet. My right hand felt as if I'd broken a bone.

Anna went and crouched over him.

'Have I killed him?' I panted.

'No, of course not.'

I heard him groan as she helped him sit upright.

'Damien,' I said. 'I'm going to get Damien.'

'I'll come too.' She came running after me, leaving Marcus sprawled against the legs of his throne.

We ran blindly out into the night, got into the car, and somehow manoeuvred the winding lanes at speed, out onto the main road. At some point, I'm not sure where, we stopped at traffic lights, and I said, 'Fuck. What if Marcus makes a run for it?'

We weren't really thinking clearly, adrenaline buzzing wildly. Anna said, 'I'll go back, make sure he doesn't.'

'I'll turn around.'

'No, there's a cab over there. You go on. Should we call the police?'

'Not yet,' I said. 'Not yet.'

She jumped out of the car, the lights turned green, I took off and I saw the cab driving away without her. But all I could think about was getting to Damien.

24

As I crossed the Harbour Bridge I looked up at the glittering ramparts around Circular Quay, wondering if Damien was sitting up there on one of those bright ledges with his newly pregnant wife, sipping champagne. And I had a blinding image of myself bursting in on them, and hurling him off, out into the night.

I parked some way beyond his entrance and walked back, breathing deeply, trying to calm myself, and reached the glass doors just behind two couples, chatting cheerfully together. One of the men spoke loudly into the speaker, and I heard Damien's name. Then the door clicked open and I was following them in. They oohed and aahed in the lobby just as Mary and I had done. Another pale figure was plying through the water in the pool overhead. I went on to the lift and pressed the button, and they all piled in behind me.

I noticed that they were eyeing me dubiously as they got into the lift, and I supposed I must look a bit dishevelled. I said, sounding unnaturally jolly, 'Twenty-eight, yes? Damien and . . .' I suddenly couldn't remember her name. My head was spinning.

'Lauren, yes,' the one who'd spoken into the entry phone said. 'Are you feeling all right?'

I wiped a hand through my hair and tucked the half of my shirt that had come out back into my trousers. 'Yes, yes, fine.' The lift was accelerating skyward.

'Quite a surprise!' I said. They looked blank. 'About the baby?'

'Baby? What baby?'

'Well—Lauren's baby.'

The women both squealed. 'Lauren's pregnant? So that's what this is all about! She sounded so mysterious on the phone!'

'Oh no,' I said. 'You didn't know? I've spoiled the surprise. Don't let on, will you?'

The lift sighed to a halt and everyone spilled out to greet the waiting Lauren, who kissed them all in turn and then stared at me with a puzzled half-smile.

'Josh?'

'Hi, Lauren,' I said, conscious of the others waiting to see how this was going to go. 'I need to have a word with Damien. It's extremely urgent.'

'Well . . . but he's not here. Someone called, his friend. He needed Damien urgently too. He left fifteen minutes ago. Is this the same thing? What on earth is going on?'

'Which friend was that, Lauren?' I said, and I realised that the tone of my voice was alarming her.

'Marcus, Marcus Fenn. Damien said he had to go over there right away, to help him, some kind of emergency. What—' But I had turned away and was thumping the lift button. The doors slid open and I jumped in.

Something had happened on the Harbour Bridge, an accident of some kind, and all the northbound traffic was being forced into one single lane. I swore and beat my hand in frustration on the wheel and the minutes ticked by as we slowly edged forward. I tried phoning Anna but got only her answering service. At last I was past the obstacle and speeding on through North Sydney towards Castlecrag. When I finally turned down into The Citadel I saw a small BMW standing outside Marcus's house. I pulled up beyond it and as I flung open my door I heard a woman's scream. I ran to the top of the entrance drive and saw the front door of the house crash open and Anna come tumbling out, silhouetted against the light. A second figure followed—Damien, but a Damien possessed, roaring like an enraged animal. He brought her down with a flying tackle and I leaped towards them, lost my footing on the slippery moss, and crashed on top of them. We struggled for a moment, then Damien disentangled himself and stumbled upright. For a second he stared down at me, eyes wild, open mouth gasping for breath, then turned and ran back into the house, slamming the door shut behind him.

Anna was lying beside me on the wet stone, choking. When I put an arm around her and tried to get her upright I felt her whole body racked by convulsive sobs. I held her as they slowly subsided. She was trying to swallow, a hand clutched at her throat, her face distorted in the shadowy light.

'Oh . . . Josh!' she finally managed. 'He tried . . . to kill me . . . his hands round my throat . . . and all the time saying he was sorry . . .'

She turned her face against my chest and began to sob again. I stroked her head, soothing her like a baby.

Finally she pulled away and said, more collected now, her voice hoarse, 'I couldn't get a taxi and decided to walk back, but then I got lost in the winding streets . . . when I finally got here the front door was still open and I went inside. In the back room Marcus was sitting in his chair, Damien crouching beside him. As soon as our eyes met I saw that he knew that Marcus had told us what they'd done. I started to back away, and he called after me to stay, softly, like not to scare me, but then getting angry. I turned and ran. He caught me in the living room . . . We fell, his hands round my neck, and he was shaking me and choking me, telling me he was sorry he had to do this. There was an empty bottle by my hand. I hit Damien with it and he looked so surprised and annoyed, rubbing his head, and I managed to get up again and run for the door . . .'

'Can you stand up? I'm going to call the police and an ambulance for you.'

'Josh!' She gripped my arm. 'I don't know if Marcus was alive. He was slumped in the chair—like he was dead.'

I tried to think. Had I killed him? I said, 'You go and wait in the car and I'll go round to the terrace to try and see.'

'I'm coming with you.'

She insisted, and we found the narrow path that led down the side of the house towards the rear. We had to push our way through wet branches and several times lost our footing, but eventually we found ourselves on the edge of the terrace. Light spilled out onto the paved surface through the French windows. We walked over and looked in. There was Marcus, just as Anna had said, slumped in his throne, his pale face tipped forward and to one side, as if asleep. He was no longer wearing the lab coat, and the left arm of his shirt was rolled up above the elbow.

And there, too, was Damien, seated in the armchair at his side, crouching forward as if trying to fix something that I couldn't make out. He raised his head and saw us, and for a moment our eyes met and he gave us what appeared to be a sad smile. I could see now what he'd been doing; his left sleeve was rolled up too, and he was pressing the needle of a syringe into his forearm.

I grabbed the door handle and tried to open it, but it was locked and of a heavy, solid construction. I rattled and banged it and called to him to stop, but he took no notice. We watched helplessly as he went on with what he was doing. I got out my phone and rang for help, then I stepped back and charged with my shoulder. The door burst inward, its glass panels shattering all over the floor as I stumbled in. Anna followed me, and I told her to go and open the front door to meet the ambulance.

I squatted beside Damien, who was staring at the broken door with eyes bright with tears, preoccupied with some internal experience I couldn't share. The syringe was empty, and I had no idea what he had taken. I asked him, but he just closed his eyes and smiled. His face had become flushed, and there was a purple bruise forming on the side of his forehead where Anna had hit him. Then something changed. His face darkened and took on a glow of sweat, and he whispered, 'I'm sorry, Josh. Really.'

By the time the ambulance arrived I'd found the bottle on the floor beside Marcus, with his hand-printed label: *Digitalis* (*Thevetia peruviana*). I gave it to the medics as they went to work on Damien. Marcus, it seemed, was already dead.

Anna drew me aside as we stood watching them. 'What are we going to say, Josh?'

We were discussing this in whispers when the first cops arrived, two uniformed men who took us out to the front room. One sat with us, taking down names and addresses, while the other spoke to the ambos. Then plainclothes police came in, and eventually Detective Sergeant Maddox.

I wondered afterwards what he must have made of the scene when he first walked in. Apart from the bodies and the smashed French windows and the deranged-looking witnesses, the whole place had an air of chaos, as if some shocking event, an earthquake perhaps, had given it a violent shake. Perhaps he was used to it, for he moved about very calmly, directing the others, then took me aside from Anna, cautioned me, and asked me what had happened. He fixed me with that evangelical eye and told me that he wanted the truth.

Well, yes. We all say we want that. Anna and I had spent the past weeks searching for it, but now we'd found it I wasn't sure it was something we could entirely share. I imagined myself standing up in the Coroner's Court and explaining that the distinguished ecologist Marcus Fenn, who had once climbed a mountain with the great Arne Naess, had decided that, in order to save the planet, one of his students had to be killed. And had then persuaded his other students to carry it out. I imagined the other people in that courtroom—Damien's wife Lauren, Owen's wife Suzi, Curtis's parents—listening to me explain how their sadly missed husband or son was in fact a murderer. I imagined the families that would be fractured by those words. Bob Kelso would be in trouble, and the others would have to re-evaluate their whole lives. Assuming they believed us.

So I told him the simplified version of the truth that Anna and I had hurriedly decided on. We had returned from Lord Howe Island without finding any definite new facts, but were still troubled by the official account. When we visited Marcus that evening to discuss it with him again, we found him working in his laboratory. He seemed overwrought, and probably drunk. He became highly emotional as we talked about the deaths of Luce, and Curtis and Owen, and he said that he was responsible for them. At one point he became so agitated that I had to physically restrain him. Much of what he said was confusing, but he seemed to imply that Damien knew the truth about Luce's death. We decided to leave and talk to Damien about this. On the way we became worried that Marcus might harm himself, and Anna decided to return to keep an eye on things.

However, in the meantime Marcus had apparently phoned Damien, who had set off for Castlecrag before I arrived at his apartment in The Rocks. By the time Anna got back to Marcus's house, Damien was there, and Marcus appeared unconscious. Damien became very emotional, physically attacking Anna and driving her out of the house as I arrived. He bolted the door, and when we eventually went around to the back of the house, we saw him inject himself, and tried to stop him.

No eggs, no phasmids, no Balls Pyramid.

Maddox asked me to enlarge on certain parts of this account, then went away and took Anna through the same process. There was a spell where he left us in order to direct a photographer and others securing the scene, and then we were taken to the police station at Chatswood. There we were examined by a doctor and a forensic officer, and our clothes were removed. Dressed in overalls, we were separately given cups of tea and biscuits, then formally interviewed on film by Maddox and another detective.

From time to time I caught glimpses of Anna, through the glass panel in a door, and passing under escort in a corridor, unreal in those white overalls beneath dazzling fluorescent light. We seemed like characters in some TV drama in which we were having to improvise the script. At some point I was allowed to phone Mary, and I explained what had happened and asked if there was a spare room at the hotel for Anna, as I didn't want her going home alone when we were eventually released. She said, of course, and drove out with a change of clothes for us, cobbled together from my wardrobe and Mary's.

It was late when Maddox released us, his final words being a rather Old Testament admonition to reflect before we met again. He clearly wasn't convinced by what we'd told him.

25

We were both exhausted the next morning when we got up after a brief sleep. There was nothing in the papers. We had a quick breakfast and Anna said she had to get home to go to work. I told her she should call in sick for the day, but she said she couldn't and I drove her out to Blacktown. There was a very brief news item on the radio, police refusing to release the name of a man found dead in a Castlecrag home the previous night. Foul play was not being ruled out.

'They're waiting for the pathology results,' I said, still not quite free of my TV character.

Anna said, 'I wonder how Damien is?' She looked very tired and drawn.

'I'll find out when I get back, and ring you.'

'Thanks.' When we reached her flat, she got out of the car and walked to the front door with all the animation of a zombie.

I phoned the Chatswood police station when I returned, and they told me which hospital Damien had been taken to. The hospital would only say that he was in intensive care, so presumably he was still alive. Then, mid-morning, the front doorbell of the hotel tinkled and Lauren walked in. There were dark rings under her eyes, her hair looked lank and she had on the party frock she'd been wearing the previous evening.

I took her into Mary's sitting room and we sat down. I told her I'd tried to call the hospital to ask how he was.

'He's in a coma, Josh. His heart stopped twice before they got him to the hospital. They're not sure at the moment whether he'll live.'

She was obviously desperately tired, but her voice was calm and level and she seemed very focused.

'I'm sorry. We called for help as soon as we could. I had no idea that was going to happen.' I also had no idea what she had been told of the situation.

'The reason I've come is because I want to know exactly what happened. I want you to tell me everything.'

The way she said this gave me pause. The young woman gushing over the news of her baby had gone. This was the lawyer, determined to get what she wanted from a potentially hostile witness. I remembered Damien saying that she was brighter than he was. I had the feeling she was considerably brighter than both Maddox and me, too.

'Of course. I don't know how much Damien has told you about the death of Luce, and then Curtis and Owen, but when I came back from London, I met Anna, who told me a disturbing thing that Owen had told her the night he died.' I went on to give her the sanitised version that Anna and I had told Maddox the previous night.

She listened in silence, concentrating on every word, her eyes following each gesture and shift of expression I made, and when I finished she sat back, still watching me, and said, 'That doesn't make any sense.'

'What?'

'You're saying that Damien attacked Anna, then barricaded himself in the house and tried to take his own life, because a hysterical Marcus had taken the blame for Luce's death?'

I felt my eyes blinking too rapidly, some TV director in my head warning me that I was looking shifty. 'I believe he had just discovered Marcus, dead, and reacted with shock.'

'No one commits suicide out of shock, Josh, Damien least of all.' She leaned forward again, drilling me with those deadly dark eyes. 'I want to know why my husband felt compelled to try to kill himself last night. You know, don't you?'

She was amazing. She'd be fantastic in the courtroom, or on TV. The eyes, the voice. I had no choice, really. She held me with those eyes, and I whispered, 'Yes, Lauren. I believe I do.'

'Then tell me.'

So I did. I told her everything.

When I got to the end I said, 'That's why he did it, Lauren—he felt he had no choice. He knew we would tell what he had done.'

Lauren sat rigid, unblinking, trying to absorb the possibility that her husband was a murderer.

Finally she said heavily, 'It's so . . . bizarre, I suppose it must be true. And why haven't you told the police?'

I explained to her. 'I thought enough people had suffered over this.'

'Then I should thank you. I know Suzi would be devastated . . . Damien's parents. So will you stick to your other version?'

'From the way you reacted it doesn't sound as if we'll get away with it.'

'Not necessarily. I spent the whole night at the hospital and only spoke a few words to the police. They'll want to hear my side of things. If I support your story, and tell them that Damien has been very depressed since Curtis and Owen's accident, they'll have to believe it. And that's not necessarily untrue—he has been different since that funeral, since he saw you again. I know he visited Marcus several times, and each time came back very low and started drinking heavily. Perhaps he guessed then that it was all going to come out, what they had done to that poor girl. I can still hardly believe it, that Damien would deliberately—'

'It was Marcus, Lauren. He could do that to people.' And then, because I'd told her everything else, I added, 'She was pregnant, apparently.'

I regretted it as soon as the words were out, and I had to turn away as tears flooded into my eyes. It was an excruciating moment.

She waited until I'd pulled myself together, then murmured, 'I'm sorry,' and left.

It was hard to concentrate on anything during the following days, waiting for Maddox to return. Once, when I was a very small boy, I had dawdled on my way to school one morning and arrived late. I joined a line of miscreants outside the headmistress's room. The door opened and we were invited in, one by one, to explain ourselves. As I waited my turn in the doorway I heard the boy in front of me offer his excuse: 'Please, Miss, my mum woke up late.' This seemed to satisfy the interrogator, who wrote something in a book and called me forward. I said, 'Please, Miss, my mum woke up late.' She wrote it down with a grim smile and I wet myself. It was my first real taste of the awful might of Authority, and now, as the days passed, Maddox took on that mantle, and I awaited his reappearance with dread, certain that he would see through our story with the same perspicacity.

As a distraction I persuaded Mary to let me take her to a

matinee of *HMS Pinafore* at the Opera House. Mary loved Gilbert and Sullivan, and the weather was fine, so I suggested we walk there, around the bay at Woolloomooloo and up through the Botanic Gardens to Circular Quay. The show was a great success; we sailed the ocean blue, sighed with Little Buttercup at her unrequited love and thrilled to the plot reversal in the final act. The only unexpected thing was the shock I felt when I realised that the name of the captain of the *Pinafore* was Corcoran. Had I known that? Was that why I'd wanted to go?

Afterwards we had a glass of champagne on the harbour's edge. I was disconcerted to spot Damien and Lauren's balcony up there between the towers, and didn't catch what Mary was saying at first. It seemed she had been to see her doctor about some symptoms, and he had sent her for tests, which had established angina, so she felt she should catch a taxi rather than walk home. I felt terrible at having made her walk all that way, but she dismissed my apology, saying she was fine really, just a little tired.

It was the middle of the following week before Maddox invited me over to the police station at Darlinghurst for another chat. I expected apocalyptic wrath, and thought it must be some kind of devious police trick when he seemed mildly satisfied. Finally I came to understand that Lauren had worked her magic on him, and he even expressed some concern that Anna and I may have been traumatised by that last encounter with Damien, whom they now knew had been deeply disturbed for some time.

There were a couple of angles that he wanted to explore. Apparently Marcus had been cooking up all sorts of stuff in that laboratory of his, including hallucinogenic compounds derived from plants. Maddox wanted to know about the use of drugs in our circle when we were students, and whether Marcus had supplied them. I told him we were no different from others of our age, and that although Marcus had supplied hash on occasions, especially to Curtis, our drug of choice had been alcohol.

It appeared that Maddox was only really interested in Marcus's drugs in so far as they might relate to the aspect of the whole case that most intrigued him, which was the hold that Marcus had had over his students, which he described as *messianic*. I wasn't sure that was the word I would have used, but maybe he was right. I found it hard now to pin down the nature of that magnetism, like trying to describe a colour or a taste.

Marcus's funeral was a very quiet affair. Damien was still in a coma and Lauren didn't go, nor did Suzi. Anna and I sat on one side, the deceased's family on the other. They comprised a cousin and his wife and their two teenage children, who were all rather amazed to have inherited the house at Castlecrag. 'Very *special*, of course,' the wife said. 'I mean, Walter Burley Griffin and everything. But *so* much work to be done. And the *stuff* Marcus accumulated!' I mentioned the Lloyd Rees print that Luce and I had liked, and offered to buy it, and they said I was welcome to it.

We didn't notice Detective Sergeant Maddox at the back of the chapel until we stood up to leave.

'He's facing the Supreme Judgement now,' he murmured.

'I suppose so,' I said.

'Your circle of friends has shrunk mighty small, Josh. You should think hard on that.' Then, as if changing the subject entirely, he said, 'I was speaking to Grant Campbell on the phone the other day. He told me about your little misadventure when you were over there recently. I really think you and Anna should consider hanging up your climbing shoes. It's a dangerous game.'

'Yes, we've come to the same conclusion.'

'Funny, it reminded me of something that came up in the Lucy Corcoran investigation.'

'Really?'

'Yes. There's a strange pinnacle of rock out in the sea to the south of Lord Howe, called Balls Pyramid. You must have seen it.'

'Yes.' I found I was holding my breath.

'There was lots of confusing information to sort out in the days after Lucy disappeared,' he went on. 'People charging all over the place, rumours of sightings and false alarms. We had to decide what was relevant and what wasn't. It's always like that with an investigation of course, but afterwards you wonder. On the day after the accident, the helicopter from HMAS *Newcastle* flew over Balls Pyramid. They spotted two people who'd landed on the Pyramid from a Zodiac off one of the visiting yachts.'

'Really? Did you find out who they were?'

'Mm. One of them had a beard, the other red hair. Sounded like Damien Stokes and Curtis Read to me. Later on I asked them, and they said they'd wanted to check that Lucy hadn't been washed up on Balls Pyramid. With the direction of the currents that would have been impossible, of course, and I took it for an innocent mistake. But then you wonder . . .'

'What do you wonder?'

He just shrugged.

'Did they find any sign of her?' I asked.

He said, 'No. Well, they couldn't have, could they?'

* * *

285

That evening I met Rory in the hallway of the hotel. He regarded me quizzically over the top of his glasses, the way he no doubt considered all dubious witnesses, then asked sombrely if I'd care to join him in a tot of whisky. I didn't, but I couldn't think of a reason to refuse.

We sat in the little bar while he poured the Glenfiddich, then he said, 'You've been to a funeral, I hear. That feller who was the tutor of those climbers, your friends.'

'That's right.' Mary must have kept him informed.

'All over now.'

'I suppose so.'

'No.' He repeated, with emphasis, 'It is all over. The coroner has accepted the police report. There's no suspicion attached to yourself or Ms Green.'

I looked at him in astonishment.

'Mary asked me to keep an eye on things. I really think this business . . .' He hesitated, then seemed to think better of what he'd been about to say. 'Mary tells me you're considering your career options.'

'Well, um, yes,' I said, and then, since he seemed to expect something more, I added, 'I enjoyed my experience in London, but I'm not sure that I want to continue in that path.'

'The Venezuelan business, eh?'

I gawped at him.

'Banker friend of mine at the club,' he said. 'He was one of the people your bank tried to cheat. He was interested when I mentioned your name, told me the story.' And he proceeded to relate it exactly as it had happened.

I was shocked, though it all seemed rather trivial now, compared with everything else that had happened since. 'They told me nothing would be said.'

He chuckled. 'No use having an anonymous scapegoat.

Wouldn't be believed. You're quite famous, apparently, in a select circle.'

I groaned.

'Sometimes these experiences can be the most valuable. And not necessarily a liability—shows you were in the thick of it. Best to move boldly forward now. Put the past behind you.'

He'd been discussing it with Mary, of course, and this was now the official line. They were really talking about Luce, and my unhealthy obsession with her death. This had to mark the end of it.

'My friend has an interest in a boutique investment company. They specialise in ecological investments—carbon trading, stuff like that? I don't pretend to understand it. But he thinks your background and experience might be just what they need. You might like to give this chap a ring.'

He handed me a card, just as Damien had once done. It had very discreet small lettering. I thanked him and promised that I would.

I assumed that was the heavy agenda business over, but then he came out with the big surprise.

'Er, Mary and I have decided to get married, Josh. Mary wanted to tell you, of course, but I asked her to allow me . . .'

It was almost as if he was asking me for her hand or something, and I couldn't suppress a big grin. He seemed discomfited by this response. 'No, no,' I said. 'I'm just so pleased, Rory. For both of you.' I didn't go so far as to say I'd love to have him as an uncle.

'I'm afraid it'll mean letting the hotel go. Mary's very reluctant, understandably, but you know about her heart, don't you? The specialist's told her she must take it easy, and I intend to make sure she does. I, too, will be retiring, from the bench.'

'I see. Anyway, congratulations.' I raised my glass.

'Yes, well . . . it's been a long time for both of us, but it's never too late, Josh, that's the thing.'

It'd be nice to think so, although Marcus wouldn't have agreed. Several weeks later I got a call from Suzi. She asked how Damien was, and I told her that he was now at home. I pictured him in his wheelchair on his ledge on the twenty-eighth floor. His brain had been severely damaged by his heart stoppages, and he had not spoken a word since. He was not expected to improve.

Suzi explained that she hadn't been in touch with anyone since she'd read about Marcus. She confessed that she'd never felt very comfortable with him. Then she asked if I'd like to call in for a cup of tea or a drink. I must have hesitated, wondering what this was all about, and she added hurriedly that she had a little problem she needed someone's advice on, and she thought I might be the one.

I called in the next morning and she made coffee. Young Thomas was playing contentedly, a far cry from the screaming child Luce and I had babysat. We exchanged news without Suzi getting to the point of the visit. Then, when we'd finished our coffees, she asked me to come with her to the backyard, which apparently was where the problem lay. Beyond a sandpit and a small rectangle of grass, Owen had converted most of the backyard into an immaculate vegetable garden. Raised beds were lush with beans and tomatoes, lettuce and silverbeet, and though weeds had begun to invade since Owen's death, it didn't look too problematic to me.

Suzi led me down a central brick path towards the back wall, against which was a compost bin and a small greenhouse.

It was filled with potted shrubs, and when I looked through the glass at them I felt a little jolt of recognition. They looked to me like melaleuca, and the last time I'd seen that tight-knit foliage, twisting like green coral, was on Gannet Green, a hundred odd metres up Balls Pyramid.

'You can't see them now, they come out at night, but Owen brought back these funny kind of stick insects from Lord Howe Island, that time that poor Luce died. He said he shouldn't have, really, and we mustn't tell anyone, especially Marcus or Damien. I really didn't see why, but he was adamant. Only, there are quite a few of them now, and I don't think I can look after them properly, and I don't want them getting out—they're big, you see, and I don't know if they bite. They're horrible things, they give me the creeps, and the thought of them getting onto Thomas or the baby . . . I almost called the pest exterminator, but Owen was so attached to them. I thought I should speak to you first. What do you think I should do?'

It was a good question. She had no idea how good. For a moment I pondered, the fate of perhaps the rarest creature on the planet in my hands. I decided that if I thought about it for a month I still wouldn't know what was the right answer, so I just went with gut feeling. Luce had sacrificed her life for these horrible things, after all.

'I know someone at the Australian Museum,' I said, 'who I'm sure will be delighted to arrange for them to be taken away.'

'Just so long as we don't get into trouble.'

Actually, it was more difficult than I'd anticipated. The nice lady at the museum thought I was playing some kind of practical joke on her, and became convinced I was from one of those candid camera TV shows. She kept peering over my shoulder, expecting a cameraman to burst in. In the end I had to tell her that Marcus had been instrumental in bringing them back from Lord Howe, and had given them to Owen to keep for him. She knew of Marcus's reputation, and had read about his suicide, and she didn't think that any TV show would be sick enough to exploit his death like that. I wasn't so sure, but at least she was listening to me.

And so arrangements were made to give the phasmids a new home, where they would be nurtured, studied and eventually returned to their island. I was there when the team came to collect them, and watched them being teased and coaxed out of their bushes, awkward, archaic but also rather dignified in their survival. There were seven of them in all, and when they were all rounded up I looked at them and thought how bitterly ironic it was that a woman such as Luce should have died for such ugly little creatures. For a moment I felt angry at the grotesque imbalance, and then it occurred to me how much Luce would have appreciated it. You might say they were her bronze sandal.

26

I am sitting now with Anna on the hotel terrace with a glass of wine, looking out at the last glimmer of evening sunlight glowing on the far side of Elizabeth Bay after several days of storms. I look at her profile, the thoughtful honest eyes, the little vertical crease at the left edge of her mouth made by her lopsided grin, the small scar on her temple, and I remember the moment, a year ago, when I first caught sight of her standing there at the reception counter.

We have been discussing some changes she wants to make to our website. I say 'our' because I am a partner in this business now, the Harris Hotel, if a relatively dormant one, enabled by a favourable loan from the boutique investment company for which I now work, following Rory's recommendation. He and Mary are the other sleeping partners, following their wedding, made remarkably boisterous by Rory's ebullient friends from the legal fraternity. The other partner, and manager, licensee and driving force, is Anna, who bought her stake through the sale of her flat in Blacktown. She lives here now, in Mary's old apartment upstairs, and I visit frequently, and often stay, increasingly for longer.

A seagull wheels in overhead. It doesn't have long scarlet streamers in its tail, nor is it doing cartwheels in the up-draught. This one looks old and battered by the storms, and when it lands with a stagger on the top of the garden wall it sags, as if relieved to have left the ocean behind. I think I understand how it feels.

She stood panting on the narrow ledge, pressing herself back against the hard surface of the rock. At her feet the second rat lay crushed in the crack in which she had finally cornered it. Five days it had taken her, days of headlong pursuit, of lung-bursting effort and numbing strain. There had been times when she had almost given up, despairing of the impossible task, and at the end her quarry, as exhausted and defeated as herself, had stared up into her face and seemed to welcome its fate.

She raised the bloody stone with which she'd crushed it, and threw it out into the void. It was all she could manage, a final gesture. She was so exhausted, so dehydrated and weary, her body so depleted, that she could barely think or see.

Then she heard a voice, far below, calling her name. She tried to answer, but her throat was parched and no sound came. They had heard the stone, clattering down the cliff to the sea, and now they knew where she was. She waited, and gradually made out the sounds of their voices getting closer, calling to each other as they climbed. Curtis, she thought, and someone else, come to make amends. She wondered how they could face her now.

There had been a time, at the summit, on the very tip

of this rocky spike, when she had given way to despair, when the thought of seeing them again had filled her with such hopeless disgust that she had decided to finish with it. How could she bring a child into such a world, where even the finest and the bravest could not be trusted or believed? She had stood on the edge of the pinnacle, arms outstretched, ready to step into the void. But it had been the child that had stopped her. It was a decision she could make only for herself, not for her child. And so she had gone on.

She looked down at a sudden sound and saw Curtis's head appear five metres below her.

'She's here!' he shouted, and gave her a cautious smile.

He clambered on up, pulling himself onto her ledge, a little to her right.

'Jeez!' he gasped, and began hammering an anchor into the rock. He clipped himself to it and called out, 'On belay,' then turned to her. 'Goodness, are you all right? Where's your gear, for God's sake?'

She just stared at him, and his face flushed and he turned away to concentrate on the other climber coming up behind him. It was Damien, she realised. He paused when he came into view, staring straight up at her, and something in his face, a kind of grim emptiness held in place by willpower, chilled her. He worked his way up to her left side, and anchored himself, and said not a word.

She looked from one to the other, seeing the hesitation on Curtis's side, the determination on Damien's. Damien reached for her, but before his hand could touch her she had stepped forward, out into the bright air.

Author's Note

In 1997 a research team reported cloning an immortality gene called MORF4. Four years later the American Geron Corporation patented an immortality gene that encodes telomerase, and in 2003 Scottish scientists discovered the immortality gene Nanog, which was reported by *New Scientist* to 'keep embryonic stem cells in a state of youthful immortality'.

At the time of writing, a few surviving specimens of the Lord Howe Island Land Lobster, the phantom phasmid, *Dryococelus australis*, once thought to be extinct and now possibly the world's rarest invertebrate, have been recovered from Balls Pyramid and taken to the mainland, where they are undergoing a breeding program with a view to their eventual return to Lord Howe Island.

*Read on, as Brock & Kolla return
with a vengeance in the remarkable*

Dark Mirror

1

Nigel Ogilvie hurried up the stairs to the Reading Room on the first floor, and made his way, panting slightly, to the big windows overlooking the square. It was a dazzling spring morning, the sun glistening on new foliage bursting from the trees in the central garden, so that it seemed as if King William on his bronze horse was prancing through a brilliant green cloud. Nigel spotted the familiar figure sitting on a bench not far from the statue, her head bent over a book, and watched as she wiped her mouth with a paper napkin, then slowly gathered up the wrapper and drink bottle by her side. He reached into his pocket for his mobile phone and took a picture, capturing the moment as Marion got to her feet and the sun caught her, setting her red hair alight. She began to walk towards the library, tossing her rubbish into a bin. Her coat was unbuttoned, and he watched the swell of her thighs beneath her dress as she strode, head up. *Lithe*, he thought, that was the word. He felt a small quickening of his heartbeat and turned away, making his way across the Reading Room to where he'd left his book earlier. Settling himself in the red leather armchair, he opened the heavy volume on his knee and waited, eyes unfocused on the text.

He was finding it hard to concentrate these days, his research not going well. The idea for the project, *Deadly Gardens*, had been dreamed up by his boss over a boozy lunch, and Nigel was convinced that it wasn't going to work. For the past week he'd been trying to make something of the gardens that Lucrezia Borgia would have known at Ferrara, Nepi, Spoleto and Foligno, but really, it was a waste of time—Lucrezia had had more pressing things on her mind than gardening. She too had red hair, if Veneziano's portrait was to be believed, and Nigel imagined that she and Marion might have other things in common—a dangerous attraction, for one.

Deadly Gardens. He sighed with frustration. He detested Stephen, his boss, a philistine about half his age, who treated him with an amused contempt that made him feel as if he was back at school. But at least the project had provided him with an excuse to hide himself here in the library. He loved the place, a refuge where he could turn off his importuning mobile phone, bury himself in the womb of a million books, snuffle about on the steel grille floors among the stacks, do *The Times* crossword and—a particular satisfaction—observe the other patrons. Poking about in the memoirs of the dead was fascinating, of course, but there was a particular buzz, a special frisson, about the leisurely observation of lives in which passions were still unresolved, and suffering still to be endured.

And here she came at last, Marion Summers, making her entrance up the main stair and looking more Pre-Raphaelite than ever, with her long flowing skirt and that mane of thick red hair and complexion so pale—deathly pale this morning—that he could make out the faint blue line of the artery ticking in her throat. She too had her particular place in the Reading Room, at one of the tables, her pile of books next to the small vase of flowers she'd brought in the previous day. He wondered where they'd come from. They were white, and more like wild flowers than the sort of thing you'd find in a florist's, rather improbable in Central London. What had she been up to last weekend? Was there an admirer out there he didn't know about?

He watched her as she approached, trying to hide his eagerness, and wondered if she would glance at him and offer one of her knowing little smiles. They were at least at that stage, although in his imagination they were a good deal further. Stephen would be irate to learn that he had certainly spent more time studying her than the Borgias' gardens. He knew her borrowing record, her home address, her working timetable, her tastes in soft drinks and sandwiches. He could recall exactly the intonations of her voice when she was puzzled, amused, cajoling the librarians who helped her track down the things she needed. And he had many photographs of her, working here in the library, sitting outside in St James's Square beneath William III on his prancing horse, and on the bus. And all this he had acquired in secret, without arousing the least suspicion.

Marion paused beside her table, splaying her fingers on its surface for support. There was a faint sheen of perspiration on her forehead, which was creased by a frown, as if she were trying to make sense of something. She grimaced suddenly, raising a hand abruptly to her mouth and reaching with the other for her chair. But before she could grasp it she staggered, and her hand knocked the vase of flowers to the floor. She doubled over with a moan and sank to her knees.

'Oh!' Her cry was cut off as she was abruptly sick, her body convulsing violently, sending the chair tumbling onto its back.

Consternation spread out in ripples across the Reading Room, people rising to their feet, craning to see what had happened. But Nigel remained where he was, eyes bright, phone in hand, fastidiously recording every detail. She was being sick again, poor thing, writhing in agony as she vomited over the red carpet.

One of the librarians was running forward. 'What is it?' she demanded. 'What's wrong?'

A man who had been seated at her table said, 'She . . . she's having some sort of attack,' shrinking back with a look of horrified pity on his face. Last to respond, the two old codgers in the armchairs in front of the fireplace had belatedly risen to their feet. Everyone's attention was focused on the epicentre of the drama, unaware of Nigel taking surreptitious pictures of Marion thrashing about helplessly on the floor, and of the shock on people's faces as they witnessed this awful scene, all of them struck by the same terrible realisation that such a thing, whatever it was, could happen to anyone, at any time, even *here* in this sanctuary.

'Is there a doctor here?' the librarian cried.

Actually there were six in the room, but none of them of the medical kind, and they were quite unable to help.

'Are you calling an ambulance?' she demanded, and Nigel froze, realising suddenly that she was staring straight at him.

'Yes, absolutely!' He dialled triple nine, feeling himself the focus of attention now as people gratefully averted their eyes from Marion. He spoke fast and clearly to the operator, feeling he was doing it rather well, and when they wanted to know his name he gave it with a little thrill of excitement—he would be on the official record.

'Airways,' the librarian said. 'We have to make sure she doesn't choke.' But that was easier said than done, for Marion's body was racked by convulsive spasms. It was some minutes before they subsided enough for the librarian to bravely stick her fingers into the young woman's mouth to make sure she hadn't swallowed her tongue. Kneeling in the mess, she cradled Marion's head on her lap and stroked her hair soothingly, the wild flowers scattered on the carpet all around. Nigel got some good shots of that.

Someone was gathering up the contents of Marion's bag, which had spilled over the floor. Nigel stooped to help. He picked up a hairbrush, with strands of her red hair coiled around its bristles, and reluctantly put it back into the bag. But he palmed the computer memory stick lying beside it, slipping it into his pocket.